IN THE BLOOD

ALSO BY DELIA REMINGTON

Out For Blood
Trial By Blood

IN THE BLOOD

BLOOD

BOOK ONE OF THE BLOOD ROYAL SAGA

Delia Remington

EAGLE HEIGHTS PRESS

In the Blood is the first book in *The Blood Royal Saga* by Delia Remington.

PRINTING HISTORY
Paperback edition / July 2017
Hardcover edition / April 2019

ISBN: 978-1-947181-11-3

Manufactured in the United States of America

Published in the United States by
Eagle Heights Press, a division of
Eagle Heights LLC., Fayette MO USA

http://www. eagleheightspress.com

To Nicki, my teacher, mentor, and friend.
I hope I make you proud.

To my friends and family who never stopped believing
and to my dogs who are endlessly patient.

And to you, for reading.
You've made my dream a reality.

PART I

PART I

The Highest Bidder

Marie Antoinette

The auctioneer was just starting the bidding when I slipped in the side door and took a seat in the back, trying to avoid notice. I scanned the room, looking for anyone who might have glanced my way, but other than the gentleman to my right who moved to make room for me, all eyes were on the stage, staring at the items on display. I knew I wouldn't have a chance to get all of them. At any rate, buying more than one might raise suspicions. No. I had no choice but to be austere, though the idea of others possessing what rightfully ought to be mine rankled me.

I have never been naturally patient. My grandmama would have said the same. But she told me over and over, thinking only of what I want and not of the consequences of my desire would be my ruination. I am only grateful she never knew how right she really was.

Watching intently, I waited, biding my time. I knew when I planned to come here which item I would bid on. One that would raise the least suspicion. There were still those who pay attention and who watch, and above all else, I had to avoid their notice.

As each item went, it pained me, knowing I could not simply take them all. But time was on my side.

At last, the item I came for went up on the block, and I watched the competition, letting them set the starting bids, laying low. Finally, my moment came, and I raised my paddle.

"$35,000 to the lady. Do I hear $35,500?"

It's not unusual in auctions of this kind for a collector to bid only on one particular item. The prices are high, a catalogue listing of all the options has been published for weeks, and many of the bidders are purchasing the items for clients. This was my saving grace.

A man in a brown suit bid against me, but I saw him sweating. I knew I would get what I came for. There was no other competition.

I raised my paddle again and calmly said, "$40,550."

The auctioneer nodded, then looked to the gentleman who shook his head, bringing out a handkerchief to wipe his forehead.

"$40,550 to the lady. Going once. Going twice. Fair warning...SOLD!"

The gavel banged, and I relaxed. I stayed in my seat

silently, putting on a pair of oversized sunglasses, waiting until the next item went up on display and the bidding started. Then I slipped out, paying the auction house and placing the item in a silver attaché case, attaching it to my wrist with a set of handcuffs. I thanked them and walked out, even as the auction was still wrapping up.

I wanted to leap in triumph, but I held in my excitement until the cab took me back to the safety of my hotel room. I barred the door, closed the curtains, and then and only then did I open the case to see what I'd bought.

I stretched out with trembling hands to pick it up from the velvet case which displayed it, and I turned it this way and that, then pressed the fabric to my cheek with delight. "Welcome home, my beauty. Welcome home."

It was only one piece of my life, but it was mine at last, and I would never let it be taken from me again. I closed the case once more and lay back on the bed, closing my eyes as the memories began surfacing in my mind.

"ANTOINNE!"

I jerk as my grandmama's sharp voice reprimands me, and I prick my finger with the embroidery needle I've been working with. "Ouch!" Sticking my finger in my mouth, I suck the blood away, looking up at her with worry. "What is it?"

"Why are you not dressed for our evening's entertainment?" She looks me up and down disapprovingly. "You've been playing with that dog of yours again. You have hair all over your clothes. What have I said?"

Sighing softly, I look at her with embarrassment. "It's a dog, not a doll."

"Precisely. Go get cleaned up. Quickly child."

I jump up from my seat. "Yes, madame," I say with a small curtsy, and I make my way toward the door in a hurry.

"Antoinne," her voice stops me.

"Yes, madame?" I say, turning.

"Your needlework," she says, looking at the handiwork I left behind.

I rush back to pick it up.

"Don't slouch. And don't run. It's vulgar."

"Yes, madame. I am sorry, madame." I bow my head and curtsy once more, then turn and walk out, this time taking my time, head held high, back straight, with a deliberate and steady gait.

I woke from a deep slumber. Those dreams of my past were almost always ones of regret or sorrow. I disappointed my grandmama. She had high expectations. What would she make of me all these years later? I still felt her condemnations. I didn't have a chance to make her proud. The world never let me.

Stretching, I sat up and checked the clock. Six thirty. Time to be going. They'd be looking for me. I only hoped there wasn't a security camera in the auction hall pointed in my direction. This trip of mine was careless. I should have used an agent. At least I didn't buy anything obvious, I hoped.

I hurried to the shower, then dressed quickly, tying my hair back wet, not wanting to waste my time on vanity, much as it went against my nature.

I knew the more time I spent, the closer they would

be on my trail, and I could not let them find me. I spent too long staying out of their clutches to lose it all because of carelessness.

I put my small treasure into my briefcase once more. No one would suspect the real value of such an item, and its worth to me is purely personal. I would have paid any price for this small piece of my past.

I scanned the room for anything I might have left behind, stripping the sheets, then taking the pillowcase off the pillow I used, turning it inside out, and stuffing them all into the briefcase. I checked the bed for any stray blond hairs I might have left behind, then, satisfied, I closed the briefcase and walked out of the room, riding the elevator to the lobby where I turned in my key-card, then stepped out onto the sidewalk. I looked carefully right and left to be sure I wasn't being followed, walked down the street for a few blocks, then turned abruptly into an alleyway. A dumpster stood nearby. I opened the briefcase and tossed the sheets and pillowcase into it.

Checking one last time for prying eyes, I pulled out my cell phone and called for a cab, specifying a location a few blocks away, urging haste, then hanging up and setting off on foot to meet it.

I didn't like New York City. Its clamor and brashness was a contrast to the way I was raised. I prefer St. Louis, my home. There has always been too much emphasis on the new in New York. The garish signs on Broadway flashed alongside the red lights of lechery, the hard lines of the buildings harsh and forbidding. I missed the welcoming riverfront, gateway to travelers, with a history that ran deep like the lifeblood of its people.

I've lived in many places, but St. Louis always had a special place in my heart, perhaps because of its French origins or the open generous hearts of its people. I couldn't say for sure, but I ached to be home whenever I went away. There, I was known as Claire Marie. Two names. It made me smile to give them both. But in New York, no one had two names. It was considered gauche.

One more reason to dislike the place.

I reached my rendezvous point, and the cab was waiting for me. "JFK, please." And I smiled at the driver, though he was too busy to notice or to think of anything but his fare. Just as well.

Reaching into my pocket, I pulled out my iPod and plugged in my earbuds, then settled back in the seat to listen to some Mozart, closing my eyes as the car wove in and out of traffic. When we finally stopped, I paid the driver, then leaned in close and glamoured him all the same, making sure he remembered nothing of me at all.

Certain I'd cut off the trail, I again put on my sunglasses, before heading into the terminal. I walked to the nearest bathroom and washed my hands, taking my time. A woman entered the bathroom. Too fat. Next was a young girl. Short. Finally, another woman entered wearing a red tank top, jeans, and a cowboy hat, all in my size. This one would do. She caught my eye, and I exerted my influence on her mind, walking with her into the large handicapped stall at the end of the row, shutting the door behind us both.

Ten minutes later, rosy cheeked, I emerged from the bathroom wearing that stranger's clothes and hat, looking nothing like myself. By the time they found her, I would be long gone.

I got in line for the security check and showed my false ID. They passed me on, and I walked to my gate, patiently waiting to board along with the other passengers, letting "Eine kleine Nachtmusik" take me to another place and time.

We taxied down the runway at last, and as the plane lifted off into the sky, I smiled down on all the little lights of New York. "Goodbye to you," I whispered, forehead against the glass. "You are much more beautiful from up here."

St. Louis waited for me and, trusting in its warm embrace on my return, I drifted to sleep as the engines whined.

Fin met me at the gate, not smiling, but I gave him one of my own, beaming at him and leaning in to kiss his cheek.

"Welcome back," he said as he took my suitcase. "What's with the getup?"

"Thank you, my darling," I said, keeping the briefcase. "Do you like it? It's the new me."

He glared and walked beside me in sullen silence all the way to the MetroLink terminal, rocking on his feet until the train arrived and we stepped aboard.

"So what was so important you had to risk it all to buy?" Fin said in a low voice once we'd found some seats at the rear of the train, far from the other passengers. He put on a show of annoyance, but I could sense his fear hidden beneath.

Leaning forward and patting his knee reassuringly, I smiled. "I got it. No one followed me."

"Don't treat me like a child. I'm not a child. Just tell me, was it worth the risk?" He felt angry, his way of showing he loved me, even after everything.

"It was to me," I said, settling back into my seat.

Fin hated traffic. He also had some notion riding public transportation was good for my soul. A car was an extravagance, he said. Greenhouse gases or some such. I grew weary of the argument, and so I acquiesced to his wishes. "I will show you when we get home. You'll see. How is Pom Pom? Was he good while I was gone?"

Fin rolled his eyes. "I hate that dog." I gave him a warning glance out of the corner of my eye, and he sighed. "Pom Pom was good. He only shredded three of my socks this time."

Smiling, I closed my eyes, listening to the noises of the people on the car, the sound of the train's movement on the rail. "Good boy," I said.

I loved my little gated community in the Central West End.

Fin scolded me once for snobbishness, but I insisted it was safer for both of us behind its perimeter fence. There was no denying that. Plus, I enjoyed my walk to work each day. Of course, the shop was merely a hobby. Anyone who paid close attention to my finances would realize I never made enough money to maintain my style of living. However, most people simply assumed I had inherited wealth. In a way, they were right.

When the train stopped at the station, Fin grabbed my bags and followed me out to the taxi stand. We didn't speak during the car ride, but as he paid the fare and we got out, I told him I was going straight to the shop instead of coming inside.

"I've got to do a few things. I'll be home soon. Thank you for meeting me, darling." Kissing him on the cheek once more, I turned on my heel and walked away, wishing I couldn't see the hurt and protest on his face.

My little shop was a delight, with the tinkling bell at the door, the ever-changing front display window, the pressed tin ceiling, and the winding arrangement of items, leading customers on a meandering path from one section to the next, encouraging a slow perusal. My assistant, Crystal Kirby, came from a small town but kept her warm personality. She had no idea who (or what) I really was, which was just as I preferred to keep it. I loved the glass display cabinets and my ancient cash register, though Fin convinced me of the addition of a computer. He was right, of course. My register was just for show. The real business transactions happened with the keyboard and mouse, but I still liked the cheery little "ding" it made when I opened the drawer.

Pom Pom was waiting for me on his little dog bed as usual. Fin had forgotten to take him home before coming to get me. He probably thought Crystal would dog-sit for me. Then again, perhaps Fin had known I'd head here first. Sometimes it seemed he knew me better than I knew myself.

I picked up the little Pomeranian and kissed his face. "Who's been a good dog? You have. Yes, you have. Did Crystal give you lots of love? Huh?"

He wriggled happily in my arms, loving the attention, then having had enough he squirmed to get free again. "All right. All right. You win."

I placed him on the carpet, and he half ran, half jumped around in circles, barking for several minutes before settling back down with his toys again.

Greetings over, I got down to the real order of business, locking the front door once more and then stepping behind the counter and through the office door, closing it behind me. I didn't want any prying eyes, even by chance. Once I knew I was completely alone, I could feel a shiver run through me. I'd gotten what I'd set out to collect and so far as I could tell, no one was any the wiser.

My shoulders relaxed, and I reached back to pull my prize from its hiding place. Turning it over in my hand, running my fingers over the embroidered pattern, I whispered to it softly, "I found you, my lovely.

You're back where you belong at last." With a smile, I rubbed the fabric against my cheek, closing my eyes. It was so long ago, and yet with this treasure in my hand, I could still feel the stays of my confining dress, and the warmth of the sun on my skin that last day before everything changed.

For those memories, the ones that made me smile, I was willing to risk everything.

Strange how we forget the details of our lives. A mother should remember what her children look like. But over the years, their features had softened in my mind. I had no photographs to remind me, and so my memory lost the crispness of reality, fading until they resembled their portraits, though no painter could ever capture the true likeness of my little ones.

As I held this swatch of fabric from my past, my children's faces swam before me, suddenly fresh once more, borne to the surface from the depths of my long memory. I staggered on my feet and dropped the handkerchief with a gasp, leaning heavily on the desk to steady myself. I hadn't expected or even hoped for such a thing. Yet as I stood there, the images receded back into the shadows of the past. I closed my eyes and tried to call them back, but the moment was over, and they were gone. It cut me to the core.

When I finally had collected myself, I bent down to retrieve the handkerchief, gingerly lifting it as though it might burn me. Where moments before I had felt warm and happy, it suddenly made me feel cold and brittle. Not for the first time, I cursed those responsible for what's happened to me, renewing my vow to be avenged one day, but the words rang hollow on my tongue, and I opened the safe and tossed the handkerchief inside, locking it away with a desperate sadness.

Fin does not, cannot, understand my obsession for buying such small souvenirs from my previous life. I have tried to explain, but he does not comprehend my aching need. He is so young. He does not understand the sort of loss I have experienced. His eyes only see the surface, the physical aspect of each item I've collected. "They're just trinkets. And you lock them away and never look at them. If you're not going to use these things or at least display them somehow, what is the point of hunting for them?

I could never be satisfied with this single purchase. I resolved one day to find an item to bring the memory of my children's faces back to me for good.

Not surprisingly, therefore, though I had only just returned from my brush with danger, I spent the rest of the evening online looking for other items for sale. When nothing else appeared, I returned home deflated, Pom Pom in tow. Fin was out. I did not know where he went in the evenings.

Perhaps it was just as well. Certainly, I was in no mood to talk.

I walked up the stairs to my be room with a heavy heart, changed into my night clothes, and slipped under the covers. Pom Pom curled up on my feet, and I drifted off at last to dark dreams. They almost always were.

Death Be a Lover

Fin

Once Marie left the house, I went inside, dropped her bags in her room, then wandered down to the library to peruse the shelves.

I never loved reading until I was dead and had nothing else to do. Now, I don't know what I would do without it. Go crazy, I suppose. Books gave me another world to live in for a while, one outside my sheltered walls where I could be human again and pretend for a while to be free.

Marie's library was extensive, stretching around the room with walnut wooden built in bookcases, that were so tall it required a rolling brass ladder to reach the top shelves, though I can't remember seeing her read any of these books herself.

She preferred to have me read aloud or simply to talk or play guitar. Once in a while, she would ask me to act out a scene for her as I read, like I was doing some sort of dramatic reading just for her amusement. I had found such requests amusing at first, but as the years passed, I began to feel like a trained pet, doing tricks, rather than a person she respected and treated as an equal, and as a result, my interest in indulging her fell off.

To be honest, I wasn't sure that she even had a hand in the selection of the books that lined the dark wood shelves. Maybe she purchased the house and kept the library as part of the furnishings. If I'd asked her, she might have said it was a gift for me, but truly, she probably hadn't thought of my needs at all in that regard. She just liked the look of them, as far as I could tell. The books on those shelves might just as well have been wallpaper. They made pretty decoration, but she wasn't really interested in what was beneath their covers.

Most of the collection was made up of classic novels and books of history and biography. I'd had time enough to peruse the library extensively, and I had my favorites.

I preferred books with action and suspense like **Treasure Island** or **Journey to the Center of the Earth**. There was something soothing in reading about other people's daring escapes that staved off the monotony of my days. For months, I'd been making my way through Jack London's works, losing myself in the tales of the far north with excitement, and it was to this I returned to find distraction from my annoyance.

For a long while I sat on the red leather sofa by the fire, reading **Call of the Wild** for the hundredth time, letting myself drift in the words and forget my anger with her.

As the time stretched out, and I became more convinced she wouldn't be returning, however, I felt agitation creep in. I read somewhere that journaling can help with long term feelings of resentment, so I'd been writing in a private blog just to get my feelings out. I knew that saying anything to Marie would be a waste of time, but at least I could purge my emotions, even if it was only to myself.

Sitting down at my desk by the window, I set down the book, got out a pack of Marlboro Reds, lit one up, then opened my MacBook and started typing where I'd left off:

I was twenty-three when Death found me. Death, my lover, my mother of sorts. She came to me unexpectedly, as death often does.

Naively, I thought myself immortal. In a way, I was right. I love her. I hate her. I cannot bear to leave her. She knew precisely what would happen when she chose me, though I knew nothing of her designs.

That Halloween night, I was reborn. Literally. While I reeled from what she had done to me, she gave me a new name, a new identity, whisked me away to a new city, and told me I could never return to my old life.

I paused to puff on the cigarette, staring out the window lost in thought.

The garden at the rear of the house was lush by modern standards, though Marie often complained she felt hemmed in by neighbors. I could see across the lawn to the formal gardens with neatly trimmed hedges, everything just so. That's how she liked it — the appearance of nature, when in fact she'd carefully planned every single blade of grass. That approach to life irritated me because I often feel she is keeping me according to her careful plan as well.

Thinking about that, I began typing once more:

I do not miss the life I had before, though I'd have thought I would. I do not miss the pressures my family placed on me to deliver on my potential. I fell into that life through no plan of my own. Music ties me to my former self. The one vestige left of my human life.

When I play, I am not me or the person I used to be. I have no self. I am a conduit for something far greater, something that transcends these paltry distinctions. There is only the music. I felt this presence before my transformation as well. It's as though the part of me I call "I" falls away, and music fills the husk I inhabit, music is my animus.

Music and Blood. My twin desires. I need them in equal share.

The first is innate, the second is her doing.

Blowing great curls of smoke, I paused there to think about her. I could've walked out. Simply left. But the thought of it pained me for reasons I didn't understand. I'd contemplated it many times. She wouldn't have stopped me, yet I also knew she'd never truly let me go. She would be there, waiting, watching, and might show up at any time, demanding my obedience. She wasn't commanding, and yet her nature commanded me.

I'd put up with all her nonsense, her games, her whims. Sometimes she behaved like a child, while at others she could be downright ruthless.

16

I didn't miss my former life. I'd let those people and the experiences I'd had fade away. I wasn't that person anymore, and really, I never had been. Everyone thought they knew me. Everyone told me who to be. I'd felt hollow. I'd been going through the motions for a long time. She'd simply given me the final push to make me leave, and I had really never looked back. No, I couldn't blame her for making me abandon my life. I'd been looking for an escape. She'd given it to me. She had simply not explained the fine print details of our arrangement. I suppose I should have asked more questions.

I balanced the cigarette on the ashtray and continued with my journal entry:

I love her and I hate her. As I love and hate myself. If I had known what she really offered that night, I would never have agreed. It simply never occurred to me what she suggested was possible.

She offered to make me immortal. I thought she was an agent or a photographer. Someone in the business. I was casual in my reply. I didn't know she meant it literally.

Foolish.

No point in recriminations. It is too late. There is but one way now, and it's with her. Thus, I bind myself to her tightly, afraid of the night when she tires of me.

I hate her, and yet I love her. And I always will.

A click of the mouse to save the document and then I closed the laptop, picking up what remained of the cigarette. She hated my smoking. Said it was vulgar.

"Yeah, well, fuck her today," I muttered. "She hadn't even bothered to tell me before she left. Just a note on the nightstand, with flight times and a heart. Right. A fucking heart. Certainly, she only drew it in order to pretend she cared."

I'd been feeling her drifting for months. She had grown bored with me. Apathy crept in little by little. She needed me still. Oh yes. She would never stop needing me. But love me? I wasn't so sure anymore. She had never loved me the way I loved her. Our relationship was never one of equals. I had accepted it long ago.

Indifference, though, was new. It killed me to see it in her eyes, and the hell of it was I couldn't stop feeling for her. Not even if I wanted to. She'd seen to that.

Stubbing out the cigarette, I looked at the screen of my iPhone to check the time. It read 8:35 p.m. in bold letters. I tossed down the phone on the tabletop. "I don't need this shit," I said. "I go and fucking pick her up after being worried sick for two days, and what does she do? Leave me with her bags. Well, fuck her. Just fuck her!"

My eyes pricked with tears of anger. I jumped up from my seat, grabbing my messenger bag and stuffing my laptop and cigarettes inside, putting my phone on vibrate, then shoving it in my pocket. I wouldn't answer her calls. She could just see how it feels.

Grabbing a sticky note from the desk, I scrawled "GONE OUT" in all capital letters and stuck the note on the mirror by the front door. I knew she always looked at herself whenever she had the chance. She couldn't resist.

I grabbed an old army surplus jacket she'd told me a million times she hated, yanked it on over my black sweater and faded blue jeans, and then stormed out the door, locking it behind myself. In order to drown out the anger, I got out my iPod, shoved the earbuds in my ears, and started for a quiet place to think, away from her. The music blocked out everything else, and I cranked it up, turning toward the area near Washington University where I could blend in and be a nameless face in the crowd.

"Fuck her," I murmured as I rounded the corner, heading in the opposite direction from Marie's shop. "Fuck her."

Surfaced

Chief Inspector

A naked woman's body drained of blood lay on the tile floor of a bathroom at JFK.

As soon as the report came into my office, I knew what that meant, so I wasn't surprised when I got the call to take my team to investigate.

Walking in, heels clicking on the tile floor, I could see the city police standing there dumbfounded and horrified by the scene. Thankfully, they'd been on the scene quickly and kept the story from leaking to the press. All I needed was a bunch of reporters descending on the airport, sensationalizing what happened.

When my "international task force" arrived, the police were happy to hand over the crime scene. The city didn't have the budget, resources, personnel, equipment, or expertise to handle a situation like this. Badges flashed, my team of "experts" and I were welcomed onto the crime scene with a nearly audible sigh of relief all around.

"Thank god you're here, ma'am. Glad you got here so fast. Never seen anything like this," said a paunched and tired cop, leading me into the restroom where several officers stood around puzzling. "Thirty years on the force. Damnedest thing I ever saw. I'm guessing this is some world-traveling serial killer's M.O.?"

I looked up from my clipboard with a scowl. "I cannot discuss an ongoing investigation. That information is need-to-know only. Why aren't the victim's hands bagged? Why are all these people standing around? What kind of homicide investigators are you? This entire area needs to be cordoned off. Get all these other people out of here. They're breathing on my crime scene and destroying potential evidence. Set up a perimeter outside. No one in or out without my say-so. Understood?"

I knew displaying a take-charge attitude from the first would establish my credibility and stifle any argument. The man might have wondered momentarily why he had never seen anything in the news about any similar incidents, but he shrugged his thoughts aside and accepted the idea it must be a high profile case. I knew what he thought. It's what they all feared most. Imagine the panic if people thought they might be exsanguinated and possibly sexually assaulted, victims of some new terrorist threat or serial killer. Travel would grind to a stop. After 9/11, no one wanted a repeat of that level of fear again.

The man backed away with a soft grunt of grudging acquiescence. I stopped him, however, telling him I needed to ask him some questions. He halted by the hand dryers while his fellow officers filed out.

I handed him some gloves and a mask, putting on my own before picking up my pen to draw out a sketch of the crime scene. He followed suit, making sure not to touch anything in the room.

"Good. Now we are alone, I need to hear your assessment of the situation so I know how to proceed." I said. "Are you certain no one staged this scene?"

He shook his head. "The minimal blood spatter over there on the wall indicates the murder occurred here."

"Did you find any evidence of a struggle?" I said, making notes on my clipboard.

"None we could see. No bruising or ligature marks. Nothing. It looks like she just walked in here and then died without putting up a fight at all. Maybe our killer drugged her, but we didn't find evidence. Toxicology report might turn up something."

I nodded. "Do you have a probable cause of death?"

"This is where it gets weird. Our vic's got two holes on her neck like needle marks. We think that's where our killer took or sucked the blood from." His nose wrinkled with obvious distaste, pointing at the body with an outstretched finger. "No idea what kind of machine could do that, nor do we have any theories how the blood would have been carried out of here in that quantity. The biggest question is why anyone would want to do this in the first place."

"Any idea what our killer used to make those wounds?" My eyes narrowed as I asked the question, gazing down at the corpse. The dead woman's eyes stared vacantly toward the ceiling.

"No idea. I never saw anything like it before. None of us has. I can't imagine what kind of weapon or medical device makes those kinds of marks. If they came from needles, they were big enough to knit with."

"Any idea of her identity?"

Shrugging, he looked down at the body sadly. "No clue. Jane Doe. No ID, no nothing."

"I see." I scanned the room and frowned at what I observed. Or rather, what I didn't.

Every investigator likes to have a smoking gun. A piece of irrefutable proof of the identity of the killer. I knew with this case, I wasn't going to be so lucky.

The undead leave no latent prints since they don't sweat. We would have to fume the room anyway for appearances, but it wouldn't give us any useful information. Still, the policemen didn't know that. They had no idea what they were up against.

My team, however, knew exactly what to look for and was efficient at gathering evidence. We had all seen other crime scenes like this one, though rarely in such a public setting. Sloppy. Whoever had done this had clearly lost his or her touch. Too many years of being immortal can do that sometimes.

Knowing what had to be done, I thanked the man and sent him outside while we did our work. He would have gotten in the way if I'd let him stay any longer.

Donning white anti-contamination suits and rubber gloves, we took photos and examined the body, taking special note of the wounds. We used UV lights to check for bio fluids on every surface of the bathroom — stall walls, floors, toilet, sinks, hand dryers, mirrors — then fumed the room and the body for fingerprints. We also gathered multiple vials of trace blood, hair, and DNA evidence from both the victim and the bathroom stall.

Having examined the entire crime scene thoroughly, I determined the body and all of the security footage for the terminal would need to be taken to our labs for extensive testing and analysis by my panel of experts. While the body and evidence were being prepared for transport, we collected detailed statements from witnesses, police, and staff. I made sure we were thorough.

Whatever they thought had happened, however, could not be allowed to remain in their memories. I had been instructed to do a complete cleanup, both of the scene and of the minds of the people involved.

By the time we were ready to depart, my techs had scrubbed the bathroom of all evidence, and the airport staff and police officers, along with all the witnesses in the terminal, came to the understanding no body existed. In fact, they all forgot about it completely. One person on the scene had taken a cell phone photo of the body. That phone came into my custody, and the owner came to believe he had lost it. As for the officials, once we were through debriefing them, they were all clapping themselves on the back for a successful safety drill while the bystanders went back to their holiday or business plans as though nothing had happened. Ignorance is bliss.

Once we were safely inside the white van and driving away from the airport, I removed a phone from my pocket and sent a text to an international number. The message read simply, "Surfaced at last."

ONE OF THOSE FACES

Sybill

Wiping down the espresso machine with a bar-towel, I looked out the window of the coffee shop, playing over in my mind the call I had that morning.

"Come home for your daddy's birthday. You never visit anymore. I'm worried about you, honey. I don't think you're eating right."

My mother always worried as though it was a hobby for her. I sometimes thought if she had just had a few more kids to spread her worry out on, she wouldn't be quite so annoying. You can't choose your family, though, can you?

The family. I remember the day I realized what that meant. I don't like to think about that day.

My father is friends with men with names like "Nick the Weasel" and "Bobby Fingers." Names most people thought were only real in movies. My father played golf with those men. They never did business at home. My father said that was rude. I just took it for granted that's how everybody did things. Now I realize my father just wanted to talk about things in an open area, away from FBI phone taps and bugs.

"Mom, I'm busy." I had sighed and rolled my eyes. Only half a lie. I'd find a way to be busy. "And I eat just fine."

"Chinese takeout isn't eating."

Her comment made me laugh. "Mom, you fed us takeout at least five days a week."

My mother had whined then, knowing she'd lost the argument. "I'd cook this time. Just come home. Your daddy wants to see you."

"He can call and ask me himself."

"Sybill, you know your father won't do that." No. Too proud to say he missed his baby girl.

"Well, sorry, but I can't. I'm busy." I'd hurried to get off the phone.

He wouldn't be put off forever. My father wasn't used to people making him wait, and he always got his way.

27

"Ahem. Can I get an espresso, please?"

The question shook me out of my reverie. A long-haired guy stood at the counter with a bemused expression. How long had he been waiting? I shook myself and put the rag away, then stepped over to the cash register.

"Yeah, sure. Sorry. That it?" I punched in the order and looked up at him fully. His eyes were mesmerizing, and for a moment I stood still as we gazed back at one another.

"Uh, yep. That's all." He brushed his hair back out of his eyes and put on a pair of black chunky glasses.

A smile came to my lips unbidden and unstoppable as I told him the amount, and he handed me some crumpled bills out of his pocket.

"You can take a seat wherever," I said, flattening out the wrinkles in the money, pressing the dollars against the wooden bar with my palm before placing them into the till. "I'll bring it out to you when it's done."

He smiled then, his expression somehow mischievous and wild, though I couldn't have said why. I couldn't help but smile back, though I almost never do it these days. "You have Wifi?" he said, walking toward a table by the window.

The question made me laugh aloud as I turned to face the espresso machine. "We're a coffee shop by Wash U. What do you think?"

"Wash U?" He quirked an eyebrow at me curiously.

"Washington University. It's just a few blocks away." I pointed at a girl with an overflowing backpack in the corner sporting a messy ponytail and Wash U sweatshirt, then laughed a little more, tamping down the grounds.

"Oh, right. Wash U. Guess I need to get out more."
He bit his lip, smiling a little sheepishly.

"No worries," I said, feeling a little guilty for embarrassing him. "The Wifi is free. You don't need a password or anything."

"Thanks," he said, nodding. With a downward glance, his hair fell over his face, and I had this feeling I'd seen him someplace before, though I couldn't say where. Maybe he just had one of those faces.

As he took a seat, he opened up his messenger bag and pulled out a silver laptop. He slung his jacket over the back of his chair, then dug out an auxiliary mouse and set it on the tabletop. As the computer booted up and the screen illuminated, the contours of his face were given dramatic emphasis with the light.

I struggled not to gasp.

Handsome as the devil. I stared for several moments before I shook myself and got to work on his espresso.

Once the coffee finished, I took it over to him, placing the tiny cup and saucer down on his table. "There you are. You need anything else, just holler."

He looked up with a smirk and laughed. "Holler?"

My cheeks were burning as I looked back at him with a smile playing on my lips. "Uh huh. Or, you know, whistle. You know how to whistle, don't ya?"

With a soft chuckle, he picked up the cup and took a quick sip. "Like old movies, huh?"

"Oh, you know…" I shrugged, "I guess I like all kinds of movies. Old, new, bad. It's all an escape. How about you?"

"Mmm." He looked back at the screen, setting the cup down on the saucer with a clink of china. "I used to be into them. Not so much anymore." His eyes flicked back up to mine. "I'm more into music these days. Live stuff. Mostly acoustic."

"Oh, well, you've come to the right place then," I gushed. "We do open mike night every Thursday. It's usually pretty good."

"Hmm. You interested in music?" He raised an eyebrow and picked up his cup again, steam wreathing around his face.

I shook my head and gave a soft laugh. "Just to listen, not to sing or anything."

He nodded as though he were thinking. "Well, thanks for letting me know. I might just have to come see what the fuss is about sometime."

Pausing, I opened my mouth to ask him a question, but just then one of my regulars walked through the door, still wearing hospital scrubs. "Hey Sybill. I need a latte, stat!"

"Gotcha! Skim milk, right?" I said, looking back over my shoulder at the intern from Barnes Jewish Hospital, then I turned my head back to face the intriguing guy once more. "Gotta go," I said, backing away with a smile.

"That's cool, Sybill," he said, then he looked back at his computer screen and started opening a program with the mouse.

A thrill went through me as he said my name, and then I felt his attention drift away as though a door had shut, and my own disappointment surprised me. Slipping behind the counter, I told myself I was being ridiculous. He was just a guy like any other. I'd probably never see him again. Who cared anyway? Someone new always came along. Still, something drew me to him. Like he'd become the center of gravity for the entire room.

As I continued working, I found myself looking over in his direction periodically. He didn't look up at me again. I never saw him take another sip of the espresso. Two hours later when I looked back over for the thousandth time to discover his table empty, I frowned. I'd never even seen him go.

With a sigh, I walked over with a tub to bus the table. Six wadded napkins. I picked up the saucer with the still full espresso and found a five dollar bill and a note scrawled on the back of his receipt left underneath:

See you Thursday, Sybill. Thanks. Meeting you made a bad day better.

Pocketing the money and the note, I took a deep breath, then wiped down the table, grinning and blushing like crazy. He'd remembered my name.

Around midnight, when we closed up, I walked home with my collar up, hands stuffed down in my pockets. People always asked me if I felt nervous being alone on the street at night. Thing is, I guess I should have been, but I just wasn't. Plus, I'd learned a thing or two about protecting myself from those old guys dad called friends. Push the heel of your palm into someone's nose, and they're never getting up again. Knee them in the balls, and they're pretty much toast. Punch them in the "snot-locker" as one of them colorfully put it. Run like hell. If all else failed, well, I had a .38 in my bag and knew how to use it.

As I walked that night, though, I had this creeping feeling prickling at the back of my neck, like someone followed me, and I hurried faster than usual, only looking back when I dared. No one was there each time I looked, but I couldn't escape that feeling until I got inside the lobby of my building and the door locked behind me. Weird, I thought. First time in three years that ever happened.

"Night, Rick," I said, waving at the guy sitting at the security desk in the lobby, and he gave me his usual noncommittal nod and grunt, not looking up from his phone.

Stepping over to the mailboxes, I fumbled with the key to open mine. Nothing but advertising circulars. Heaving a soft sigh of disappointment, I threw the papers into the blue recycling bin, then walked over to punch the button to call the elevator.

I relaxed as I rode up to my apartment, loosening my scarf and unbuttoning my coat from the heat of the building. My imagination had run wild. That's what I told myself. I should have been wondering why, but the thought never occurred to me.

Safely inside my cocoon, I tossed my keys and emptied my pockets on the kitchen bar, threw my bag and coat on my love seat, and headed back to shower. I smelled like coffee and cigarettes and while I don't mind wearing that smell during the day, I don't like to take it with me to bed.

The water massaging my scalp, warming my skin after the cold night air, relaxing every muscle, I scrubbed and loofah-ed until my skin glowed.

Finally clean and new, I stepped out to dry off, wrapping myself in a fluffy robe and twisting a towel around my head.

Barefoot and smiling, I padded into the kitchen for a glass of water before bed. That's when I saw it again. Under the pile of change and wadded bills from my tips, I found the note from him, and it made me smile once more. I picked the little scrap of paper up and read it over, my thumb touching my name in his lettering. He wasn't the first guy to scribble a note to me at work. Usually, it included a phone number and his name, along with an offer to "show me a good time." I threw most of those out.

This one was different, though.

He remembered my name. He'd actually really been listening to what I'd said about the open mike night. He'd thanked me. I found myself wondering what had been so bad about his day. And what was his name?

My brain burned with curiosity.

Finally, even though it didn't make sense, rather than toss the note in the trash, I put it up on my fridge alongside my Chinese fortune that had told me, "You will soon make a new acquaintance who will change your life completely." I stared at the two pieces of paper next to one another for a few seconds, then started laughing softly at myself. "Yeah right. Change my life. Whatever."

Shaking my head, I turned off the light and went to bed.

I've Got a Secret

Fin

She glowed. All her tattoos and piercings just made her even more beautiful. Her body was so fragile and small, but she had decorated it to show her ferocity. And her hair, black as night, made those china blue eyes of hers stand out like pieces of the brightest sky. She was a stunning study in contrasts.

"Sybill." My lips said her name silently as I walked out of the coffee shop. I shoved my hands down deep in my pockets as though warding off the chill, echoing the actions of the people I passed, though I haven't truly felt the cold in years. Not since the change. We do love warmth, though. We crave it.

I felt tempted to stay there, basking under her gaze, feeling human again just for a fleeting precious few hours. However, a glance at my watch reminded me I had only an hour before the public library closed, and I wanted some more music to fill my voracious appetite. Marie would buy me whatever I wanted — movies, music, books, clothes — she had a seemingly inexhaustible fund to draw upon, but I knew where much of her money came from, and I felt dirty each time I held something bought with it.

Moreover, I hated owing her. It made me feel trapped somehow, bound even more tightly to her with golden chains. The library existed for everyone, rich and poor alike, as an equalizer.

I stayed a while, perusing the collection, picking out a few old folk CDs, plus some more recent indie artist music that might be listened to by flannel-wearing hipsters, stuff I called "Grunge Light," though only in my head. For a few moments, I also paused in front of the New Books display before walking over and plucking one of my favorites from the Recommended Reads shelf. I had read it before. Several times, in fact. But I loved picking it back up and reading it all over again. Arms full, I carried my selections to the desk and waited patiently for the librarian to scan them all.

When she handed me back my checked out items, she looked at me sharply. "Anyone ever tell you, you look a lot like that actor...what's his name Christian Slater? But, you know, the younger version."

I shrugged, not making eye contact, shoving everything down in my bag. "Yeah, I hear that sometimes. Not as much as I used to, though." Then, I looked up and smiled before making sure she promptly forgot my face. I hated using glamour on people, but I had no choice.

Chewing my lip, I went back out into the night. My hunger rose, but I didn't want to give in. Still, I couldn't face going back home yet. Marie might not have even had time to notice I had left, and I wanted her to feel it. Feel the emptiness. Understand just a little of how she'd made me feel when she left.

I walked the streets, thinking about the nearness of Forest Park. It would be so easy to find what I needed there. So easy.

Forest Park is the largest city park in the entire United States. Our house sat on its doorstep. Marie had made her choice carefully, just as she calculated everything else she did. With a steady nightly stream of winos, addicts, and sex-trade junkies, all hiding in the dark, if a few of them went missing, well, the city cops felt like it was their own damn fault for being reckless. Make it look like a mugging gone wrong or an overdose. That's all I had to do. Easy. No one much would miss them.

I never asked Marie how she could justify it to herself. In life, I'd been vegan. Ha. What a laugh and a half. Vegan. Try being a vegan vampire. Good luck with that.

Yeah, okay, I could kill a deer or something. There were plenty of those in the park, but they tasted bad. It would keep me alive, but it wouldn't stop the craving. I needed blood. Human blood. All my moral principles were pointless. I found my only consolation in the thought I was cleaning up the streets. Plus, I didn't need it as often as you might think. Once a week sufficed. Marie had a blood supplier and kept the refrigerator stocked.

Unfortunately, the refrigerator was too far away, and I felt famished.

No. I refused to give in. Instead, I clenched my jaw and walked to a bus stop, taking a seat on the bench and getting out my book, just like anyone else waiting for the bus. I pulled up my coat collar, trying to look as though huddling for warmth, and I lit a cigarette, reading, not looking up at the people who passed by.

As each person drew near, I could hear the "thump, thump, thump" of a heartbeat beneath their tender flesh. The blood called to me, pounding in my ears with a tantalizing rhythm.

To distract myself, I found one of my favorite passages and read it aloud in a soft whisper, knowing no one would be listening. No one listens to someone waiting at the bus stop. My stomach rumbled then just as the bus pulled up to the curb, and I knew I couldn't get aboard without doing something awful. Something impossible to contemplate. Something monstrous.

"God dammit," I growled, stuffing the book back in my bag. I couldn't wait any longer. I felt dangerous. I blamed her for that too. She never warned me. Never told me what it would be like. "Damn her to hell."

Leaping to my feet, I shoved my way past the commuters. The park. Just get to the park. Not far.

That night, I found just what I needed on the footpath near the skating rink. Just outside the lights, he lurked in the shadows, shooting up. I felt his pain, his desperate loneliness. He wanted oblivion. I gave it to him.

As the warmth of his blood flowed through my veins, for just a few fleeting moments I sensed the cold, felt nearly human again. Then he went still, and the feeling passed. I dropped his body by a tree, licking my lips before turning back to walk out of the park once more. Snow began to fall.

My feet took me down late night avenues, and I didn't look up to even notice my surroundings until I found myself across the street from the same coffee shop. What am I doing here? I slunk back into the shadow of an overhanging awning as I gazed over at the storefront. The lights shut off inside, and two people walked out together.

Sybill stood there, locking the front door. Another employee was with her. They exchanged words, then parted. She walked off alone away from all the bus lines. My eyes narrowed in surprise. Surely she must live close then.

Following her was the last thing I'd planned on. Yet I haunted her footsteps all the same. I told myself it wasn't stalking. I was simply making sure she got back home all right.

Why did it matter to me? I couldn't tell you. All I know is it did.

I had an idea in my head of the type of apartment a coffee shop girl with tattoos lived in. Someplace run down on a dark street. Imagine my surprise when she stopped in front of an expensive high-rise building, got out her key-card, and walked in the front door. Those apartments had to cost more per month than she made in three months as a barista. How did she pay for that? Did she live with someone rich? Somehow, I didn't think so. She had an air about her of someone who lived alone, maybe with a cat, maybe not.

Sybill was turning out to be a mystery. One I wanted to figure out.

Lighting a cigarette, I stood at the corner in the shadows for half an hour or so before turning away at last. Time to go home again.

The night bus passed me as I waited to cross Euclid Avenue, and when I finally slipped into the tree-covered path leading the back way through the gardens, I smiled to myself. For the first time in a long time, I felt excited to see what tomorrow would bring. I had a secret. Its name was Sybill.

THE LEGACY OF DREAMS

Marie Antoinette

"**M**ama! Mama, there are bad men outside!"

In my dream, my children were clinging to my skirts and crying as a hammering of fists and bodies and weapons shook the doors. I dropped to my knees, huddling on the floor beside them, holding them close. "I know, my darlings. Shh... it's going to be all right. Don't you worry. The brave soldiers will keep us safe."

My husband paced anxiously, rattling his sword in its sheath at his side. He only wore it for show. He had no real talent for swordplay, and against men such as these, he had no chance at all. We were all counting on our gallant men-at-arms to protect us and still believing the people had simply forgotten their place or lost their

40

minds. Surely the church, the magistrates, the military, our powerful friends and allies would stop this foolishness. Our pleas for calm and common sense would prevail. I still believed we would all gather round and laugh one day at the nonsense of this revolution of theirs.

Watching the scene as if in slow motion, my mind began screaming at my dream self to run, to escape, to take the children and use my power to get out of there. Why did I wait? Why had I listened to all those men who were so foolhardy?

Yet in my dream, I was trapped and forced to watch in agony all over again as the doors broke open at last and hordes of angry men and women rushed toward us, baying for blood. They killed some of our men, then ripped my children from my arms, took my husband and I, and placed us in chains, dragging us off to prison. We wept as they spat and cursed and threw all manner of filth at us, but we never fought back. How could I not see what they had in store for us? It never occurred to me they would actually mean to kill us all. What a little idiot I had been then. Naive. Trusting. Weak. It made me sick to see myself that way.

Frustrated and furious, I shrieked at my dream self, "NO! NO! NO! Get out! Get out, you fool!"

With a jerk and a gasp, I awoke, wringing the covers in both hands, and I could still feel the echoes of my cries throughout the house. I'd woken myself up with this nightmare. The nightmare I lived through over and over, wishing each time, things would end differently.

They never did.

The terror, the rage, the panic came back to me afresh once more. I wanted to kill them for what they did to my family. To me. Whatever my own crimes in their eyes, both real and imagined, my children were innocent. They did not deserve to suffer.

Once, I thought to end it all and find a way to truly die, but then I discovered the name of the one responsible, and I made a vow. I would not rest until he paid for what he had done.

He incited the mob against us. He fanned the flames of rebellion. His hand held the puppet strings of weak men, and he laughed at our pain. Hundreds died at his goading, hundreds brought to slaughter beneath the cruelty of Madame Guillotine. He killed his own kind and reveled as their blood soaked the streets of Paris. No, I could never forget or forgive.

As I sat up in bed, I wondered what had brought on the dream. Something always triggered it. Perhaps my hasty trip to retrieve my rightful property. The handkerchief. The one I'd held the morning they came to take me away to my eternal punishment.

Then I remembered. My chambermaid…what was her name? I could no longer recall. I felt a little shame. She gave so much that day.

I begged the men for a few minutes alone to pray. "Please, gentlemen, only a moment. Let me make my peace with God."

I had looked them in the eye as I made the request. The chief among them caught my gaze and agreed, closing the door to my prison cell for what I knew would be the briefest of reprieves. But I had just enough time, and I was desperate enough to do the unthinkable.

Taking my chambermaid's hands in mine, our eyes locked, and I glamoured her into doing exactly as I bid her. Compliant and calm as she traded clothes and wigs with me, she took that handkerchief with her, and when the door opened again, I convinced them with my glamour she was indeed the woman they sought. As the men led her away, I followed out into the yard. They were never the wiser.

She made a pretty, if short, little speech before she died, and when her head landed in the basket, her hand dropped the handkerchief. I'd forgotten that little detail. I'd been in too much haste to escape to let it register in my mind. I'd gotten myself lost in the crowd who'd come to see the spectacle and then disappeared into the shadows, stolen a horse, and ridden away as fast as ever I could out of the city and into history.

But now, the memory came back to me with all its resultant guilt and heartache. She lost her life because of me, in my service, and I did not have the decency to remember her name.

I owed her both my life and my vengeance.

Fin asked me once when we were traveling together what made me so afraid. Why I checked for cameras, carefully ensured not to leave behind any evidence of my existence in public places. When I told him the truth of my identity, who I hid from, he stared, dumbfounded. Impossible, he said. All the history books gave accounts of his death.

I laughed. "You're supposed to be dead too," I said. Hundreds of books, plays, and films told the story of my death as well. Yet, here I stood, walking and talking just the same.

He knew of my wealth, yes, and I was clearly much older than I seemed. My accent gave me away as a foreigner. I was a vampire. However, he did not know my story. His legacy. Not until I explained. The impossible had happened. His existence proved it. He was the child of Marie Antoinette, Queen of France, the last of my bloodline. I had chosen him above all others to carry on my legacy.

My dream reminded me, both of all I had lost and of what I owed. Of who I am and of what I must do. Of all I fear most and of all that can be taken away.

"Fin?" I called out in the dark house. Surely he is back by now, I thought. Dawn approached. "Fin? I need you."

Pom Pom came up immediately and buried himself in my arms, but Fin never appeared. I'd hurt him. I could see it clearly. I hadn't meant to, yet I had done it all the same. I'd frightened him and I'd left him alone without warning, thoughtless of his feelings, and he felt broken-hearted about it.

With a sigh, I hugged Pom Pom to me, kissing the top of his head tenderly. "What am I going to do, eh? I've been a bad, bad mama, haven't I?"

Pom Pom only whined, but it still sounded like an answer, and one I didn't want to hear. I needed to make it up to Fin and win back his trust. I resolved then and there, no more spur -of-the-moment trips without talking to Fin first. No more auctions. I'd placed us both at risk with my recklessness. No wonder he became so furious with me. If the wrong people recognized me or traced me back here, then neither one of us would be safe ever again.

"You'll forgive me, won't you boy?" I said to Pom Pom,

and he licked my nose happily.

I only hoped my conversation with Fin, once we finally had it, would go as smoothly. Something told me I wasn't that lucky. I also felt certain expecting Fin to be my lapdog might lead to some serious problems in our relationship.

With the little dog snuggled up close to my chest, I fell asleep again, this time deep and dreamless, and I never even heard Fin's return.

KEEPING THE COLD AT BAY

Fin

Softly, I heard Marie knocking on my bedroom door. I covered my head with the blankets and groaned.

"Fin? Fin, darling, it's me. Can't we talk?" Her knocking, insistent and annoying, became like a gnat buzzing in my ear. Trying to ignore her didn't work, though. I heard her pleading question from the doorway, and it irked me.

"Go away."

Paying no attention to my command, she walked right in anyway.

"Oh come now, darling. You don't mean that. Not really."

I sat up in bed, scowling toward the door. "What, you're an expert on what I mean now? I definitely do mean it.

46

I'm warning you. Go away."

"Tsk." She shook her head as she pushed her way into the room. I saw her take in the untidiness of the room. Clothes were strewn about on every flat surface, and a cursory glance showed her three empty cups I'd had blood in. "Look at the state of this place. Really, my dear. I can't let the maid in to see this. What will she think?"

"There you go, judging me already, and you've only been standing there for a few seconds." I closed my eyes and gritted my teeth, sitting up a little more. "I don't want the maid in here. I don't want you here. What part of 'go away' was unclear? Now fuck off!"

"There is no need to be vulgar."

Propped up on my elbows, bare to the waist, the blankets covering my lower body, I saw her sniff the air. Her nostrils flared. "Who is she?"

Oh shit. She knows. How does she always know? I pushed back the covers and swung my legs over the edge of the mattress, not caring if she saw me naked or not. She had seen it all before. "Who?"

I began rummaging for a clean pair of boxers and pulled them on before looking for a pair of jeans draped over a nearby chair.

The disapproval on her face nearly made me laugh. "You know who. Don't play coy."

"I'm not playing anything. You're the one who plays games, remember?"

"Lying is an ugly habit, darling."

I avoided her eyes, giving my attention to the buttons on my fly. "Ha! Pot, meet kettle." Barefoot, I walked across the room to pull a rust colored t-shirt from a pile on top of the dresser.

"Mmm. No, cryptic doesn't work for you either, darling. Let's just be direct, shall we? It will save an awful lot of time for us both."

Yanking the shirt over my head, I tugged it down roughly before looking back at her. "Yeah? Well, I tried the direct approach, but you ignored me. Go away. I thought I was pretty clear."

A deep sigh escaped her lips. "You're trying to protect her from me.""

"Am I? Is that what I'm doing?" I stepped over to the bedside table and pulled a pair of unmatched socks from a pile there. "How's it working so far?" Taking a seat on the edge of the bed, I began putting on the socks, not looking at her again.

"Not well. You just admitted there is a 'her' to protect."

I couldn't help smiling. I knew exactly what to do to throw her off guard. "I admitted nothing of the kind. You're slipping, old girl."

That term made her wince.

"Don't call me that." She stared at my mismatched feet. "Are you really going to wear those?"

A low rumbling chuckle welled up in me. "What? Old?" I glanced at her face and took pity on her. "Yes, I am aware my socks don't match. Somehow, I have forty seven socks, all missing a mate and none of which match one another. Don't ask me how it happened because I really don't know. I'll be wearing boots anyway. No one will see. It doesn't matter."

She stood there silently for a moment before she spoke at last. "I'll buy you some new socks. Ones that match."

I shrugged, searching around for my boots. "They're just socks."

"I want to anyway."

The change in her tone made me turn to face her. "Look, I'm sorry, okay? There's nothing going on. I'm just...I don't know. Restless, I guess. Don't worry about it."

Gliding across the room, she reached out to touch my cheek. "It's my job to worry about you."

Her sudden tenderness shocked me. I couldn't remember the last time she touched me like that. I stared into her eyes, wondering what brought it on. "I'm fine. I'm sorry for being a jerk earlier. I didn't mean it."

"I'm sorry too." For a second, I thought maybe she would take me in her arms and hold me close, but she hesitated and the moment passed. "You know you can always talk to me, right?"

I forced myself to nod and smile, using my actor's training to make it believable. "Sure."

She didn't push me, though I'm sure she knew I was lying. "Good." She stepped back and glanced around the room. "By the way, your boots are under the bed."

"Boots?" I'd forgotten I had been looking for them, and it took a second before I understood what she meant. "Oh... thanks." Sheepishly, I walked over to the bed and reached down to pull them out.

She reached out to scoop up a couple of the cups to take out of the room with her. "Are you sure you won't let me send the maid in to tidy things up a bit? Really, darling, it's in an awful state."

I realized she was not going to let it go. I also realized that her actions meant she still loved me, and I relented. "Okay. Fine. Have it your way. But tell her to stay out of my things. I'm not going to hang around while she cleans either. I'll go to a coffee house or something for a few hours so I'm out of her way."

Filled with gratitude at my peace offering, she smiled. "Of course, dear. I'll send you a text message when she's through and the coast is clear."

A twinge of guilt came over me. I tried to hide my excitement at the prospect of seeing Sybill again, bending to the task of putting on my boots to keep the thought from showing on my face. "Sounds good."

Taking the third cup in her hand, she walked with them over to the open door and left the room without another word.

It was a start. I hoped, in time, we could overcome the wedge between us. I missed the closeness we used to share. Not the romance, but the intimacy. In the past, I used to tell her everything. Someday, I hoped I would again.

Snow came down softly as I walked to the coffee shop. Trying to appear casual, I strolled into the coffee shop where she was working. As she stood there, stunningly beautiful in front of me, I couldn't remember what I had planned to order, and I ended up repeating what the customer in front of me had said, feeling like a parrot and trying not to seem embarrassed.

She was so witty, I was dazzled. All my words seemed inadequate and awkward to me, though she smiled and laughed anyway. The line was long, so I stepped to the side to wait while she took other orders. When she looked up and said the name of some coffee drink, it took a second to register that she was speaking to me. Trying to hide my nervousness, I took the cup and saucer, then smiled before turning away in search of a seat.

"Thanks" was all I was able to stammer out, feeling like an idiot and wondering why I never seemed to be as clever and charming in person as I was in my mind. Finally, I realized the pointlessness of me being there. I wasn't going to find the courage to say what I wanted. Truth be told, I wasn't really sure what I wanted anyway.

Every scenario I ran in my head was a non-starter.

I couldn't tell her what I was, obviously. Besides the certainty that she would run away screaming, I would be putting both myself and Marie in danger. And anyway, there wasn't a single way I could see to explain the truth about myself that would end well.

For all my wishing to be just a normal person, I wasn't anymore. What good would gaining her interest do? Did I think I could take her on a date? Ridiculous. Even if I did, how would I manage to stop the craving to kill her?

The best outcome I could imagine was a simple continuation of this odd acquaintance, but the tension between us was too strong to maintain that relationship for long. There was no point to my staying, so I packed up my things, left a tip, and walked back out into the night.

I wasn't ready to go back home just yet, however.

Instead, I wandered the streets, people watching, keeping my distance, standing in the shadows in the way I have always done since Marie turned me. Before the night ended, I stood below her balcony again, looking up. I never felt so alone.

I returned home just before dawn, covered in snow, and after shedding my coat and boots, I went straight up to my room, to sleep.

Curling up in bed for the day, I could hear the sounds of a snow plow on the street and the roar of a snowblower clearing sidewalks in the neighborhood. I burrowed further down under the duvet to block out the noise, punching down my pillow.

Marie thought me strange for it, but I insisted on using an electric blanket. While I couldn't feel the cold, I did love warmth. It let me pretend for a while I was still alive. I turned it up to the highest setting and let the heat seep into my bones.

My mind drifted to Sybill, and I wondered what she would be doing that day. Would she be working? Did she take classes at the university? Did the snow make them cancel classes? Was she lying in bed trying to find the warm corners of her blankets? The thought made me smile, and as I slowly fell asleep, I could almost imagine she lay there beside me, keeping the cold at bay.

Person of Interest

Chief Inspector

With a headset hooked on my ear, I paced in my office. My door was closed, and my blinds were shut tight. Though the wee hours had crept up on me, the time didn't matter to me at all. I dedicated my life to my purpose.

Confidently swaggering, I said with self-assurance, "Yes sir. The humans on the scene were pushed into forgetting what they saw. You have my assurance, there will be no further investigation by local authorities."

During a long pause, I listened to the voice on the other end, and then I said firmly, "A vampire definitely committed the killing. Our team examined the bite marks, and we are certain the vampire glamoured the victim. That explains the lack of evidence of struggle or defensive wounds."

With lips pressed together tightly, I listened again, then went on, "We are narrowing down possible candidates, though without dental records for comparison, it's a matter of conjecture at this point. Unfortunately, our records are not helpful in this regard. No one has ever recorded a kill with this particular bite signature. However, we have quite a bit of data we believe will prove useful once we've had a chance to complete analysis.

I picked up the case file from my desk and opened it as I continued. "We know our killer is female based on items from the crime scene and other circumstantial evidence. We believe the perp stole the victim's clothing, and we are certain she carried out this theft in order to provide a quick change in appearance. Unfortunately, despite all our efforts, our experts who analyzed the camera footage from the airport were unable to get a positive visual ID. The perp seemed to be aware of camera locations and managed to avoid showing her face."

I paused as I listened to the voice on the other end, pressing the earpiece tighter with a finger, nodding periodically.

"Yes, sir. I understand sir. We do have some circumstantial evidence leading us to believe one candidate stands out above all others. I didn't want to speculate until we had more positive proof."

Nodding again, I concentrated on the voice on the phone, then began pacing once more as I answered. "Very well, sir. According to my team, we believe the person of interest is most likely The Widow Capet, based on the height, weight, build, clothing, and shoe size of the victim. We presumed she died many years ago, as you know, but we have good reason to believe those reports are false and instead she has been a fugitive for several decades. Her file says she was last seen in the 1940s, but witness testimony in this case leads us to believe she is indeed the vampire responsible for this event. We do not yet know what might have led to her appearance in New York."

I stopped and listened, and gradually a smile grew and spread across my lips. "I see. Yes, that might be exactly what drew her out. I'll put my people on it. We will gather data from the location and then look for corroboration with the airport evidence. I should have a definitive answer for you within the next couple of days. I will contact you once we can confirm."

One more pause, and then I nodded a final time. "Understood sir. Thank you."

As I hung up, I walked across the room to my desk and began to write on a Post-it note. "Auction. Video surveillance? Witnesses? Payment?"

Pulling the note free, I held it between my fingers and thumb and strode from the room to give my orders.

A few hours later, the team returned from the auction house with bags full of evidence. They went over video and witness testimony as well as copies of the receipts from items sold.

Finally, a technician walked into my office to report to me. That information made me grin from ear-to-ear. "You've done well. The Master will be pleased indeed. Thank you."

Thus dismissing the technician, I made another call to the same number, this time from my desk chair. "Sir, we have completed our initial comparison. Though we still cannot be absolutely certain of the identity of the person in question, the evidence is pointing toward The Widow Capet as our Number One Suspect. The handkerchief sold at auction to a woman fitting her description for an amount that raises eyebrows even among collectors. She paid in cash. The purchaser collected the item in an attaché case and walked out with it. Surveillance footage from security cameras on the entrance of the building were able to get a number for the cab she took upon leaving the premises. We are in the process of garnering records from the driver to see where she went. Since most cabs in the city have cameras in them, we should be able to gather visual data as well."

I paused when I finished my report and listened carefully as the voice on the other end spoke to me.

"Yes, sir." I nodded. "Yes, I will, sir. Thank you, sir."

Again I paused, and this time what I heard made me puff up a little with pride. "Thank you, sir. I am honored to do my duty." One more nod, and then I said, "Yes, sir. Right away. Good day, sir."

With that, I hung up and then went back out to inform the team of The Master's pleasure with the speed and quality of their work, as well as his high expectations for continued success.

It's all in the Past

Fin

The scattered fragments of a dream still lingering on the edges of my consciousness, I had awoken with a start, and I wondered if I had said Sybill's name aloud in my sleep. She'd been a part of my dream. I was sure of it, though the details were fuzzy. That's just what I needed. If Marie heard me, there would be no end to the questions. I lay in bed, arm over my face, trying to decide what to do.

I listened hard for any sound of Marie in the house, but I soon realized she had left. I must have slept late. She had already left to work at the shop. Relief washed over me, and I smiled to myself, luxuriating a little longer under the covers, wishing

I could go back to that dream once more and find Sybill. I would take her in my arms and never let her go.

But dreams aren't reality, and I finally gave up chasing them and got out of bed to head to the shop. I needed to face up to Marie and try to make peace if I could.

"You were back late last night," Marie barely glanced up at me from her chair behind the computer as I walked through the front door of the antique shop she called her second home. "It's All in the Past" painted in gold letters on the storefront windows was a reflection of the way she liked to keep things, always focusing on the present and never wanting to talk about the past unless in absolute necessity. I came to a grudging acceptance of this attitude of hers once I knew her true identity, though it still rankled to know she had not trusted me enough to confide in me much earlier.

Guitar strapped to my back, I strolled in with a shrug and a murmur of acknowledgment, not explaining myself at all. Maybe I should have told her right away where I'd been and what I'd done, but I wanted to keep Sybill my secret as long as I could. If I mentioned her, Marie would become resentful of my interest. Her jealousies never ended well. Another man might have found it endearing to have a woman like Marie jealous over him, but I knew it wasn't a sign of her love for me so much as a need for her to control me. If my attention wasn't all on her, then whatever intrigued me became a threat in her mind. My computer, my music, anything that drew me away from her. I didn't want that for Sybill. Better I never see her again and just have the memory of her in my mind than to bring down the wrath of Marie upon her.

Eyes downcast, I walked behind the counter, then took a seat at the stool behind the glass cabinet with small pieces of jewelry. Usually, Crystal sat there, but her shift had long since ended, and she'd gone home.

Sometimes, I wondered if Crystal ever knew more about us than she let on. She always asked me questions about my life –where I went, who I saw – friendly questions, but I always gave her vague replies, and I'm sure she had to know something was a little off. Still, as far as I know, she never questioned her boss' strange hours or resented working alone during the day while Marie took over at night.

Opening the guitar case, I spread the instrument over my knees, strumming it absently, pretending Marie wasn't glaring at me, and I stubbornly refused to look up.

"Not speaking to me, I see," she said with a dramatic sigh. "I suppose I deserve that. I should have told you what I was doing. I just wanted to protect you. But I didn't think about how much you would worry, my darling. I truly didn't. I never meant to hurt you. I'm sorry."

I clasped my hands around the neck of the guitar in front of me, staring down at my fingers as I tried to think of a response. "I see," was all I could safely reply.

She fluttered her eyelashes then at me pleadingly. I used to find that expression sweet and charming, but now I saw it as a coquettish trick to make me do what she wanted. "Please, Fin. I can't bear thinking I've hurt you so much. Won't you forgive me? Please?"

Though her tone was wheedling, it had something of steel behind it, and I could feel her pushing me in a way

I found hard to resist. In my mind, I cursed her, but I felt helpless against her power over me. "Was it worth the risk?" I said, the soft way I asked the question making it clear I'd already given in.

Reaching out to touch my arm, she whispered conspiratorially, "Do you want to see it?"

I didn't, though she wouldn't want to hear me say so. "Sure," I said, my voice full of defeat as I returned the guitar to the case and zipped it shut.

With a girlish squeal of delight, she leapt from her seat and grabbed my arm, dragging me back to the office. She closed the door behind us, then opened the safe. I don't know what I expected her to bring out of there, but I certainly never thought she'd done all this for a handkerchief. She placed it in my hand. I touched the gold silk with delicate embroidery on the fabric, and examined the lace around the edges. "Um...?" I blurted, my eyes searching hers for what to say.

"I know it must not look like much to you," she said, reaching out to touch an embroidered flower reverently. "You'll think I'm a sentimental fool."

"No," I lied. "It's...it's pretty."

She burst out laughing. "Oh my darling, I would have bought it even if it was in tatters. I made it, you see. This is my needlework from when I was a young girl, full of hope and dreams of my life to come. Each stitch was a prayer for love and happiness. I kept it with me when I married him...Louis, I mean. And when I became a vampire, I had it with me then too."

Her voice became soft and full of emotion as she went on. "When the people imprisoned me and put on trial, I had it then as well. This handkerchief held the tears of my disappointment and loss of everything I loved. The day I at last had to abandon that life to become someone else in order to survive, I lost this piece of myself. Someone else died on that scaffold in my name, holding this handkerchief as the guillotine fell."

"Oh," I said simply, but the depth of understanding behind it felt overwhelming.

A tiny smile crossed her lips. "So I had to have it, you see. I had to. When I saw it on that machine of yours, saw someone else might buy it in my place, well…I couldn't allow that. It had to be mine."

I nodded, handing it back to her. "How much did this cost you? Cost us?"

Immediately, I regretted the question.

"Is that all you can think about?" she snapped, turning away to put the handkerchief back in the safe. "What's it to you? It's my money, isn't it? I'll spend it how I want."

The tone in her voice made me feel this was an old argument, though never one she'd had with me until now. "What I mean is, won't someone notice if you overpaid for it?"

"Nonsense!" she said. "Who else cares about a silly handkerchief?"

She pushed past me to go back out into the store, and I followed, catching her elbow to stop her as I said, "Your enemies might."

I could see from the fear in her eyes she'd thought this same thing. "I was careful. I promise." But she was holding something back. I could sense it, though what it might be remained a mystery to me.

Letting go of her, I sighed and nodded. "All right then. If you say so, I believe you. I'm sure I'm just being paranoid."

She touched my cheek with her cold little hand and smiled, her fangs showing. "You don't have to worry, darling. No one will ever hurt us. I won't allow it."

"You can't know that for sure," I whispered. "Just promise me this is the last time."

Her smile faded, and she pulled away. "Don't try to tell me what to do, darling. I had enough of that in my life. I won't take it from you."

"I'm not trying to...ugh!" I ran my hand through my hair in frustration. "Look, you're the one who said we had to stay hidden. Keep our heads down. You said they were still looking for you. Do you want them to find us? This is dangerous for both of us, don't you see?"

Instead of answering me, she turned and walked away, going back behind the counter again and picking up Pom Pom. She gave him a kiss on the nose, and I knew she was reprimanding me without her saying another word. She treated me just like her annoying dog, thinking with a condescending pat on the head she can make me roll over and heel to her commands.

"Fine," I said, walking over to face her across the glass cabinet. "Have it your way. You'll do what you want regardless. But I like it here, and I don't want to have to leave because of this bullshit."

"Oh pish-posh. We're not moving, are we?" she said to Pom Pom, holding him nose-to-nose with her, talking in a sugary baby voice that made my skin crawl. "No, we're not. No, we're not."

"I'm going out!" I said grabbing my guitar, shoving it in the case, then turning and stomping to the door.

"Be home by dinnertime, you hear me?" she commanded.

Waving my hand over my head, not turning to look back over my shoulder, I said, "Later!" I shut the jingling door and walked away down the street.

Part of me empathized with her. I could understand the mixture of pain and nostalgia this piece of her past stirred up in her, and I knew though she often hid her feelings behind a mask of placid calm, deep inside, her emotions were visceral. Still, if she really did have enemies who wanted her head, even after all this time – enemies who, according to her, were merciless in their pursuit – then why risk everything we had for such trinkets? I missed things from my past too, but I knew full well if our roles were reversed, her anger with me would have been incendiary.

I lit a cigarette and tried to calm myself. That night, I intended to perform at least one song at the open mike night. *Will Sybill be there?* I felt foolish for the thought. What did it matter? I'd never be free to find out if my feelings were returned. Shoulders sagging, I nearly turned back and went home. But then, as I thought about the way Marie would react, I became filled with a righteous fury. *How dare she keep me hostage to her own little whims? Didn't I deserve to be happy? Surely she hadn't turned me just to keep me prisoner forever.* "I'd like to see her try," I muttered.

My belly full of rebellion, I turned toward the coffee shop, determined to take a stand. If Marie could do as she pleased, then so would I.

I knew what song I would sing. People in this generation had likely never seen the movie in which I'd performed it, but I knew it showed off my voice and my skill on the guitar to great advantage. If I ever wanted to play something to impress Sybill, this was it. The song was catchy and humorous, and I'd sing it straight to her.

I always knew how to fix a girl with my gaze and hold her captive. I didn't need vampire glamour to do it. I planned to use all the natural charms I had. If Sybill fell for me, I wanted it to be real, not coerced. I needed it to be me she wanted. Just me. No funny stuff. It terrified but also electrified me. I'd be vulnerable on stage, but at least I'd be myself.

One Step Up, Two Steps Back

Sybill

I felt him walk into the coffee shop before I ever saw him, like my whole body was tuned to his frequency. I gave a little shiver, goose bumps rising on my skin, and when I turned, I didn't feel surprised at all to see his eyes meet mine across the counter. With a soft smile, I leaned forward to greet him, "Well, hey there Espresso, right?"

He nodded and smiled back, pushing up his thick black glasses. "You're good."

"Yeah, well, that's why they pay me the big bucks." As I got out the cup and saucer, I looked over in his direction and said, "You going to drink it this time?"

He laughed a little self-consciously, looking down and then back up at me. "You don't miss much, do you?"

"Nope," I said, shrugging as I tamped down the grounds. "But I figure it must not have been because you didn't like the coffee since here you are, back again. You just forget you had it?"

"Something like that," he said, a secret smile curling the corners of his mouth.

I poured the fresh coffee into a shot glass and then into his cup, wiping off the machine with a bar towel, before handing him the espresso. "That'll be $2.50."

As he dug in his wallet for his money, I watched him carefully. "No laptop this time, huh? You come to play tonight?"

"That's the plan, yeah." He handed over the cash, stuffing a dollar into the tip jar. "There a sign-up sheet or something?"

I pointed across the room. "See the guy in the Rastafarian hat? He's got the clipboard."

He chuckled again. "Blond dreadlocks? I thought those went out with grunge."

"Some things just won't die, I guess. Good luck."

"Thanks, Sybill," he said, starting to walk away.

"Hey, what's your name anyway?" I blurted, immediately kicking myself and blushing a little at my rudeness.

He paused and looked back at me, licking his lips thoughtfully as though deciding how to reply, before he answered. "Fin."

I tilted my head with a smirk. "Funny. You don't look like a Fin."

Chuckling, he raised an eyebrow. "Oh? What does a Fin look like?"

"I dunno," I shrugged. "Irish maybe?"

"You saying my name is wrong because I'm not a redhead?" He ran a hand through his hair, still laughing.

Again, I shrugged, starting to wipe the counter with a bar towel. "I'm just saying you don't look like a Fin."

He bit his lip and looked down and then back up again, "Well, I'll just have to work on it, huh?"

"Nah. You look fine…Fin." And for some perverse reason I don't even understand, I winked at him then, making him laugh softly once more.

"Well, thanks…Sybill." He stood for a moment longer, gazing back at me, then turned and strode away across the room.

Inside, I kicked myself with embarrassment. *What the hell are you doing? Way to go. Make fun of his name. Now he thinks you're a flirt and a weirdo. Great.*

But his name did seem wrong somehow. I've been around people who lied about their real names. His name sounded hollow, rehearsed, not natural. Plus, it really didn't suit him. I was just being honest.

I found myself wondering why he would lie. Was he homeless? Didn't seem likely with his expensive laptop. A runaway? Possible. A criminal? No way. I can spot those guys a mile away. Maybe he was in witness protection. Nah. That seemed pretty unlikely. He must have his reasons for lying. Maybe he just didn't want me to know his real name because I seemed creepy or something. No. Not with the way he looked at me. He definitely had secrets, though. It roused my curiosity, and I found myself glancing over repeatedly while I tried to concentrate on my job.

When he finally took the stage, he sat unassumingly on the stool, pulling the mic over toward his face, and his hair hid his eyes as he introduced himself. "My name is Fin. This song was written to be sung by a woman, but…you know…I like it, so oh well. Sing along if you know it."

He chuckled a little nervously, and then he began to play, flipping his hair back. I expected something a little folksy, but when I realized he'd chosen a country song, I stopped in my tracks and stared, laughing in spite of myself. The song described a man who "done her wrong," and soon the audience laughed and clapped with him.

He was good. Really good. His voice sounded soft and clear, and he played from the heart. Then, when he reached the chorus, he looked straight up and sang directly to me, his smoldering eyes fixed on mine, making my knees go a little weak. I felt breathless, my pulse pounding when he finished, and the audience cheered and stomped for more.

After a moment, he waved and thanked them. "Okay, one more. This one's one of my favorite songs." I hope you like it."

The second song was intimate and full of longing for forbidden love, and his voice wrapped around my heart and tugged. Once more, when he reached the chorus, he met my eyes and sang only to me. I froze in place, knowing he meant every word. When he strummed the last chord, I heard a collective gasp from the audience before they began to clap, some of them even rising to their feet. He thanked them again, then got up, waving away their calls for another, and walked off stage. Several people clapped him on the back, and some of the women watched him with desire in their eyes, but he simply put away his guitar and walked over to a table in the corner where his espresso waited.

He sat through the rest of the performances politely, clapping and giving each of them his attention, but I felt so stunned and distracted, I kept making mistakes for the rest of the evening. He never looked back in my direction while the other acts were going on, and I started to think perhaps I'd imagined the look he'd given me.

Finally, the emcee got up and thanked everyone for coming, made a short speech reminding people of the next open mike night, and then bid them goodnight. The crowd began to disperse, trickling out in huddled groups to return wherever they'd come from, bundled in scarves and hats. I walked out with the tub to start bussing tables and cleaning up. That's when I saw him still sitting there, watching me curiously.

"So what did you think?" he said, taking off his glasses and cleaning them on his shirttail.

"Of?" I said, playing for time so I could think of something clever to say.

He laughed. "I guess I asked for it. I meant what did you think of my songs. Probably not your kind of thing, I'm betting."

"I…I liked them," I stalled, cups clanking together in the tub.

"Ooh. Ouch." He stood, pulling on his jacket. "You 'liked' them. Well, you fish for complements, I guess you gotta accept whatever you get."

Placing the tub down on a tabletop, I stopped and looked up at him, fixing him square in the eye. "You were remarkable."

He paused, gloves in hand, and blinked at me in surprise.

"What? Come on," I said, starting to pick up a few more dishes. "You know you're good. You can't be that good and not know it. I'll bet you've played a lot bigger places than this."

Running his hand through his hair, he looked away before saying, "I just like music is all. I never tried to make a career out of it or anything."

"Well, that's your own choice, I guess, but you and I both know if you wanted to, you could be famous." I looked up, lifting the tub to take it behind the counter.

He shook his head. "Famous is overrated."

"Yeah, right," I laughed, walking back to load the dishes into the dishwasher. "Anyone ever tell you you're weird? No offense. I like weird."

"None taken," he laughed, putting his glasses back on. "I've been called weird plenty of times. Weird is fine with me. Better than some other things I've been called. You're not so normal yourself."

"Ha. Touché, Mister I-don't-wanna-be-famous." Pouring the detergent into the dishwasher, I turned the machine on and looked at him again.

He walked toward me, his crooked smile making me melt. I could barely meet his eyes with that expression on his face. He made me feel as though he were undressing me right there, and I felt embarrassed knowing my emotions were so naked. I never could hide my feelings well. Clearing my throat, I started cleaning the equipment. "So, this what you do for fun? Sing to girls in coffee shops and make up fake names?"

"Are you always like this?" he said.

"Like what?" Polishing the espresso maker, I kept my eyes on the job.

"So confrontational."

I looked up, struck. "I'm just honest is all. You can't tell me you weren't singing that song at me. I saw you. You were looking right at me."

"Not the whole time," he said, and I heard a teasing tone in his voice.

"Oh really?" I tried to hold back a smile, but without success. "I beg to differ."

"Well, if you noticed, then you had to be looking, didn't you?"

I laughed and grinned. "Yeah, you caught me."

"I like you, Sybill." The look on his face seemed suddenly vulnerable, and I thought for a moment he might ask me out. He shifted on his feet and then lifted his guitar. "I…I'll see you around maybe."

"Wait. You're leaving?" I came around the edge of the counter, cutting him off before he reached the door.

He pressed his lips together and stood for a moment before saying. "This isn't going to work, you know."

"Oh? This what? I thought we were just talking."

"No. We're doing the tango with words, you and me He paused again, then went on. "I like you a lot. More than I should. I ought to go."

My forehead furrowed, and I stepped a little closer. "You married or something?"

"What?" he gaped in surprise. "No. No, I'm not."

"Girlfriend?" I searched his face, trying to understand.

"No. I don't have a girlfriend. Not anymore."

Anymore. Hmm. And he felt the need to talk about her still, which meant maybe he wasn't quite over her yet. I could tell he wanted to tell me something else, but he didn't come out with it. "Well, you're not gay. No gay guy looks at a woman the way you were looking at me all night."

He burst out laughing, looking out the window into the darkened street. "No, I'm not gay."

"Well, okay then. So what is it?" I don't know what made me press him. I just felt compelled to know the truth.

With a sigh, he shook his head, still not looking at me. "You wouldn't believe me if I told you."

"So that's the way you want to do this? Give me those eyes all night long and then go away without explaining? Look, you gonna ask me out or what?" Hands on hips, I gazed back at him, a challenge in my eyes.

He laughed again. "Ask you out? To do what exactly?"

I shrugged. "I don't know. Whatever. But you don't just do this…whatever it is…and then drop it. I know you're into me."

"Yeah," he said, turning his face to mine once more. "Yeah, I am. But it's not a good idea. Not for you, anyway."

"Well, that's my decision, isn't it?"

"Listen, I don't know what I'm doing here. I just…." He searched my face as though he'd find the answer hidden there.

"Okay, fine. I'm asking you out. Want to come back to my place?" I spoke the words, shocking myself, but not willing to back out of it or show my own surprise.

He stared, jaw dropped. "Back to your place? Uh…y-yes.

I would. But...not now."

I took a deep breath and smiled with triumph. "Okay then. When you're ready, you give me a call." I took his hand and wrote my number on his palm. His fingers were cold, almost icy. "You better put on those gloves of yours. It's cold out there."

His hand lingered there in mine for a second, and then he pulled it back as though he'd been burned. "Right. Cold. Brr. Okay. I...I gotta go. I'll call you."

Nodding, I leaned in to kiss his cheek which felt also chill to the touch.

"Night, Fin," I whispered in his ear.

"Goodnight, Sybill," he said softly as I pulled away. He gazed into my eyes for another long moment before he walked out the door.

I heard a whistle behind me, and turned to see Antony watching. "Girrrrrrl! That dude's got it BAD!"

Blushing, I threw the bar towel at him. "Mind your own business."

"Yeah, yeah," he laughed, catching the towel with a wink. "Whatever. I saw what I saw. I ain't blind. And I ain't never seen you look at nobody like that."

"You need me to help you finish cleaning up?" I said, pointedly not responding to his jibes.

"Aw naw, baby girl. You go on. Do what you do. I got this. Ain't nothin' left but moppin'." He waved me on. "I'll see you tomorrow night."

"Thanks. You're the best." Beaming, I took off my apron and went to get my coat and bag from the back.

As I headed home, my feet hardly touched the ground, and my mind practically spun with thoughts of Fin. I laughed aloud at his name all over again. "There is no way that is his real name," I muttered to myself. "No way."

Back in my apartment, I felt too wound up to sleep, so I changed and went into the second bedroom I'd turned into my art studio. Turning on my stereo, I cranked up the volume and got to work, starting on a fresh canvas.

Daddy never understood what I liked about painting or why I'd want to make that my major, but all his pushing to get me to choose something more practical — business or computing — only made me more determined than ever. Painting was my release. I could paint things I'd never dare say.

This time, I didn't stop till almost dawn, so tired I fell asleep there on the love seat in my studio, still wearing my paint-speckled clothes.

Past is Prologue

Marie Antoinette

On Fridays, I luxuriated under the covers, listening to the bird songs and the noises of the city just outside my window. The sounds reminded me life still went on, and I couldn't help but smile. Like everything in my life, it felt bittersweet. Thinking back on my past, I couldn't remember a time when there I didn't feel at least of hint of sadness in each pleasant thing. Always, there were those who would ensure joy seemed transitory.

Happiness ended. It seemed as though the universe required this knowledge as payment for allowing us to have hope.

Many vampires my age found this realization overwhelming. They sought, and found, ways to bring their

75

lives to an end. A few of them asked how I kept myself from succumbing to a similar fate. My simple answer was it wasn't my time. But this was the child's answer. In truth, I honestly did not know. I could only say I lost nearly everything that ever mattered to me at such an early stage it made me cling to what remained and strive to make the best of the situation. All that remained to be taken from me was my life, and I would be damned if anyone forced me to relinquish it.

Each sadness held an opportunity. Each loss a chance to find something new to hold on to. I learned that even as a child, before I ever became one of the immortals. I learned that lesson the hard way, and I never forgot. It served me well these long years.

Fin was still young enough to feel the pain of shrugging off his humanity. He carried it still around him like a cloak. I tried to be patient with him. I knew full well how the loss of it could smother the good within us. However, once he let go of his human-ness and embraced the self which still remained and would never fade, then he would no longer feel such anger toward me. Only the pain of growth made him so frustrated. He blamed me for stealing his humanity, but he did not yet fully understand how I had set him free. One day, he would thank me, not just for allowing him to live forever but for changing him into something infinitely more than he could ever have been.

Remembering one of the chapters in my past, before I had qualms about being caught hunting, I couldn't help smiling. Once, I was not nearly so safe around humans. I used to love playing with my food.

For Fin's sake, I all but abandoned my old ways. He made me see my recklessness, and only the fear of discovery made me tame the wildness of the creature within.

Fin returned late, and I could hear him humming to himself from my seat in the library. I didn't recognize the song, but I knew it bespoke of a change in his temperament. I sat idly stroking Pom Pom's ears, and when he entered the room, I pretended not to have noticed him, barely looking up until he sat down beside me before the fire. "You seem pleased with yourself. I trust you're in a better mood than you were earlier?"

"I am, yes." A secretive smile hung about his lips and made me curious, though I knew better than to press. Not yet, anyway.

"Does that mean you've forgiven me?" Batting my eyelashes at him, I gave him a contrite look, and I hoped, coupled with his improved mood, I could prevail upon him.

I knew he saw through me, but his eyes twinkled good-naturedly all the same as he said, "You know I can never be angry with you for long. Just promise me it won't happen again? Please?"

Throwing my arms around him with gratitude, I gave him a loud and playful kiss on the cheek, "Oh my darling. I promise. I won't go anywhere without consulting you again. Cross my wicked little heart."

Relief washed over his features, and he wrapped his arms around me then. Then I smelled it…smelled her. Beneath the scent of coffee and cigarettes I smelled a lingering perfume mixed with something definitely human. I didn't detect the scent of death or even of blood, however. That meant he hadn't fed on her, only been close to her. Raising my head to look him in the eye, I said, "Who is she?"

"Who?" He did his best to seem surprised.

"Oh come now, darling. I'm far too old for that kind of tomfoolery. The human, of course. Who is she?"

"Tomfoolery?" he snickered, then shook his head. "It's nothing."

I raised one eyebrow, looking at him nonplussed. "Men only say that when it's something."

He chuckled and kissed my forehead. "I found a place to play guitar. Some silly girl hugged me after. I assume she liked it. Simple as that."

The sweet playful smile on his face convinced me I should let it drop. I smiled and put my head back on his shoulder. "Well, you are talented. Poor thing couldn't help herself, I'm sure."

He didn't reply, but he didn't need to. We simply lay there on the sofa for a while in silence, arms entwined, just enjoying the closeness between us, watching the fireplace flicker. It had been years since we were lovers, but we were both the only family the other had, and the bond between us ran deep. I played with his fingers, he stroked my hair, and when at last the time came to go upstairs to rest, I went smiling to my room, content and glad at last we were back to the way things ought to be between us.

Getting to Know Me

Fin

We were walking hand-in-hand together, Marie and I, through a clearing in a pine forest. I could see mountains in the distance, and I recognized the place from a childhood family vacation – The Grand Tetons.

The sun beamed down on us, warming our skin, and she gave me a tender, almost childlike smile. "I understand, you know," she said, and I couldn't remember what we'd been talking about earlier. I swallowed hard to give me time to think, not sure how to reply, looking off into the distance toward the view and squinting. "Oh silly, of course I understand. It's time. I don't know why I didn't see it before."

"Time?" Turning my head back to face her, I puzzled over her meaning. "Time for what?"

With a tinkling laugh like a girl, she hid her mouth with her hand delicately, giggling at me. "My poor dear boy. You know exactly what I mean."

My forehead furrowed, and I let go of her hand, embarrassed and annoyed. "No, I really don't. Pretend I'm stupid and tell me, why don't you? You know I don't like your games."

"Oh my darling," she relented, reaching out gently to touch my cheek. "Time for you to leave me, of course."

Startled, I jerked back, blinking with denial, yet inside, I knew she was right. In a pained whisper, I choked, "I could never leave you."

At that moment, a rumbling began beneath our feet. Trees began swaying, though I felt no wind. I took hold of her, knowing I could not protect her from a possible earthquake. Then came a terrible roar and a lurch, and beyond the mountains I saw a plume of fire and smoke rising with a fury.

"He's coming!" she squeaked in terror against my chest.

"Who?" I asked, fighting my rising panic.

But before I could ask her who she meant, we were consumed in flame.

I jerked awake, sitting upright in a panic. The dream had already faded, but I knew something...no...some*one* terrible was coming. And I knew one more thing. Marie expected me to leave her.

Wondering whether the easy acceptance I'd felt from her in the dream was a reflection of her true reaction or if was it simply wishful thinking, my brain seeking permission and forgiveness, I felt disturbed and anxious. I had to see Sybill. I had to find a way to tell her the truth before Marie found her first.

A glance at the clock told me it was still early, for my kind, anyway. The coffee shop would still be open for a few more hours, and I hoped Sybill would be there. Again, I heard Marie's voice in my mind. *It's time.*

Filled with a sense of urgency as though I were already late, wanting desperately to leave the house before Marie awoke, I threw back the covers and got up, not bothering with a shower but simply throwing on a sweater and jeans, lacing up my boots, then running my fingers through my hair to brush it out of my eyes. Grabbing my glasses from the nightstand, I pushed them up my nose, then took my messenger bag with me as I hurried out of the room and down the stairs two at a time. As I yanked on my coat, I paused for a moment to look at my reflection in the hall mirror. My face looked haunted, unshaven, and my sunken eyes reminded me of my hunger. It had been too long since my last feed. For a split second, I envisioned sinking my fangs into Sybill's sweet pale neck, and my stomach gave a lurch that snapped me out of it. No. Not her. I'd never do that to her.

Shaking off the image, I turned back to the kitchen and opened the refrigerator. Bags of fresh blood filled the shelves. I took one, bit in, and drained it quickly. Though it was still cold and made my nose wrinkle with distaste, I swallowed the blood down just the same. It would keep the hunger at bay, and that was all I needed. I tossed the bag into the garbage.

Then, licking my lips, I left the house as quickly and quietly as I could manage, shutting the door with a soft click before running toward the crosswalk at Kingshighway. Pulling up my hood, I hitched my messenger bag up on my shoulder, hoping I wasn't too late to catch Sybill before she went home for the night.

Traffic made me impatient. Every car in my path became a delay. I had to see her. I forgot to pretend to feel the cold, leaving my coat open as I ran, gloveless, scarf-less, not caring as humans stared openly at me.

I only stopped when I arrived at the coffee shop. That's when I sensed how strange I must seem to the people who passed me on the street. I'd run for blocks and blocks, but I wasn't even breathing hard. In fact, I wasn't breathing. I'd forgotten to pretend that too. Snow swirled in whirling eddies, but none of it melted on me at all. A live person would have had steam rising from exposed skin because of the exertion. If I could have blushed, I would have. Instead, I ducked around the corner, buttoned my coat, stuffed my hands down into my pockets, then raised my shoulders as though huddling inside my collar from the winter chill. I shook my head to scatter the snowflakes, then hurried into the coffee shop, stamping my feet on the mat by the door and making a show of shuddering.

She stood near the windows, bussing tables. Must be a slow night, I guessed, so she kept busy by cleaning. I sniffed and she looked up, and the smile of recognition on her face lit up the room.

"Well, hey there, stranger," she teased. "What brings you out so late?"

I grinned back at her. "You."

She blushed then, and only the presence of the other humans in the room kept me from scooping her up in my arms at that moment. She looked so lovely, I wanted to hold her forever, to kiss her, to taste her...no. Not that. The smile faded from my lips, and I looked away. "Sorry," I muttered.

"Don't be," she said softly, stepping in close, reaching out to touch my arm. I could feel the heat from her body through my clothes.

"I shouldn't bother you while you're working. You're busy." I couldn't bring myself to look at her, fearful my desire would be naked in my expression. I worried my fangs would show despite my best effort to hide them. I wasn't ready for her to see the monster in me. Not yet.

"Pssh," she laughed. "That's a laugh. We've had five people in here all night, including you. I'm just about to pack it in. They can close without me. Want to get out of here?"

The question made me look up in spite of all my fears. "Yes," I said, not thinking as the words came tumbling out of my mouth. "More than anything."

Her bright blue eyes opened wide with surprise for a moment, and she bit her lip smiling at my reply before answering. "I'll be just a minute then."

I stood there on the wet doormat, watching as she went to collect her tips and put away her apron. She whispered something to her coworker, then disappeared behind the employee door for a moment. When she came back, she had on her coat and hat, her purse slung crosswise over her chest.

Pulling on her gloves, she looked up into my eyes. "Let's go. Lead on, MacDuff."

"Lay on," I corrected, opening the door for her.

"Huh?" She raised an eyebrow at me as she stepped out onto the sidewalk.

The door closed behind us, and I laughed softly. "Never mind. How do you feel about a walk?"

"You don't have a hat or anything," she said. "Aren't you going to freeze?"

I shook my head. "I'm all right. It feels good to me."

"Okay then," she shrugged. "Walk it is."

She took my arm, placing her hand in the crook of my elbow, and I thought I might die of happiness right then and there. Though I'd come with every intention of telling her all about me, now I had her at my side, I couldn't think how to begin the conversation, and I started strolling toward the park, my mind an utter blank.

"So…how's things?" she said after we'd walked a block and a half in awkward silence.

"Fine. Good. How about you?" Distracted, I stared at the falling snowflakes as they fluttered down in the glow of the streetlights.

"Mmm. So we're going to have one of those conversations. I get it. Okay. Well, this is where I say I'm great, thanks." I could hear the slight annoyance in her voice. "Now we've got that out of the way, how about you tell me what you really wanted to say."

"I…I don't know what you're talking about."

"Oh yes, you do, Mister Cryptic." I looked over and saw her roll her eyes. "You didn't walk all this way in the snow at this time of night just to talk small talk. So why don't you just spit it out and be done with it?"

We crossed the street as the light blinked caution, hurrying our steps until we reached the curb. "I don't know how to say it." I blurted.

"Well, how about just straight up, no chaser, huh? Just say whatever it is. What's the worst that can happen?"

I laughed at her bluntness. "First there's the screaming, then the running…"

She laughed too, not realizing I was serious. "I promise not to do either one. Scout's honor."

"Since when were you a girl scout?" I smirked, teasing her, starting to relax a little.

"Oh, you don't know. I made a really cute Brownie. Had the uniform and everything. Lasted all of about six months until they made us sell cookies. I sucked at that and quit."

Chuckling, I looked down at her, "I'd have bought your cookies."

"Subtle, mister," she grinned. "Very subtle."

"That's just the kind of guy I am." We crossed another street, and I realized without meaning to, I'd walked toward the house. My house. The one I shared with Marie. I couldn't take her there. Could I?

"Right. So where are we going, anyway? Or are we just wandering aimlessly? Not that I'm complaining, of course, but it is chilly." I looked down and saw her shivering.

I hesitated. Marie would have gone to the shop by now to go over the books. "I…would you like to see where I live?" Nervously, I stammered on, looking down, "I'm not…I mean it's warm there, is all. We don't have to, if you don't want."

Her smile reached her voice as she said, "I'd like that."

"I promise, I'm not going to try anything," I babbled.

"Well, that's a disappointment." Her laugh was warm, and I looked over at her with relief.

"It's this way," I whispered, pointing across the street.

"You live in Westmoreland Place?" she said, her eyes full of surprise.

I simply shrugged and nodded sheepishly, crossing as the light changed.

"Huh. You're full of surprises," she blinked. "How come you never told me you were rich?"

My eyes slipped sideways to meet hers. "You're not the only one with secrets, you know."

I saw her defenses rise once more, and she looked up at the gates as I unlocked them and we passed through. "I don't have secrets."

"Right." I laughed. "Neither do I."

The shady street hid us from view of the traffic and blocked some of the noise. Our footfalls through the deepening snow were the only tracks we could see. We didn't say anything more as we walked, and soon we stood in front of the house. Number 16. "This is it." I whispered.

"You live here?" I could sense her awe as she spoke. "Wow."

I tried to laugh it off, heading toward the front door, but I knew the affect the house could have. "You get used to it."

"I don't know if I'd ever get used to this."

"You'd be surprised what you can get used to," I said, turning the key in the lock and opening the door for her. "Ladies first."

She stomped her feet on the porch before walking in, and I followed, shutting the door behind us. It echoed with the emptiness of the tomb. Her gaze traveled up and up and up as she looked around the room. "This place is enormous."

"I guess so." I took her coat and hung it in the closet beside mine. We both stepped out of our wet boots and left them to dry on the rug by the door. "Come on. I'll show you my favorite room."

Taking her hand in mine, I pulled her down the hall and into the library. She gasped in the doorway just like I knew she would, and I smiled, letting her stop and take it all in before leading her on inside. "This is…wow."

Outside the windows, the snow still fell, and I realized the house must feel cold for her. "Have a seat," I said, gesturing to the leather sofa on our right. "I'll light the fireplace. It'll just take a second."

Marie had converted the fireplaces to gas when she bought the place. She didn't trust wood burning fireplaces. Too dangerous, she said. She did like the appearance of a fireplace, however. She'd bought the most expensive and realistic gas hearth set she could find, and the switches were conveniently hidden. I turned them on, and the fire blazed into life, casting a golden glow over everything in the room, including Sybill and me.

As I turned back around, her fragile beauty struck me. She was so alive.

She folded herself there on the end of the sofa, legs tucked up under her like a little bird. I couldn't take my eyes off her as I sat at the other end, smiling at her with awkward admiration.

"Well…I'm here. So…what did you want to talk to me about?" She looked at me with expectation and hope, and I gathered myself before I could reply.

"Promise you won't run away screaming?" I said.

"We've been over that." She smiled. "Just tell me."

I shrugged then, giving her a sheepish grin. "Okay. But remember, you asked for it." I took a deep, unnecessary breath, my nervousness making me feel almost human again. "I…I'm not who you think I am."

"Uh…okay. I don't know what that means, but I kind of figured out you gave me a fake name." Her head tilted to the side as she looked at me with curiosity.

Nodding, I clasped my hands on my lap. "I can't tell you my real name. Not now, anyway. Maybe someday, but not now. It's not safe."

"For you?" she said.

"Or for you," I said. "It's dangerous for both of us."

"Why? Who's after you?"

"I…I can't tell you." I looked at her earnestly, hoping she would see the truth in my eyes.

"Are you in witness protection or something?" The look on her face told me she wanted to believe me, no matter what I said.

I shook my head, looking toward the flames. "No. Nothing like that. Well, not exactly like that. There are…people…looking for me. I can't explain any more. Not right now."

"What do they want?" The worry I heard in her question broke my heart.

"Honestly, I am not sure. But I had to leave everything, my home, my family, my friends, and my name. I can't ever go back to my old life. It's over. I'm not the man I used to be. Not anymore." Until I said it aloud to her, I hadn't realized how much it still hurt.

Her hand stretched out to touch my knee gently, and I looked down at it in surprise as she spoke. "I want to help you."

"You can't." I whispered. "I made my choice a long time ago. It's done."

She pulled back and looked around the room before speaking again. "You don't live here alone, do you?"

"I wouldn't call what I do here living, but no. Someone else is here too." I looked back at the fire for several moments before I could gather myself to face her. "She's not my wife or girlfriend or anything, if that's what you think. It's not like that."

"You telling me you live with your mother?" Her eyebrow rose dubiously, and I couldn't help but laugh at her question.

"In a way, sort of. I guess." I shrugged, giving a sigh.

"I see," she nodded, and her voice held a supposition I didn't quite understand. "So, let me get this straight. You've got some kind of Mrs. Robinson type who took you in, gave you a safe place, and now you're feeling like you don't need her anymore. Is that it?"

I laughed then, shocked. "Um…wow. You don't pull any punches, do you?"

"I call 'em like I see 'em," she said, shrugging her shoulders. "Big house. Fancy furniture from France. And you dress like a poor college student. Only thing that makes sense. I'm guessing you just don't know how to leave after she's given you so much. Is that about right?"

Suddenly, I felt defensive, as though she judged me, "Why did you want me to tell you everything again? Seems like you've got it all figured out on your own."

"Oh, now don't be sulky. You were begging to say it. You came all the way down there to find me so you could tell me. And by the way, you haven't told me I'm wrong yet." I heard a hint of tension and sarcasm in her voice. Maybe even jealousy.

"You're not wrong. She is older. And yes, I was her…lover. For a while. But she's the one who got tired of me, not the other way around. She's like that. I do still need her, just…not the way I used to. I loved her." The word tumbled out of me before I could stop them. "She's impossible not to love. You'd love her if you ever met her. Which, by the way, is a bad idea, so don't even think about it."

"Why? Is she jealous or something? Think she'll rip my head off," she snapped.

"That's exactly what I think. Yes." I said honestly. "I wouldn't be surprised one bit."

"Hmm. Now I'm curious." Her eyes narrowed in a way that made me nervous.

"Don't be. Please. I'm telling you, it will be bad. Very bad." I pleaded, hoping she would listen.

She sniffed disapprovingly. "Bad for who? For you? Because that whole 'being the other woman' thing isn't really me. Just so you know."

"I'd never ask that of you," I said. "And no. Bad for you. She wouldn't let it go. Not ever. I don't care what she does to me, but I care very much what she does to you."

Her eyes rolled again. "Then what the hell did you bring me here for, huh? You want me, but you don't. You want to leave her, but you can't. You need to tell me everything, but it's not safe. Look, maybe I should just go. I didn't come here to listen to you be all angsty and weird. I thought...I thought maybe, just maybe, you were going to tell me how you feel. Instead, you're giving me more of the runaround."

She got up to go, and I caught her hand in mine to stop her. "I did want to tell you how I feel."

"Oh? Then what happened?" Her body tensed, and I knew things between us were standing on a tipping point. Whatever I said next would determine the way we would be with each other from then on.

"Then I realized how much I...I love you, Sybill. Or at least, I could. Not like they tell you it is in movies, but the real deal, you know? It scares the hell out of me. I'm not good enough for you. I'm not what you think. Once you know everything, you'll probably walk out and never see me again. I don't know what it might do to you if I decide to be with you...if you decide to say yes. I'm terrified because I can't help myself."

Her jaw clenched, and she stared at me without speaking for several moments. I thought she might hit me.

"Say something," I begged. "Tell me to go to hell. Something."

"Just shut up, Fin. Whatever your name is. Shut up." She leaned forward then and kissed me fiercely, taking my face in her hands. Her kiss stunned me at first, but then my body took over, and I pulled her to me, kissing back with an urgency that ached. She straddled my lap, knees on either side of me, and she pushed me back against the sofa, her body pressed against mine, soft in all the right places. Her lips felt warm, and so did her tongue. My hands found her hips and the small of her back, and the weight of her body felt like heaven to me. Though I'd never expected this kiss to truly happen, now I never wanted this moment to end.

Our lips parted finally because she needed to come up for air. She looked down at me, panting. "Well, that was worth the wait."

I chuckled, still holding her hips in both hands, not wanting to let go.

"Good to know. I'd hate to think I'd lost my touch."

"Oh, you've got the touch all right."

She smiled seductively at me, then winked before reaching down between us and making me gasp. My eyes fluttered closed, and I felt the prick of my fangs.

That made me put a stop to things immediately. Pressing my lips together, I pushed her back and slid her over onto the sofa, then stood, looking away. "I should get you back."

She gave an exasperated sigh and slumped in defeat. "I don't get you. I really don't. Are you sure you even want me at all?"

92

"That kiss didn't convince you?" I said. "Because I thought my feelings were pretty damn clear."

"Okay fine. Then what is it? I don't understand." She paused as though puzzling something out, and then a look of shock came over her. She covered her mouth with her hands as she went on. "You have AIDS, don't you? Oh god. That's it. You're dying, and you can't figure out how to say so."

I burst out laughing, though her guess was closer than she realized. "No, I don't have AIDS! I can assure you I'm definitely not dying for a very long time. For god's sake, I'm trying to be a gentleman. Is that so wrong?"

"Wrong?" Her face scrunched up as she looked at me. "No. I'm just not...used to that, I guess."

I could see she didn't quite buy it. She knew I held something back. With fingers outstretched, I brushed her cheek tenderly. "I'm just trying not to rush things. We hardly know one another. I don't want to mess this up."

Still, I saw doubt in her eyes, but she didn't press the issue further. "Hmm. Well, I guess that is true. I haven't exactly told you much about me, have I?"

"No, you haven't. Then again, I didn't really ask either." I shook my head. "Tell you what. Why don't I walk you back, and you can tell me whatever you want me to know? Then we'll be even."

She got up from the sofa with a smirk, mollified. "You worried she's going to find me here?"

"Not really," I lied, switching off the fireplace and walking with her back to the foyer, "though it would probably be best if she doesn't all the same."

As we put on our boots and then I helped Sybill put on her coat, I imagined the expression on Marie's face if she were to walk in on us at that moment. The mental image made me move a little faster to button up my own coat and hurry us out the door, this time remembering to grab a hat, scarf, and gloves so I looked properly bundled against the cold.

"So," I began, our feet crunching in the snow, "what do you do when you're not serving coffee to weird guys with glasses?"

Just as I hoped, she laughed, looping her arm in mine again. "Well, I'm an art student at Wash U, which my dad hates."

"Why would he hate that you're creative?" My own parents had encouraged creativity in all of us, myself included, so the thought her father wouldn't appreciate her abilities didn't make sense to me.

Her breath hung like smoke in the air as she spoke, "Because it's not computers. Or accounting. That's what he always wanted."

"But if you're not good at it…."

"Oh, but I am," she said. "I'm good at both of those. I just…I know why he wants me to do them, and I refuse. I won't be who he wants. I just won't."

"Does that mean you're being an artist just to spite him?" We stopped at the gate on Kingshighway, and I looked down at her, puzzled.

"Whose side are you on, anyway?" she laughed, poking me playfully in the shoulder with a gloved finger.

I raised both hands in surrender, ducking back behind them. "Ow! Yours! I'm on your side! Stop that!"

"Ha! Darn right!" She nodded, and then we walked on through the gate to wait for the light at the crosswalk. "Anyway, I like it. Art, I mean. I think I'm good at it. It's more... challenging, I guess. Math and computer programming always came easy for me. I can just do it. Like breathing. I might get frustrated with my work sometimes, but afterwards, I feel like I've learned something and become stronger."

"Hmm. Math always seemed like kind of a puzzle for me." I shrugged. "Weird since I'm good at music, huh?"

The light changed, and we began walking again. "You're all right, I guess," she teased.

"Well, good enough for coffee shops, anyway." I smiled at her jibes. It made me feel good she felt so comfortable around me. That she trusted me enough to laugh at me and know I wouldn't take offense. "So what is it you were afraid your dad would want you to do?"

She sat quietly for a few moments, and I thought maybe I'd asked the wrong question. Finally, with a sigh, she stopped in the middle of the sidewalk, still looking away, and whispered, "Swear to me you're not from the feds, just pumping me for information."

Her face turned up to mine in the half-light of street lamps, searching my eyes with sudden anger, and I blinked at her in confusion. "The feds? What are you talking about?"

Glaring and growling, her eyes narrowed, and she stepped forward until we were almost nose-to-nose. "Look, you won't tell me your real name. You won't tell me who you are or what you're doing here. You show up at my work and come at me like a goddamned heat-seeking missile. You're a total fucking enigma designed to charm the pants off me, but you won't have sex with me when you have the chance. Now you're taking me for a goddamned walk in the most non-walking friendly time and place possible, nonchalantly asking me about my friggin' dad like people do this all the fucking time. I just put all those things together in my head and realized I almost trusted you enough to tell you something I shouldn't. So yeah. Swear to me. You better make it good because I'm about five seconds away from either beating the shit out of you or screaming 'rape' at the top of my lungs. You get me? Swear! Or I swear to fucking god, I will make you sorry you ever saw me."

My eyes went wide with shock. "Jesus! What the hell, Sybill? We were just talking!"

"Talking, my ass! You're trying to get dirt on my dad! Man, you must think you are such a great actor, huh? Almost had me fooled, you fucking bloodsucker!"

Stunned, I gaped as she unwittingly spoke the truth, staring open-mouthed as she went on. "Aren't you going to say anything? Go on. Tell me why I'm wrong."

My mind reeled. "Sybill...I..." But I couldn't think of what to say, I felt so shocked.

"I...?" She stared for a moment, waiting, but when I said nothing else, her eyes narrowed as she stepped back. "Right. Well, guess what? You won't get anything from me! Go back to wiretapping. We're done here."

She turned on her heel then and started stomping away as fast as she could through the deepening snow.

For a moment, I stood there alone in silence, confused and hurt beyond anything I could have imagined. Her retreating figure radiated wreaths of steam from her breath, and I watched as she slipped around a corner toward her apartment. I gasped as my stomach gave a lurch. I knew then I couldn't live without her. "Sybill!" I called. "Sybill wait!"

I ran after her desperately, but she had already gone into her building by the time I caught up. I shook the door handles futilely, and watched on as she got into the elevator and disappeared from view. "Sybill!" I screamed, but she couldn't hear me anymore.

My eyes scanned up the building, and for an insane moment I wondered if I could scale up to her balcony. Of course, I could, but it would reveal my true nature to her, and that would only make things much worse.

As I walked dejectedly back home, I went back over our conversation trying to understand what made everything go so wrong. I finally decided whatever she hid for her father had to be the reason she always seemed on edge. She might want to defy him, but she'd fight to the death to defend him. Her loyalty made her even more appealing to me. It made me love her all the more to know she could care so deeply and selflessly for someone. If I could only convince her I didn't pose a threat to her father, I thought, then maybe, just maybe, one day she could love me that fiercely.

Who is this Masked Man Anyway?

Sybill

W hat in the hell was I thinking? I was so furious with myself. I said so much more than way too much. Nothing that could be used in court, but definitely more than enough to justify an ongoing investigation. God! I thought him so different! I stormed away from him, leaving him standing alone and miserable on the sidewalk.

But as soon as I stepped inside my building, I began to have second thoughts. When I stepped into the elevator and remembered his stricken face, I realized my pride was all that kept me from changing my mind and rushing out to him.

The devastated shock I saw there made me bite my lip to hold myself back, and I kept hearing his voice calling my name.

I knew I acted like an ass. But knowing something and admitting it are two different things.

Back in my apartment, I went to my studio intending to paint, but I couldn't concentrate. I kept thinking over that kiss. He had meant it. I could still feel his lips on mine, taste him on my tongue, feel his hands as he pulled me to him. He couldn't fake the passion behind our embrace.

He'd been so cold. His lips. His hands. I remembered how he'd walked all the way to the coffee shop without a hat or gloves, just to see me. I blushed with a twinge of guilt. He felt so driven to see me, he had not even thought about it. I'd been foolish. He might have something to hide, but an undercover agent? No. I don't know what had made me make such an awful accusation. Maybe I just felt angry because he clearly had secrets. I didn't like knowing he still lived with a woman he used to date. Just thinking of another woman with him made me angry. It sounded like she must have been holding something over him in order to make him stay.

Still, knowing that didn't make me feel any better. I will never be someone's dirty little secret.

Funny how it didn't really bother me not to know the truth about his past nearly so much as I hated he couldn't or wouldn't tell her the truth about me.

That's when it hit me. I'd fallen for this man whose name and history I didn't even know. Far from feeling just a passing flirtation, I had real, strong attraction to him. In spite of all he'd told and not told me, I felt drawn to him. I knew then I had to find him and explain how I felt. Tell him I'd been wrong. Swallowing my pride might take everything I had, but I couldn't help myself. I wanted…no, I needed him. He had to be mine. Simple as that. Nothing else mattered. Not pride. Certainly not the "other woman."

I wanted to throw my coat over my painting clothes and run back out in the snow to his house, call his name outside the windows like some silly romantic movie. I didn't even like those movies, yet here I was, sappy and aching for him in a way I'd never been for anyone else. Then I remembered his face. How much hurt I'd seen there.

However, as much as I wanted to, I couldn't make myself go to him at three in the morning, I told myself. He would think I'd gone crazy. Plus, what if "she" was there? I didn't want to make things even more complicated. No. I would wait until a sane hour. I cursed myself for not having gotten a phone number from him. I'd have to wait and see if he came to the coffee shop. If he didn't, well, then I'd go over there and risk coming face-to-face with her, the woman he hid me from. I'd apologize, and then...well, I didn't know afterward. I only knew I had to do it.

Thinking over everything between us, I walked to the sliding doors to the balcony and looked out on the still falling snow. For a fleeting second, I wished I'd see him standing below like Romeo, gazing up to catch a glimpse of me. Silly childish notions. I thought those sorts of ideas were long ago purged from my cynical soul. Then again, maybe I didn't feel so cynical as I liked to let people think. Deep inside, in spite of what

I might say and do to the contrary, I was still the little girl who wanted the fairy tale with a handsome prince to come whisk her away from it all. Chuckling at myself, I stepped away from the window once more, shaking my head at how ridiculous my friends would find me. The only kind of "princess" I was didn't come with a crown.

That night when I finally went to bed, I kept running over in my mind what I would tell him, trying out different ways to say, "Forgive me." None of them satisfied, and I woke feeling exhausted and wrung out emotionally.

The alarm blared far too early for my taste, but I got up groaning anyway. I stood in the shower for a long while, trying to wake up and prepare to face the day. Taking my time, I made myself look fierce, my eyes smoky and seductive. I'd go to see him, determined to be strong and confident even as I made an apology.

Just as I poured a dash of soy milk into my first cup of coffee, my phone buzzed, and the girly part of me leapt up, my heart pounding, hoping desperately to hear Fin on the other end.

No such luck. The screen read "Daddy." With a disappointed sigh, I answered. "Hey, Daddy. I'm just heading out. What's up?"

"Your mother tells me you're not coming over to the house to have cake. Is that right?" Nothing like getting to the point. His booming voice made me jump each time. He wasn't yelling. He always spoke loudly, and he nearly always got what he wanted as a result.

"Daddy…" I started. "I've got a lot going on, that's all."

"So much you can't tell your old man Happy Birthday?" He didn't whine, but he may as well have.

"Daddy, you know I've got classes. Plus, I have to work." I winced, knowing how lame that sounded.

"Work." He said it just like that. Simply and dismissively. "At that coffee joint. Ain't they got nobody else workin' there but you? Your cousin Artie, he's comin' to town special, all the way from Chicago. You live what, ten minutes away? You can't take an hour out of your busy schedule for the party? I thought I raised you better."

I knew then he wouldn't let it go. I'd get the full-on, no-holds-barred, guilt-trip-o-rama. I sighed, but Daddy knew he'd gotten under my skin.

"You know, one day, I'm gonna die, just like everybody else. You ought to show some respect now before I'm in the grave." I could hear him pacing over the phone, and I pictured him in his wood paneled office, treading the oriental carpet down.

Rolling my eyes, I relented. "Okay, Daddy. I'll ask. I can't promise, but I will try."

"That's my girl." His chair squeaked over the phone, and I knew he'd stopped pacing, sitting back down in satisfaction. "How's things going, princess? You need money?"

"No, Daddy," I said with a shake of my head. "I'm doing just fine. Thank you."

"It's no problem. I'd do anything for you, princess. You know that. These coffee shop bozos treatin' you good? They pay you like they should? I could talk to 'em if they ain't."

Oh lord. That's just what I needed. My dad, the mafia don, calling my bosses and telling them how to treat his baby girl. "They're great, Daddy. I love my job. Really. You don't have to worry."

"Good. That's good. Okay then. Well…you be safe, okay? Watch out for yourself."

I couldn't help but laugh. "Oh, Daddy. I know you've got someone watching out for me all the time. I'm staying out of trouble."

"Hey, I got to keep an eye out for you, don't I? What kind of father would I be if I didn't?" It warmed my heart to hear him say so. I could hear his smile over the phone. "I love you, princess."

Smiling, I said softly, "I love you too, Daddy. I gotta go. I'll call you later."

"All right. You just let me know when, and I'll send Bobby to pick you up."

"Oh god, Daddy." I moaned.

"What? Bobby's a good driver. He only had that one accident on I-44, and that wasn't his fault." He paused, and I heard the chair squeak again. "Wait did Bobby do somethin' to you? Say something? You just tell me. I'll have a talk with him."

His words made me panic. "No! Daddy, no! Bobby's perfectly nice! I just don't need you to send someone to come get me, that's all. I can take a cab."

"Pssh. It's on his way. Forget about it."

I couldn't help but laugh. Could he be any more cliché? Then again, there every cliché had a grain of truth, didn't it? "Okay, Daddy. I'll let you know. Now, I really have to go."

"Okay. I'll see you later." He hung up. Daddy always had to have the last word.

I sighed deeply. Conversations with my father always wore me out. I should have known I'd never win against him on the birthday thing. Family was sacred to him. I remembered him telling me time after time, "Blood takes care of blood. Always, baby girl. Never forget it."

Truly, I had an hour before I had to get to class, but I packed up anyway and left early. The city had done its job to clean the streets, and now the white clean blankets of snow that had covered everything the night before were shoved to the gutters, grayed with salt and dirt. The slate gray sky made me glad I'd bundled up tightly.

My art class helped me center myself. I looked forward to each one. The professor played classical music, Bach and Mozart and Vivaldi, and we worked on our projects without much talk. He simply came around to observe and make comments on our technique. I felt so grateful that day. I couldn't have handled a lecture class after the conversation with my father. I still had several more days before my current project would be complete, but it was coming along nicely, and I lost myself for a while in the motion of the brush, the sensuousness of the colors. All my other worries fell away, leaving just me and the canvas. When at last the professor said, "Time's up" and turned off the music, I felt surprised to see it was growing dark outside already. Relaxed, I put away my materials and gathered my things before heading off to work.

That night, I determined, I would resolve the situation with Fin. I had made up my mind. Once I made a decision, like my daddy, I'd be determined and see things through, no matter what. One way or another, Fin and I were going to be together.

THE DEVIL'S IN THE DETAILS

Chief Inspector

I led my investigative team into a New York hotel. I gave the clerk a smile and caught his eye. Quickly and without any fuss or discussion, he gave me complete access to the computer area. I knew the date we were looking for, and it didn't take long before I narrowed down the rooms we would need to search to ten. A woman staying alone for one night.

My team scoured the security footage to find a female who fit the fugitive's description, narrowing it down again to three of the rooms from that night. Reviewing the notes from the cleaning service, a maid found one of those rooms the next day with bedding missing.

"We've got her," I said, a smile crossing my lips. I turned to whisper something to the clerk, and he handed over the key-card gladly, smiling benignly and telling us each to "have a nice night" as we walked away. He then began humming tunelessly to himself, forgetting completely we'd even been there, tapping his fingers on the counter with boredom at such an uneventful evening.

Upstairs, we scoured the room for any trace evidence. The fugitive had been thorough. There would be no DNA to gather from the bedding or fingerprints from the furniture in the room. No, I knew she'd been careful, and the cleaning service had taken care of any such evidence she might have missed. However, I knew I had another chance. One the suspect had perhaps overlooked.

In the notes written by the maid, she'd indicated fresh towels had been placed in the room and wet ones were removed. That meant the suspect had taken a shower.

My team removed the cover on the shower drain and fished it, pulling out hair trapped in the pipe. The hairs were placed in a test tube and then into an evidence bag before replacing the drain cover. I had reason to be happy indeed as we exited the room.

Back in the lab, the individual hairs were teased apart to separate them, then tested for DNA and compared against a known sample from the suspect. In her human life, the fugitive had been careless, giving out locks of her hair as gifts to nobility who visited court as signs of her favor. The testing took time, but at last one hair, golden and long, proved a match with the sample. A pleased lab worker came to my office to give me the news personally.

Sitting behind my desk, I heard the results and thanked the lab workers for their efforts, promising a reward. As soon as the door shut and left me alone in my office once more, I allowed myself a gleeful little dance in my chair. "Yes! I knew it!"

Excitement filling me, I quickly called The Master, knowing I would have pleased him well.

His voice on the other end answered, and I could not contain my joy as I said, "We have definitely found her, sir. She is alive."

I listened carefully, then nodded emphatically, "Yes, sir. We are certain. There is absolutely no doubt. DNA does not lie."

Making notes, I waited while he spoke, then said, "My people are already narrowing down the search for her destination city. It won't take long now, sir."

He said something more, and I smiled. "Yes, sir. This day has been a long time coming. We will have her in custody soon, I assure you. I will contact you as soon as we know the exact location."

I liked what he said next. My leadership pleased him. Filled with pride, I said, "Thank you, sir. Yes, sir. It is a pleasure to serve, sir."

When I heard a click on the other end of the line, I hung up, still full of confidence and self-satisfaction. I allowed myself a few moments to cherish my success before I at last rose to call the team into a meeting. The Master had given us orders, and I took those instructions seriously, just as I expected them all to do.

We would find her. The Widow Capet. Madame le Deficit. Marie Antoinette. The fugitive queen. She would face the judgment of The Master at last.

Map of the Human Heart

Fin

I had known inevitably Marie would smell Sybill on me. I suppose I should have anticipated the reaction she gave.

Leaning in close, she sniffed then wrinkled her nose. "You reek of human. The same human, in fact." Her forehead turned down in a frown. "Yet you have not tasted her. I smell none of her blood on you at all. What is this? Twice in one week, the same female? I taught you to glamour. Convince her to leave you alone. It's disgusting, that smell."

My jaw dropped open, offended by her tone. Sybill smelled heavenly. "You giving me an order, my queen?" I hoped she heard the sarcasm dripping from my lips.

Her head snapped back at me and she glared. "Do not be impertinent, darling boy. It does not suit you. You heard me. I do not wish to smell that scent again."

I had never seen her so angry. If it were possible, her face seemed even more pale than ever, as though the fury she felt stole all the blood she'd drunk for the last few days. Still, I stood my ground. I had expected a fight. I had not expected to be ordered about like a dog. In the coldest voice possible, I leveled my gaze right back at her, and said an emphatic, "No."

She blinked several times as though I'd slapped her. "I beg your pardon?"

"You heard me. I said no, and I mean it. I won't." I braced myself, planting my feet solidly in preparation for attack. "You have no right to make demands like that."

"I have every right!" Her nostrils flared. "I am your maker, and I am telling you to get rid of her! You will do it! You will do it tonight!"

Shaking my head, I stood my ground. "I won't. She is my friend. You've taken everything else from me. You cannot have her."

Eyes narrowing, she gnashed her teeth. "You are a fool. Humans cannot be our friends. They are food. They are useful. They can be pets, even. But friends, never. I can smell her on your skin. On your lips. You are mad if you think you can ever have anything with her."

"Well, then if this is madness, commit me."

Her tongue clicked. "You love her."

Even through my anger, her statement startled me. "I…I care for her. There is nothing wrong with that."

"There are a million things wrong with that. It's sick. You can bring her nothing but death. You know this. If you…care for this…human, then you will tell her it's over. For her sake, if not for yours and mine."

"How does my having her in my life affect you?" I knew this question would hurt her, but I didn't care anymore.

I had expected her to cry. To gasp in shock. I did not expect her to answer so calmly and seriously. "Because she will know our secrets, and humans can be glamoured. Our enemies will find her eventually, and then they will find us. Is that not reason enough? Now, do as I say. End it."

Knowing she was right and being willing to admit it were two different things. I stared at her, clenching my jaw, considering my reply before I said at last, "So what if I do love her? What if I chose to make her one of us? What then?"

She scoffed, rolling her eyes at me. "Oh please. This is an infatuation. You and I both know that. If you simply must, then fine. Take her to bed. Get her out of your system. But mind you, do it quickly. Then glamour her and let that be the end of it, for all our sakes. For hers too. You know what they will do to her to get to us. You don't want that on your conscience."

"No." I sighed. "I do not."

"Darling, the sooner you take care of this, the sooner we can get on with our lives."

I practically sobbed as I said, "This isn't living."

That hurt her deeply. This time, her eyes did tear up. "I have given you everything. Everything."

"I never wanted it! This never-ending emptiness, day after day. I can't stand it!" My voice cracked with pain.

This time, she did gasp. I knew I'd cut her deeply then. "How can you say such a thing?"

Shaking, I said, "You did this to me. You can't keep me your captive forever. I am so lonely. It's just you and me. I've lost everything. All because of you. I...I loved you so much. But you don't love me. You love your things. All your little collections from the past. You never loved me. You just needed me. But need isn't love, Marie. It isn't. I need to be loved by someone who loves me back."

Blood tears spilled down her cheeks as I spoke, and then she whispered, "I have always loved you."

I shook my head. "No. You loved the idea of me. You loved what I did for you. But not me."

She stepped forward and reached out a hand to touch my face. "I admit I do not feel what a lover feels for you. You are right. But that never lasts, my darling. You are so young. You don't know. You are still full of the fire of passion, but that fire will turn to ash. It always does. But if we are lucky, when the fire dies down, there is still love. A long lasting love. I love you as a mother does a child. I love you as a brother. You are a part of me. We share the blood, you and me. That can never be broken. You will always be mine, as I will always be yours. Not romantic, but more than that. It's a love that is forever."

Throwing my arms around her, I held her close and cried. I cried for the life I'd lost. For the love I'd had that faded. For my innocence now gone. For the truth in what she'd said. I did love her. But as a son loves his mother. As a sister. The only family I had. That bond had sealed us to one another for eternity.

At last, my tears subsided, and I pulled back, my heart bittersweet. "I love you. But I cannot live the way we have forever. I need to try. I need her. I can't help myself. Is there no one you ever felt that kind of love for? A love so unexpected and dazzling, you would give up everything in order to keep it?"

She laughed, though it was tinged with a deep sadness. "Oh my darling, I have never stopped feeling it, but it is pointless. He is lost to me forever. You are so young. I hate to see you hurt in that same way."

"Isn't that my decision to make? Nothing will hurt me more than the ache of regret. If I never try, I will never know. I will regret losing her for eternity. Forever is a long time. Don't make me face it, always asking myself 'If only…' until the end of time. It will make me hate you eventually. I don't want that."

Her eyes dropped then, and she turned away. I thought I had brought on another argument, but she only said quietly, "Go to her. You have a week, but that is all. Unless in that time, you have told her about yourself, the whole truth, and convinced her to join us of her own free will, then you must make her forget you and leave her forever. We cannot risk longer than that."

I stood stunned for a moment, not sure what I had heard at first. "Does…does that mean you're giving me your blessing?"

She shook her head, still looking away, and I heard that same bitter laugh. "I must be insane. Go, before I change my mind."

My hands trembled as I reached out to touch her shoulder. "Thank you."

"I said go!" she roared, flinching, and I knew more than just my desire to be with Sybill drove her to such anger. I also knew if I asked her to explain, her pain would only increase. I patted her shoulder once more and then left without saying anything more.

Quickly grabbing my bag and throwing on my coat, hat, scarf, and gloves, I went out into the darkened street, leaving her there alone with her brooding thoughts, moving as swiftly as I could, without attracting attention, toward where I hoped Sybill would be, though it was late. I would do anything to convince her to listen. Beg, cry, get on my knees if I had to. I just needed her to hear me out.

The swirling snow enveloped me, but I might have been the only person out on the street who did not feel the cold, a black smudge against the blinding white, but the darkness and I were one, and only the street lights gave me away.

"Please be there, Sybill." The words were a whispered prayer that fell from my lips, silenced in the frozen winter night. "Please be there."

In my haste, I found myself running into someone and knocking her to the ground. "Oh, sorry," I muttered, reaching down to help her up, but my eye still gazing down the street.

"Fin?" Her voice startled me beyond anything I could have imagined.

When our eyes met, I felt a thrill rush through me. "Sybill?" I pulled her to her feet so our noses nearly touched. "I…I needed to talk to you."

She laughed. "I was coming to see you. You didn't show up before we closed."

"I tried to hurry...."

"Shh...." She stopped me talking with a gloved finger to my lips, then she stretched up on tiptoes, and her lips were on mine. We kissed there on the sidewalk in the cold, the warmth of her body sending a thrill down my spine. I don't know how long it lasted, but when at last we broke apart, she panted for breath again.

"Can we go to my place to talk?" she said. "It's cold out here."

I took her hand and beamed down at her with joy. "I'd go anywhere with you."

Blushing, she laughed a little and squeezed my fingers. "Come on. It's not far."

Though I could describe the place perfectly, she didn't need to know that, and I didn't want to sound like a stalker. Day after day, I had dreamed of walking into her building with her, and I tried not to let my excitement show, though I'm sure she could tell. When she opened the front door, I hesitated. "Come inside," she pleaded, tugging at my hand.

Another thing she didn't need to know. At least, not yet. I still had time to tell her. I smiled at her invitation and did as she asked.

We walked across the lobby to the elevator and, as we waited, I pulled her hand to my lips and kissed her fingers. She blushed a little more, and I thought my heart would burst from happiness.

In the elevator, we stood side-by-side, holding hands, staring at the number display as we went up. You could feel the tension between us, drawing us together, though neither of us wanted to make the first move. So we waited. The elevator "dinged" and the doors slid open. She let go of my hand to take her key from her shoulder bag. We walked down the corridor, and then she stopped in front of one of the doors to unlock it. A jingle and a jangle, and then the door swung open.

"Please, come in." Taking off her bag, she walked in ahead of me and tossed her keys on the kitchen bar. I followed slowly, eyes scanning the room, and closed the door gently behind me. Her bag, she placed on one of the barstools. "You want something to drink?" she said from the kitchen.

I shook my head. "No, thank you." I felt thirsty, but not for anything she would find in her refrigerator.

She turned around, twisting off the cap of a bottle of water, and smiled up at me. I could tell she wanted to slow things down between us, and I felt grateful to her. I wanted to take my time with getting to know her. I wanted to take forever.

"Let me just say I'm sorry…" I began, but she cut me off, lifting a hand to shush me.

"No. I'm the sorry one. You've got to think I'm crazy." Stepping forward, I could see sincerity in her eyes. "It's just…I don't talk about my father. For good reason."

"You don't have to tell me," I said.

"Oh, but I do. I want to. You deserve to know. You want to have a seat? This might take a while."

She gestured toward the living room, and I followed her in. We sat on either end of her sofa, facing one another. Curling one leg under her, she took a sip of her water before setting it down on the coffee table. I waited patiently as she prepared herself for what she wanted to say.

"My father," she said, "he's...he's in organized crime." She laughed a little before going on. "I've never really said it aloud. Sorry. He's got a lot of people who want to find something they can prove so they can send him to jail. He's good at hiding things. Hiding money, bodies, even his identity if he thought they were getting close. So I've learned to live with secrets. To live a double life. In school, I told everyone my father was a businessman. He is. Just...not the kind of businessman they knew about. I learned to tell half-truths. That's how I knew you gave me a fake name. I can spot a lie, even a practiced one, a mile off. You have to be really good to fool me."

Nodding as she talked, I watched her expression and saw how much pain and effort it caused her to admit the truth, but also I could see she felt relieved at last to confide in someone.

"When I was five, Daddy used to have me look out for the cops as he drove me to kindergarten. Can you imagine? A five-year-old being the lookout. Only I couldn't call them cops. They were 'the bobbies' since no one from here would know what that meant. That way, if I slipped up at school and told a teacher or another kid I'd been 'looking for the bobbies,' no one would be alarmed and call social services. That's still one of my dad's favorite stories. Me looking for the bobbies. He laughs each time he tells it. I used to laugh. I don't anymore. Not since I found out what my father really did. What he was capable of. What he wanted me to do."

She looked down at her hands and took several deep breaths. I fell silent, still watching, letting her tell it her way.

"He seemed like a good father. Loving, fair, affectionate, read to me at night. He always said he was proud of me. All the

117

things daddies ought to be. But." She shook her head, still staring at her hands. "But he is also ruthless, conniving, and unforgiving. Only at work, mind you, but he took his work seriously. He still does. If someone crosses him, they will regret it. His justice is swift and final. I never knew that side of him until I grew much older. I wish I had never known.

"He pays for this apartment, as you might have guessed. He's paying for my tuition. He insisted on both of those things. He wouldn't have his little girl in debt or living in squalor. But I refused let him push me into taking more. It's never good to owe my daddy anything. He will use it to make you do what he wants. Even me.

"He knew I was good with numbers and computers. He called me his little Einstein. He encouraged me in both these things. He wanted me to be an accountant. His, in fact. He had my job all lined out, waiting for me on graduation. He wanted me to manage his offshore accounts. Find ways to hide his money electronically. His legacy to me.

"I didn't know other people's fathers didn't have money hidden in the Caymans. How could I knew what 'normal' even looked like? Who would he trust more than his own child?"

A tear ran down her face, and she brushed it away. "At thirteen, he had me learn about his accounts and how to launder money. Thirteen. I should have been at dance lessons or soccer, but instead I sat inside at the computer learning about the business from a guy they called Frankie, though I think his real name was Robert. They called him that because he counted all their Franklin hundred dollar bills, I think. Anyway, Frankie used to handle all the finances. At least until Daddy caught him skimming money. If it had just been a little bit on the side, Daddy would have let it go. But it turned out to be a lot more than what Daddy could forgive.

"At age sixteen, Frankie had been teaching me for three years. I remember, I sat in Daddy's office with Frankie, going over the books. Daddy came in with some guys I'd seen only a couple of times before. They never spoke to me. Frankie looked up and had the strangest expression on his face. He went so pale. I'd never seen anything like it. No one said anything. But Frankie got up quietly. He didn't argue. He didn't cry. He just walked over and looked my father in the eye. They stared at each other for a few seconds, and then Frankie sighed and looked away. Those two men walked out of the room with him, and my father looked at me and said in a voice I'll never forget, 'Frankie's got to go, princess. You ain't seen him. Not all day. Go up to your room. I'll be in to tell you goodnight.' Then he left. Just like that. I never saw Frankie again.

"Two days later, I saw on the evening news some guy found his body over in Alton, Illinois near the warehouse district. My mother stood at the counter making meatloaf, and she dropped the pan on the floor. Hamburger meat and ketchup splattered all over the tiles. Daddy just looked at me and said 'Guess we're eating out tonight, huh?' That's it. No reaction. His money-man just died, and he just thought about his stomach. That's when I knew. Frankie didn't just die. Daddy had him killed."

Her lip trembled and more tears fell. I whispered, "I'm so sorry."

"It is what it is," she said with a sniffle. "Daddy told me a couple of days later he wanted me to take Frankie's place. 'You're smart, princess. You can do it, I know.' But I shook my head and said I wanted to go to college. He agreed so enthusiastically. 'You can be an accountant. Or a computer whats-it. You'll do great, princess. You're good at that stuff. You're a whiz.' Every compliment just made me feel sick. I couldn't stand knowing Daddy had groomed me for taking Frankie's job. That's when I cut my hair. Got tattoos. I told him I wanted to be a painter."

"And he let you?" I said quietly.

She laughed through her tears. "I'm his baby girl. We fought. Oh, believe me, we fought. But he loves me. Whatever else happens, he loves me. So he had to let me make my own choices. He still hopes, I think, I will change my mind and come back to work for him. He figures this art thing is a fad, and I'll get bored with it or not be able to make a living and then I'll need him."

"But you don't want that." I finished for her.

"No." Her voice sounded emphatic. "I do not. I don't ever want to work for him again. I won't betray him. He's my Daddy and I love him, but I won't be a part of what he does."

I nodded and said "Of course" but inside I ached. She would never understand about me. I was a killer. I'd had to be. It was in my nature. And I couldn't ask her to live another lie. Asking her to join me and keep my secrets would make me as bad as her father. I couldn't be that selfish. I had to do as Marie had asked and let Sybill go. Even if it broke my heart.

With a sad smile, she looked up at me, wiping her cheeks with her fingers. "Well, guess it's your turn. I showed you mine. You show me yours."

She laughed, trying to break the tension.

"Oh, you don't want to hear all that," It sounded just as wimpy from my lips as it had in my head.

She raised an eyebrow, and I could see I'd hurt her. "I just told you my deepest, darkest secrets, and now you're telling me you're not going to trust me with yours? That's not fair, and you know it."

I bit my lip. Sybill was right. I owed it to her, even if it meant she would hate me. I owed her the truth. "I'm not good at this sort of thing," I said. "If I tell you the truth, I'll be putting my…Claire Marie at risk."

There. I'd said her name. Not her real name, but close enough.

"That's the woman you live with, right?" she said, tilting her head at me.

I nodded. "Yes. If I tell you my secret, it will be telling hers too. I don't want to be the reason something terrible happens to her."

Leaning forward, she patted my knee. "Look, I'm not telling anyone. I'm good at keeping secrets. I swear, no matter what, I won't tell anything you say to me to another soul."

"It may not be so easy," I said. "The people who want to find us will make you talk."

She shook her head. "No way. I swear. I never go back on my word."

"You don't know what you're promising," I said.

"Yeah, well, my Daddy could have you taken out if you were bad to me or if he thinks you might tip off the feds, so we're even." She laughed, but I knew she meant it.

I laughed with her, giving in. "All right. But don't say I didn't warn you."

"Duly noted. Please, just tell me, and get it over with. I promise, no interruptions."

"Okay then. You asked for it." I took a deep breath, and though I didn't need to, the action made me feel more human. "Have you noticed anything different about me? Out of the ordinary?"

"You mean besides the fact you sat here for forty-five minutes and listened to me tell you about how my dad is in the mob? Naw. You're perfectly normal." She laughed once more.

"I'm serious. Things that seemed strange or just a little off."

Her face took on a worried expression. "Well, you're a lot less…handsy than most guys I know. Stand-offish almost. Cautious. Like you're afraid of what might happen if you touch me."

I nodded. "Good, anything else?"

"Um…" she shrugged. "You're a night person, but where I work, that's not a strange thing."

"Right. That it?"

"Well, you don't seem affected by the heat and cold the way most people are. I mean, the other day you walked around for who knows how long without a hat or gloves, and tonight you're still wearing your coat in here when I'm practically roasting. You know, you could take it off and stay a while."

I laughed in spite of myself, looking down and then starting to unbutton the jacket. "I completely forgot to pay attention to that. Sorry." I tossed the coat onto a nearby chair and then looked back at her, pushing my hair back with one hand. "Better?"

After a brief appraisal, she nodded, smiling. "Much. Oh, and you are maybe the sexiest guy I've ever met. Not weird, just something else I noticed."

"If I could blush, I would," I said, a smile making its way across my face. "Look, there's a reason for all those things, but you're going to have trouble believing me."

"A reason why you're sexy?" She smirked. "I thought it was just you."

Looking down, I shook my head. "I am trying to tell you something important. And yeah, your reaction to me might be a part of it as well, though I hope not. I hope you're right. I never consciously tried to make you feel that way for me. If anything, I made an effort not to do so."

"I don't understand," she said, forehead furrowing.

"I know." I paused, took a deep breath, then looked up at her over my glasses. "Promise me you won't scream."

She backed up a little, but still held her ground. "Uh... scream?"

"Don't worry. I won't hurt you. Just promise." I had to work at it not to glamour her. My every instinct told me how easy it would be just to push her a little, but I wanted her reactions to be natural, not forced.

"Okay. I promise."

I could tell she still felt nervous, and I gave her a reassuring smile before I took off my glasses and set them on the coffee table. I closed my eyes for a moment, thinking about blood, the last kill I'd had, letting myself drop my façade of humanity. My fangs extended, and when I opened my eyes again, I let her see them. Her hands covered her mouth to stifle a gasp. She backed away from me, putting her feet on the cushions in a defensive posture, pressing her body against the arm of the sofa. She trembled, eyes wide, and the monster in me thrilled to hear her heartbeat pounding faster, faster, faster. I practically salivated at the thought of tasting her, and I had to struggle not to pounce upon her right then and there. "This is what I am. Do you understand now?"

She nodded frantically, shaking like a little rabbit, and I gave her a terrifying smile before I closed my eyes again and willed myself back into my disguise once more. The fangs retracted, and my demeanor returned to the quiet face she'd come to know. When I knew it had passed, I opened my eyes and put my glasses back on. She stared, quaking, stunned speechless.

"That is why I don't feel the cold. Why you only see me at night. Why I felt so reluctant to…get close to you. I don't want to hurt you. I wouldn't hurt you for anything. I didn't want to frighten you. I'm sorry I have. I wanted to keep it from you. I told myself to just leave you alone, but I couldn't help it. I tried to stay away, but I felt drawn to you in a way I don't even understand. I've never felt for anyone the way I feel for you, Sybill."

"Y-you want to…eat me?" she said, still trembling.

"No! Well…yes, the monster does, but no. I don't want to. I would never hurt you. It's the human in me that wants you.

124

You're the most amazing person I've ever met. Astounding. I love you. I'm not afraid to say it. I know it may be the last chance I have, so I'm saying it now. I love you, Sybill. But I need you to know me. All of me. Even if it means I lose you forever. I need you to know."

I could see a million questions swimming behind her eyes all at the same time, overwhelming her. She blurted, "Wha-how? I mean, what happened? How did you...what are you? Is this a joke?"

Answering her questions in order, I said, "Claire Marie bit me, as you might have guessed by now. Then she fed me her blood, just like in the movies, and made me a vampire. No, it's not a joke. I wish, but no. Though I sometimes feel like I am a joke in all this."

"O-okay." Her voice sounded flat and tuneless as she went on, obviously in shock and struggling to process what I'd said. "Right. Vampires are real. Right."

"I know. It's a lot." I didn't know how to help her accept what I'd said. "I didn't want this, in case you're wondering."

Several times she nodded, obviously overwhelmed. Since she seemed unable to speak coherently, I went on. "That's why I have a fake name. I had to leave everyone and everything I'd ever known. That's the price I had to pay."

"Uh huh," she said, her voice a monotone, eyes like saucers.

"Sybill?" I reached over to touch her gently. "I'm the same person, you know. Nothing has changed. I'm still me."

She looked at my hand as it touched her knee. "You're... you're not...alive. Your hand is cold because you're not alive.

Everything is different."

With a sigh, I pulled back in disappointment and looked away. "I'm sorry. I had to tell you. It went too far. I didn't have a choice. I never meant to upset you. I can fix it, you know. If you want. Make you forget. You can go on with your life and forget all about me."

That seemed to snap her out of it. "Forget you? How could I ever forget you?"

I couldn't help but smile. "I can make you forget me. It's one of my special gifts. I can influence your thoughts, your feelings, your memories."

Her face went pale, and I knew exactly what she thought. "No," I said, cutting her off at the pass. "I haven't done that to you. I want something real with you. I could make you want me, but that is so hollow. It makes me sick even to contemplate doing such a thing to you. It's like rape, in my mind. Plus, I want someone who wants me for myself. Using glamour would mean I would always wonder if you really cared for me. I don't want to doubt."

After a few moments of contemplation, she looked at me seriously and asked the one question I had most dreaded. "Who is it you're afraid of? Why are they after you?"

"That story is not mine to tell. It's Claire Marie's. It is her enemies who would love to see us both dead. Me, because it would hurt her. I know they will have no mercy if I am found. They see her as a traitor to our kind."

"Why? I don't understand." She leaned forward, putting her hand on the sofa beside me. I could feel the warmth of her body, and it calmed me somehow.

"I don't know all of the history. It is an ancient grudge. Claire Marie has only told me her side of things, and even then she only explained what she felt safe to tell me. The things she felt I needed to know in order to avoid drawing attention and danger to our door. She said she wanted to protect me by keeping the information secret. That way, if someone captured me, I wouldn't be able to tell them anything."

"That doesn't seem fair," she said softly. "How can you protect yourself if you don't know everything there is to know?"

I shook my head. "Fair has nothing to do with it. It's her decision, not mine. I just have to obey."

Her eyes searched mine. "Can you tell me who you are? Or used to be, anyway?"

I laughed bitterly. "You wouldn't believe me, and if I told you, I'd need to glamour you into forgetting. Unless...no. I shouldn't say it."

"Unless what?" she scooted further forward, closing the gap between us. It made me a little nervous, but my hair stood on end with excitement.

"Sybill…" I whispered, reaching out to touch her face with my cool fingers. She gave a shiver, but didn't move away. Her skin warmed beneath my touch, and I saw a blush rise to her cheeks. "Oh, Sybill. I wish things could be different. I wish you could have met me before all this. I'm so sorry."

"For what?" Her voice hushed and tender, she gazed into my eyes with fascination.

"For being so complicated. For bringing all my dangerous problems into your world. For not being the man you thought or expected me to be."

"Did you do it on purpose?" she said, looking at me with eyes deep and dark and curious.

I shook my head just a little. "No. Of course not."

"Well, then you don't need to apologize." She moved in closer still until we were brushing noses. Then, before I could say another word, she kissed me. Her lips were soft, and they brushed mine with a feather touch. My hands cupped her face, and I gazed down at her. She looked so beautiful and so fragile. I could kill her without effort, and I drank in that human weakness with loving eyes. "Can you still feel anything for me? After what I've told you? Can you possibly love me now?"

"Oh, Fin. I don't know all of your story, but I'm certain you would never hurt me. You've had plenty of opportunity. If you wanted to kill me, you could have done so a long time ago. I think you're telling the truth. It terrifies you, but you've told me anyway. You've put yourself at my mercy. I know enough to be dangerous to you. But you are still here. You trust me. That is the definition of bravery, in my book."

I shook my head, not taking my eyes off her. "Not brave. I love you, Sybill. I won't lie to you."

"I know." She gave me a soft smile. "I am overwhelmed you chose to tell me. You believed in me enough to be honest, even when it might cost you everything."

"I hoped it wouldn't."

My eyes flickered down to her lips, and I licked my own unconsciously. I couldn't help it. I wanted to kiss her.

She saw the gesture and laughed a little. "Shut up, Fin."

Then we were kissing once more. Her hands were in my hair, and our tongues touched in tantalizing ways.

We kissed slowly, taking our time, and I let her take the lead, moving our intimacy forward at the pace she chose.

Then those lips blazed a trail of fire to my ear, her fingers tugging my hair, and she whispered, "I want you. I just need to know…is there anything you need to tell me first? Say it now, because I plan to make love to you in every room in this place if you'll let me."

At her words, my fangs extended, and I moaned softly. I pushed her back gently so I could see her face. I let her see the fangs there, gleaming dangerously.

Curious, she ran her thumb along my lip before touching one of them.

"Sharp," she said, and I felt her pulse quicken with a mixture of fear and desire.

"I promise not to use them unless you ask me to," I said, my voice deep with passion, wanting to be sure she understood what I meant.

"Does it hurt?" she said, still stroking my lip.

I shook my head. "Not unless I want to hurt you, which I never would. I understand tattoos are a pleasurable sort of pain to some people. It's much like that." And I took one hand and traced the outline of one of her tattoos with my finger.

Her eyes perked up, and I felt her body react to my touch. "I promise not to ask unless I mean it," she said, and then she kissed me again, fangs and all, her tongue exploring them, making me shiver. I breathed her in, her lips, her hair, her skin. She smelled intoxicating, like cinnamon and caramel and coffee…and blood.

As she pulled off my sweater, her fingers slid up my chest

and sides, making me gasp with pleasure at her touch. She threw it to the side, and then her lips were tracing down my neck, testing to see my reaction. I bit my lip and tasted my own blood.

Soon my hands were beneath her sweater, exploring her body. Then the sweater came off, tossed to the floor beside my own. Her skin was soft and smooth and delightfully warm. I couldn't get enough of touching it, feeling the muscles flex beneath the skin, her blood making the blush in her cheeks spread to her chest. Oh, she was more beautiful than anyone I had ever seen.

I took off her bra, then laid her down on the sofa beneath me and began to tease that tender skin with my lips, my tongue, and my teeth, loving it every time she sighed. My long hair brushed her skin, and her eyes closed, her head pressing back into the cushions as I continued making my way down toward her belly. When I reached her belt buckle, I lifted my head, pausing to look at her for permission. She opened her eyes, dark and liquid with desire, and nodded, whispering, "Yes." I smiled then, and keeping my eyes on her, I took off her jeans until she wore nothing but a pair of red panties.

"You're beautiful," I breathed, gazing down at her in awe. "So beautiful."

She panted as my lips brushed her inner thigh. I pulled off her panties then, and she cried out, arching her back with pleasure, hands gripping my hair as I savored each successive quiver and moan I elicited from her. At last, when I'd driven her almost to a frenzy, she reached for me desperately and opened the zipper of my jeans. When she reached inside to stroke me with those warm fingers, I thought I would go insane. I couldn't wait anymore. I kicked off the rest of my clothes, and then kissed her as I entered her.

We both made an aching cry as our bodies thrilled to one another. Her thighs and hands clasped me to her, and we moved together, thrusting, hungry for more. When at last we reached the height of passion, we clutched one another tightly. I uttered her name, deep and full of satisfaction. She shouted "Yes!" with a throaty cry, and then we exploded together with shuddering gasps.

For several long moments, we lay together, not wanting to move. I felt happier than I'd ever been. "I think I love you, Sybill," I whispered, kissing her throat. "I love you."

She gave a contented sigh, her fingers stroking my back, and then she whispered back the words I never thought I'd hear her say. "I think I might love you too."

I lifted my head and kissed her with joy, and the kiss soon deepened. "I want you again," I said, my lips brushing hers.

"Yes," she said simply.

I lifted her up and carried her, her thighs around my waist, into her bedroom, stumbling blindly, still kissing, and we fell upon the bed together, making love again, this time with even greater urgency. I claimed her body with kisses, enraptured as she pulled me into her with a need matching my own. And when we were hovering on the edge of orgasm again, she moaned, "Bite me. Do it now."

She cried out as my fangs pierced her shoulder, her nails pressing into my back, and when I tasted her blood on my tongue, I growled and shuddered. Moments later, overcome with waves of pleasure, we clung to one another in amazed ecstasy.

I retracted my fangs and then collapsed on top of her with a sigh. Her arms held me close in a gentle embrace, and we lay there amazed and sated.

Finally, with a little sigh of pleasure mixed with longing, I lay down beside her, pulling her close. I held her to my chest, her head on my shoulder, stroking her hair. "Does it hurt?" I said.

She laughed softly. "I can promise you, I feel no pain at this moment, though I'm not sure I'll be able to walk right for a day or two."

"Is that a complaint?" I joked, kissing the top of her head.

"No way," she said. "You're welcome to do that to me again. All of it. My god."

Chuckling, I said, "I'm going to remember you said that, you know."

"God, I hope so," she smiled. "You'd better."

I stayed there with her until she fell asleep, watching as her breathing slowed and deepened. Her heart beat against my chest, and I could feel her breath on my skin. For the first time in my life, I felt at peace. At last I slid out of bed and wrote her a quick note:

I have to go before the sun rises. I swear I would stay if I could, but you know why I have no choice. You are amazing and startling and I am yours, totally and without reservation. Call me in the evening tomorrow. I love you.

Yours always,
F

At the bottom of the page, I scrawled my phone number, breaking all the rules for her, and I didn't care. She was the only thing that mattered. I put the note on the pillow, then gathered my things, dressed, and left as quietly as I could. My heart soared as I walked out onto the street and turned toward home. The thought she loved me sustained me all the way back to number 16.

Marie hadn't returned home yet, oddly. I climbed the stairs and went to my room to shower. The scent of Sybill clung to me as her body had done, and though I found it delicious, I knew it wouldn't be wise to flaunt it in front of Marie. She might have given me permission, but that doesn't mean she wouldn't be overcome with jealousy all the same. I didn't want to give her reason to be upset, and I hoped soon I might be able to introduce Sybill to her and get her blessing.

The water felt warm and wonderful, and I stayed there for a long time, so happy I sang.

In My Shoes

Marie Antoinette

My daytime assistant Crystal still sat at the shop going over the receipts when I arrived that evening. "Well, hey there, boss lady! How's it going?" When she heard the bell ring at the door, she looked up with a big smile, blue eyes crinkling with genuine friendship.

"There's my Sparkle girl." The nickname was an inside joke, and suited her personality. "I am well, thank you," I replied with a grin.

Being a vampire meant never being ill, but Crystal had no idea of my real nature. Some people who ask how you are do so out of lip service, but you got the feeling from Crystal she really cared. I liked that about her. It's one of the reasons I trusted

134

her implicitly. "How are you?"

"Oh good. Sold that big oak wardrobe today." Her eyebrows lifted with excitement and pride as she put away her paperwork. "The guy paid $5000 cash. Can you believe it? He'll arrange delivery later in the week, he said. Want me to take the deposit over to the bank so it's not sitting here in the register?"

"That's fantastic!" I exclaimed, then shook my head. "No, don't worry about the bank. I can take the money to the night deposit when I leave. It's snowing out there, and you don't need to be out in that. Just get on home, and be safe."

"You sure?" She stepped back from the counter and took her coat from the back of the chair, putting it on and pulling her hair out from under the collar before zipping up the front. "I don't mind. It's on my way."

Smiling at her, I shook my head. "I'm sure. Be careful on the sidewalks. It's slick down by the corner."

She patted my shoulder, then gathered her purse before pulling up her hood. "Thanks, boss lady. You take care, okay? I'll see you on Friday."

"Friday it is," I said. "See you later."

I waved her out the door and waited until she disappeared from view before I settled into my seat behind the counter.

Though I'd told myself I wouldn't look at the auction lists again, I just couldn't keep my promise. I wanted to prove somehow even if I couldn't control Fin, I could still make my own decisions about how and when to spend my money, thank you. I was not Madame le Deficit.

I turned on the computer. *Just a peek. I'll just do a quick search to satisfy my curiosity. That's all.*

Fin had put me on a listserv for auctions of antiques, particularly French pre-revolutionary style items. My clientele expected a certain degree of elegance from me and, of course, I'd made that period of decor my specialty. Only Fin knew how I'd become such an expert on the time period. The style had come back in vogue among the wealthy of the Central West End, and I became the primary purveyor of the artifacts they desired.

I had a list of clients on the lookout for rare and interesting items, so I needed to regularly check the listserv. I told myself scrolling down to read the items up for bid was just part of the job, and if I should happen to find something of personal interest, well, I couldn't help the coincidence, could I?

It is the lies we tell ourselves which become our ruination. That is a lesson I should have learned years ago, but perhaps enough time had passed for me to forget the truth of it.

Ordinarily, I skipped over the clothing items. None of my customers collected them, and those items never sold in the store. However, something made me scroll through the headings. Nostalgia, perhaps.

Whatever the reason, I paused when I saw "Marie Antoinette's shoes" in the list. I did love shoes. They were a particular weakness of mine. *Perhaps they are replicas.* I tried to dismiss my impulses and move on.

However, I'd only know for certain if I looked. *I'll just see if they've found the real thing or if they're fakes.*

Foolishly, I clicked to see the item photographs. There, below the written description, I saw them. My favorite green striped shoes. I'd had a dress made specifically to match them. I'd bought feathers for my hair, dyed that precise shade of green.

136

Deep inside my heart, I felt an ache, a need, an urge to have them, to wear them once more, if only in private.

They were mine. They had to be mine again.

Bids started at $15,000. *So much for such silly little things.* I heard Fin's voice in my head echoing the chastisements I'd heard in my past and it made me furious. *How dare anyone judge me for wanting fine things?* I was the Queen of France, and though the title had been stripped from me long ago, I still felt angry beyond measure at what I had lost. *Who claims to own these shoes?* I wondered. *Anyone in possession of them attained them through theft. How dare they put stolen goods up for auction as though time had given them the right?*

I clicked to place a bid without thinking, and when someone bid against me, I bid again. And again. And again. For almost an hour, I watched a back and forth volley of bids around the world, all vying for a piece of me.

When at last I knew I'd won, I stared at the screen in triumph. Then suddenly, it came crashing in on me what I'd done. I'd just bid over $60,000 for a pair of shoes. That kind of money had to attract attention. I would have to give them my personal information in order to claim them. Suddenly, I shook with fear. *This auction could have been a set-up. Who owned it? How did they find this item in the first place? Could they trace the purchase back here to me, to the shop, to our home? How could I be so stupid? I'd put our lives at risk, all for a pair of shoes.*

Leaving the contact and mailing information screen blank, I grabbed my cell phone from my purse and dialed the only number in it, Fin. I needed his help so desperately. He'd be unbelievably angry when he knew what I'd done, but I would weather the storm of his fury. Fin always knew what to do.

"Marie? I'm home already," he answered. "Where are you? Still at work? Isn't it late for antiquing?"

"Fin, I need your help. Please, come to the shop right away." No point in sugar coating it. "I've done something…oh Fin, please."

My voice must have sounded desperate, because he didn't argue or question the way he usually does. He simply said, "I'll be right there. Don't move." He hung up.

Though I know only a few minutes passed while I waited, I paced until he arrived, wringing my hands with worry. He unlocked the front door of the shop, and I ran to him, throwing my arms around his neck as I sobbed, "Oh, Fin. You'll be so angry. Please don't be angry. I couldn't bear it."

His arms held me close and, his voice full of compassion, he whispered softly, "Just tell me what's wrong. We can fix it, whatever it is."

I clung to him for a few moments more, dreading to have to speak the words, then I pulled back a little and looked him in the eye. "You were right. Of course you were right. I just wanted to have my things back, that's all. I didn't consider…I just didn't think."

"What did you do?" The warning in his tone made me wince.

With a worried sigh, I walked with him over to the computer and showed him what I'd bought. "They were on auction, you see? An online auction. I didn't think about the risk. I mean, no one could see me."

"You didn't think spending that much money would attract attention?"

He said it so quietly, but I could feel his fury.

Pleading with him, I took hold of his arm, begging for understanding, "I got caught up in the excitement. I didn't mean to. I just couldn't stop. Oh Fin, what can I do? They want my contact information. I can't fill that out. I'll lead them right to us."

He looked at the screen and then back at me. "They will be able to find us anyway. You've given them your credit card number."

"But that's in a false name, of course." A weak defense, I knew, but I had nothing else I could say.

Taking me by the shoulders, he sat me down and looked at me seriously. "You've taken a huge risk. A risk that affects both of us."

"I know," I said, looking down at my hands. "But what can I do now? How can we fix this?"

"We?" he laughed. "Kind of late to ask about we, isn't it?"

"Please, don't be cruel." I said, lifting my eyes back up to meet his. "Just tell me something can be done. I don't want for us to have to move again. Not after everything. I'll do anything you say. Please. Just tell me, and I'll obey."

I saw mercy in his eyes then, and I knew he would do whatever he could, whatever it took, to make sure we were safe.

He began walking back and forth, pacing and thinking aloud, "First of all, you need a post office box in a false name. Do you have one?"

Biting my lip, I thought for a moment, then I remembered, "I do, but it isn't here in the city. It's an old one. I haven't used it in years. I still pay for it, though."

"Good. Use it." He paced some more, still talking, "There's nothing more we can do about this purchase. However, we can make sure this sort of thing never happens in the future. We will need an Internet security expert to come and help cover your tracks electronically. They would have to divert any data from your ISP."

"I-S-what? Oh, I don't even know what you're talking about, though I suppose it doesn't matter."

"Internet Service Provider," he said, his voice understandably a bit testy. "We will need to find someone who can hide your transactions. Make them untraceable."

"Oh, of course. But who could we could trust? What we're asking them to do is illegal, is it not? Homeland Security and all that nonsense."

"Yes, I am certain whoever we hire would have to break several laws."

His expression was a mask of anxiety, though I could see his mind working madly to think through the problem. Abruptly, he stopped pacing and looked at me. "It's nearly dawn. No time to solve this now. We need to rest for the day. Tomorrow evening, I'll see what I can do."

Relief washed over me, and I nearly wept. "Oh thank you, Fin. I knew you would know what to do. I knew it. Thank god for you. I don't know what I would do without you."

With a sad smile, he pulled me close and kissed the top of my head. "Come on," he said. "We need to go. I'm not spending the day in here."

We gathered up Pom Pom, leaving everything behind in the shop, forgetting the deposit. I turned the little sign to "CLOSED," and hurried home.

Lost and Found

Sybill

When my alarm went off, I hit snooze and lay there, still half-asleep. I smiled at the dream I'd had, though I couldn't quite remember how it ended. Then the alarm sounded again, and as I turned it off, the whole of the night before came flooding back. Fin and me, I didn't dream it. I could still feel him on my skin like echoes of our lovemaking. Automatically, my hand went to my shoulder, and there were two small marks which ached a little to touch, though not as much as I had expected. Impossible. Crazy. But then again, I had proof on my body. Fin was a vampire. For several minutes, I stared at the ceiling and struggled to process everything we'd told one another. I must be insane.

142

With a sigh, I rolled over, and there on the pillow where he'd slept beside me lay a note. As I read it over, I felt my heart skip a beat. He loved me, and however impossible the whole situation might seem in the light of day, it had happened. Most importantly, I knew I loved him, more than I had ever thought it possible to love anyone.

I read the note again and laughed at the absurdity of the idea he might be sleeping in a hole in the ground or in a coffin or a refrigerator. Did he drink blood from a "Kiss the Librarian" coffee mug like Spike? Ridiculous ideas. Then again, you could write a book on all the things I didn't know.

Thinking about it wouldn't give me answers. Setting the note back down on the pillow, I got up and decided I needed a shower to let go of all those questions for now. Of course, that didn't work. All the vampires I'd ever seen in movies and television shows came swarming to my mind as I let the water beat down on my back. We hadn't talked about the logistics of his...condition. What were the rules? His limitations? His weaknesses? His supernatural abilities? I wondered if he could fly or turn into fog or a bat, if he had super-speed or strength.

My fingers massaged the shampoo into my scalp while I continued my curious list of unanswerable musings. The whole daylight thing must be true. His note implied it, as had his story. He could glamour people, and I believed he told the truth. He felt cold to the touch, so that was true too. Silver? Crosses? Garlic? Holy water? Did those affect him? Was he really immortal? How old was he? I rinsed and conditioned and loofah-ed myself until my skin glowed, and by the time I turned off the water,

I had decided all this wondering wouldn't bring me any answers. I would just have to ask him to tell me.

I dried my hair, running scenarios for that conversation over in my head, and the results made me frown. I couldn't just call him up and demand he tell me all that stuff over the phone right then. If I said "we have to talk," well, that was just asking for trouble. But how do you bring all that up in a casual way? "By the way, how do you feel about garlic?" Pretty sure that would just make everything awkward.

"Oh, just stop being such a girl!" I yelled at myself, stomping into the kitchen to make breakfast.

While my bagel toasted, I turned on the TV. The local news team told about a body of a teenager found in the park by the skating rink. The cold weather had preserved the remains, the idea of which made me shiver. So far, the police were releasing no details, but they were asking anyone with information to call Crime Stoppers. I turned the TV back off, not wanting to hear any more. Only a few blocks away. Too close for comfort.

Apparently, my parents had seen the same newscast, because a few minutes later, as I spread my bagel with peanut butter, my mother called me all in a state, asking did I lock my doors at night, and on and on. I did my best to reassure her, trying to change the subject as soon as possible, telling her I was just fine and the kid probably was a runaway or a junkie or a gang banger, all of which I could assure her I definitely was not.

It took several minutes for her to wind down, and though I didn't say it, I did think about how the parents of that teenager must have gone through the same panic attack when they realized their son had gone missing. Then again, not everyone's parents cared about their children's welfare. For all my parents' shortcomings, I always knew they were looking out for me and worrying about keeping me safe.

That poor kid. How did he get out there? Did someone kill him somewhere else and then dump his body at the park? Was it a mugging? A suicide? An overdose? What had gone wrong in his life to lead him to that place they found his corpse? I had to believe someone must have cared about him, worried when he disappeared, and would be devastated to find out he died.

Then my mother said something that made my blood run cold. "You know," she exclaimed, "a friend of your fathers who works in the coroner's office said the whole thing is like some sort of cult or serial killer or something. That kid had no blood left in him."

"Wait. You mean like they'd slashed his throat or something? Gross!" I shivered. Knives gave me the creeps.

"No! That's what's so weird! No blood on the ground or anywhere. Just gone. Like they took it! Isn't that crazy?"

I fell silent for a moment. Someone took the blood. "Yeah. Crazy."

"I wonder if it's a Jeffrey Dahmer type. You know, a cannibal. Or some wacko like that guy who tried to eat that other guy's face off down in Florida. I know they said he'd been on drugs or whatever, but I swear I think there's really monsters out there. Vampires and zombies and who knows what else."

"Mom, just stop!" I couldn't listen to any more of her ramblings. "Sorry. I…I have to go. I'm fine. I'm sure the police will figure this out, okay? I'm fine. Really. Gotta go. I'm late."

Before she could say anything else, I hung up. I stood there stunned and nauseous, staring out the window across toward the park a few blocks away. I could just make out the tree tops between the buildings. I could hardly breathe for the panic. No blood. Someone took it.

After a long while, I realized how badly my body trembled. By that time, I knew I couldn't go back to class or to work. I called and made my excuses, and then I wandered back to my room and sank into bed, hugging my pillow to my chest and trying to shut out all my thoughts. At last, I fell into a dreamless sleep, and when I woke, the sun had set. Yesterday, I had looked forward to the night, but now I knew it was full of vampires, one of which surely would make his way to me. Where I would have been happy, now I felt afraid.

CLOSING THE NET

Chief Inspector

Across the country, newspapers and online news sources splashed sensational headlines: *Bloodsucking Killer At Large, Manhunt on for 'St. Louis Vampire,' Cult Slaying or Would-Be Vampire: Forest Park murder baffles police, Mysterious murderer lurks in the shadows of the Arch.*

I rubbed my hands together with excitement. For years, I had been waiting for this lead. I had no need to contact my superior. The Master would have seen the news himself. I knew what needed to be done. Once I had our quarry in custody, I would contact him, and he would be well pleased.

Running on Empty

Fin

In my dream, I walked hand-in-hand with Sybill, crossing through the park in the shade of some large oak trees. Though the sun shone down, the air felt heavy with imminent rain. We paused under the leafy canopy, and I pulled her close to gaze into her eyes. "I've never been so happy," I said. "It's as though she made me a vampire only so I could wait for you to be born."

She took me in her arms then and held me close, kissing my cheeks, my eyes, my lips. For a moment. I felt complete satisfaction.

First I heard one drop fall, then another. I felt so enraptured with her I didn't notice initially. But as she pulled back from me, I could see red drops of blood spattering her hair, landing on her shoulders. As I gazed on it in horror, the sky opened up, and the red *rain fell over everything, covering the grass and the trees in a deluge of blood. Sybill screamed. I tried to enfold her in my arms, to cover and protect her, but I couldn't. We were drenched with it, and I woke from the dream gasping, "I'm sorry! Oh god, I'm so, so sorry!"*

———————————————

For a long time, I stared at the ceiling, trying to calm myself and release the sense of dread that nearly choked me.

Outside the house, I could hear a storm battering at the windows. *Just a dream. The noise of the rain must have crept into my thoughts as I slept. You're overreacting.* The conversation with Marie and her paranoia about discovery had gone to my head.

Marie was still asleep. I could sense it. That meant I had time before she awoke to slip out of the house and find Sybill.

I couldn't help wishing she and I could just run away from Marie and from whatever or whoever was looking for her. But how could I abandon the only mother I had left in this world? The agony and guilt I would feel would spoil any happiness I might share with Sybill. I could never leave Marie.

Anyway, running wouldn't work. All her foolishness surely could be resolved by someone clever enough to hide the electronic transactions. I thought back about the conversation in the shop. I knew the obvious answer to our problems. What I didn't know was whether asking for the help we needed would spoil any chance I had of being with Sybill. I hoped with all my heart that it would not.

As thunder crashed outside and the rain continued to beat down from above, I threw back the covers and rose to put on my favorite sweater and jeans. I took my phone from the charger, pulled on my coat, grabbed an umbrella, and texted on my way out the door, "I'm coming to see you at work to talk to you about something, if that's all right. Be there soon."

I'd walked halfway to the coffee shop when I got her reply. "Come to my apartment," she said. "I have the day off."

The idea of that made me smile in spite of the downpour, and I veered off happily in the direction of her building, anticipation mounting in my cold dead heart. I longed for a taste of her skin, the feel of her lips on mine, the warmth of her body, the smell of her hair. With each step I took, I became increasingly impatient to hold her in my arms. The night before, she had promised to make love to me in every room of her apartment, and we still had a few places left on the way toward that goal. I wanted her more than anything or anyone in my whole life. Only a few weeks ago, I had been so alone, and now my heart and soul were filled with the thought of her until it seemed as though I might burst with joy. I couldn't imagine life without her. I don't remember how I made it to her door, but I am sure I must have run the whole way.

She buzzed me into the building, and I rode up the elevator alone, watching the numbers tick by with each floor, biting my lip to keep from laughing aloud at my own impatience.

When I saw her face, all my excitement turned to worry. Up to that point, I'd been so focused on seeing her I hadn't thought how odd it was for her to be home rather than at work.

She stood in the doorway, still in her pajamas, her skin pale, with puffy dark circles under her eyes as though she'd been crying, and she didn't lift her gaze to meet mine.

"Sybill?" I said, my voice full of worry as I looked at her.

"Sybill, are you all right?"

Her lips pressed together, and she took a ragged breath before answering. "I don't know if I am or not."

I stepped forward to touch her cheek, but she shrank back from me and shook her head. "Don't. We…we have to talk."

"What's happened?" I said, a million awful scenarios swimming through my mind. Maybe her father died or perhaps she had decided she didn't want to be with me after all.

After another moment of thoughtful awkward silence, she opened the door a little wider, "You'd better come inside."

Walking in, I watched her shut the door behind me, and my forehead furrowed with concern at her hunched shoulders and shuffling step. Sybill wouldn't look at me. She just turned and walked into the living area and sat with one leg curled under her on the sofa. I followed close behind, and I couldn't help but reach out to touch her hand as I took my seat. "Sybill, what is it? Please, tell me."

She flinched, but this time she didn't pull away. Instead, she inhaled deeply and looked up at me. Her eyes pored over my face. "I have to ask you something. Please understand. I have to know."

"Anything." I nodded.

"Did you kill that boy in the park?" she blurted, staring at me.

"Wha-what?" I blinked, panicking. "What boy?"

"Don't fuck with me!" Her hands balled into fists, and her voice shook. "Just answer me! Did you kill him?"

"I-I don't know what you're talking about," I lied, grateful my body couldn't break into a nervous sweat. "I told you, I get my blood from bags we keep in the fridge. I don't need to kill anyone."

She burst into tears then, covering her face with her hands.

"Sybill, please. What's this about?" My arms reached out to her, and she buried herself against my chest, sobbing.

She couldn't speak for a few moments, but when she finally looked up at me again, I saw relief in her eyes. "I knew it couldn't be you. I knew it."

"Back up. What brought all this on? I don't have a clue what you're talking about." I squashed down my own rising panic and made myself focus on her.

"On the news. This young guy, they found his body in the park. All his blood...someone took it." Tears streaked her cheeks. "I'm so ashamed. How could I think you would do that? It's just you're the only vampire I know. It made me panic. I know it's stupid. I don't even know if it's a vampire who did it. Please, forgive me."

"Where in the park?" Stroking her hair, I forced my voice to sound calm, but inside I reeled with what-ifs.

She shrugged, snuggling against me once more for comfort. "I don't know. Somewhere near the skating rink, I think. Off in the trees. The snow had kept his body frozen. It's just so gross to even think about."

I said nothing, just kept running my hands through her hair, trying to think about what to do. DNA. Would they find any of mine on him? If they did, they would never believe the results. I died. I didn't have a twin. I wanted to believe the police would see it as a dead end, but something told me I couldn't be so lucky.

"Are there others?" she said in a tiny voice.

"Hmm?" For a moment, I didn't know what she meant.

"Other vampires. Are there any others here in St. Louis who could have done this?" Again, her eyes searched mine, looking for reassurance.

I shook my head. "Other than Claire Marie and myself? I don't think so. At least not in this neighborhood."

She pleaded with me then. "Are you sure?"

Her question frightened me, and I snapped. "Look, Sybill, we don't have some kind of 'Vampire Clubhouse' or something. Sorry to disappoint you. It's not like we check in with one another or have a secret knock. I just told you I don't think so. Can't you just let it go?"

I could see the hurt in her face, and she pulled away from me then and muttered, "I'm sorry." That phrase cut me deeper than any knife.

"No, Sybill," I said, lifting her chin so she faced me. "I'm sorry. You're right to be frightened. I shouldn't have burdened you with my problems. It's all my fault." That was as close as I could come to admitting the truth. I'd killed that boy in cold blood, literally, and I'd thought I could escape without being caught. I'd been foolish and selfish, and I was dangerous to her. "I should go."

"Please," she whispered, "don't leave. I'm sorry I accused you. I'm so ashamed. Forgive me, please."

Twisting the knife.

I leaned forward and kissed her forehead gently. "There is nothing to forgive. I want to protect you, that's all. I need to go talk with Claire Marie about this. She will know what to do."

Deep down, I knew what Marie would say, and I dreaded her words. All my plans of arranging ways to stay here were worthless. I'd finished what she'd started by revealing our location to those who were hunting her, and the time had come to stop hiding and run. I knew one more thing. It would mean losing Sybill forever.

But for that moment, Sybill didn't need to know. I could be strong for her and smile. All my actor's training had taught me that. How to smile when you were screaming inside and make others believe the lie.

"I'll be back soon," I told her as I rose from the sofa and stood, the look on my face telling her things would be all right. "Don't worry."

"I'll try," she said, but I could see the struggle behind her eyes.

I crossed the room and had my hand on the doorknob when I heard her call out to me once more.

"Fin? What did you came here to talk to me about?" She tilted her face toward me, still trying to be strong.

Shaking my head, I smiled again. "It'll keep."

I opened the door, not wanting to look back as I walked out, afraid it would be the last time I saw her face.

"Fin?" She called again, but I kept my eyes firmly averted, determined not to break down for her sake. "What is your real name? Can't you tell me now?"

I hesitated.

"I love you," she said, and her voice cracked as she spoke

the words. "I just want to be able to say it to you. The real you. Please? I won't tell a soul. You know you can trust me."

With a sigh, I turned to look back at her, closing the door again. She was so beautiful, a mixture of strength and fragility that dazzled me completely. I loved her with my whole heart. I gave her a smile, a real one this time, and answered, "I'm Raul. Raul Griffin."

Her eyes were huge as she stared at me, looking me up and down, trying to fit the name with the face.

"What, you never saw a dead actor before?" I laughed nervously, feeling embarrassed at her scrutiny.

"You're...you're not kidding." Though framed as a statement, it felt almost a question.

"This is the part you don't believe?" I said. "You're willing to believe everything else...vampires, stake-in-the-heart, the works, but not my real name? Man, that's a bummer if you're willing to believe in the supernatural but not in who I am. Look, go ahead and ask me anything, anything at all. I'll prove it to you."

"I...I don't know what to ask." She looked pale, staring back at me with incredulity. "People saw you die. Like on the street."

"Yeah, well, turnings are a bitch," I shrugged, defensiveness rising in me. Her eyes were boring into me, and I couldn't stand there any more. I needed a smoke. Something to calm my nerves. I'd hadn't hoped for this reaction from her. "If we're going to do this, mind if I have a cigarette?"

"Knock yourself out," she said.

"Thanks." I crossed the room to the sliding door that led

onto the balcony and opened it in spite of the storm outside. The rain and wind blew louder than I'd expected, but I stepped out anyway, ignoring the cold wind that blew the rain toward me in gusts. I took off my glasses and put them in my pocket so they wouldn't get rain-splattered. "You know they cast me to appear in Titanic as Jack? Instead, I died, and that lucky son-of-a-bitch DiCaprio got the role."

Undeterred, she followed me, stopping in the door-frame just out of range of the rain. "Do you even need those glasses of yours, or are they just a prop?"

I laughed bitterly. "Why? You think I look stupid in them?"

"I didn't say that. I just thought, if you're a vampire, doesn't that give you like super eyesight or something?"

"Doesn't cure me being almost blind in one eye, no." I sniffed and sneered, digging in my pocket for my cigarettes. "Hate to disappoint you. I've been that way all my life. If I'd been born with only one arm, I wouldn't suddenly grow one like a starfish either. Doesn't work like that."

Tilting her head to one side, she stared curiously. "Which eye?"

"My right, okay? I can't wear contacts. Never could. They bug the shit out of me."

She shifted topics then, crossing her arms over her chest. "They said you died from an overdose. People said you took speedball in the bathroom at that bar...the place that actor guy owns."

"The Garden of Paradise. Ironic, huh?" I shook my last cigarette out of the pack. "Yeah, that's the place. What, did you study the news footage or something? You some closet tabloid reader?"

"They've shown your life story on TV a thousand times. I caught it once or twice."

I tried to light my cigarette, but the damp and wind made my lighter keep going out. She didn't believe me, and I stood there getting soaked.

"God damn it!" I threw the cigarette and lighter over the railing with annoyance, then turned back to face her. "Look, why would I lie about my name? Who wants to be that guy? I'm the poster child of how not to be famous. There's online forums about it. It's not like I can go on there and say, 'No, asshole, it didn't happen like that. I met a woman in the bathroom and got turned into a vampire instead. I'm actually still alive, sort of, and spending eternity alone.' I can't even tell my own mom. Jesus. My friends had to watch me die in the gutter, and I have to live with that for the rest of forever. I can't even say I'm sorry."

My fingers pushed my wet hair back, not bothering to wipe away my tears, and I looked at her as she stood in the open doorway. "Instead, I wake up in the morgue, and the same blonde woman who bit me is standing there, yanking off my toe tag, telling me I have to leave with her. I sit up, and my chest hurts like hell, you know? I lift up my shirt to see what's wrong, and someone must have sliced me open because there are deep cuts there, like really fucking deep, and I'm terrified, you know? And my heart ought to be pounding away, but I can't feel it at all. Then as I'm staring, I realize that those cuts are healing right before my eyes. Like special effects in some kind of horror movie. I'm staring like 'This can't be real,' you know? 'This cannot be happening.'"

I paused and wiped my cheeks with the back of my hand, sniffling before I went on. "So this woman, she's got this John Doe dragged over to the table next to me, right? She's putting my toe tag on him, Then she starts stripping off my clothes to put on this stiff, and I realize he looks kind of like me, I guess, if you're not looking closely. I'm freaking out, and I'm all like 'Who the fuck are you, lady?' Then, she just shoves some hospital scrubs in my hand and tells me there's no time. I've got to hurry up and get dressed before they come back. I try to ask her who the hell she's talking about, you know, but she won't answer. Then I try to tell her no and to leave me the fuck alone, but I can't. Like physically, I can't. The words won't come out of my mouth. I have to do what she says, and I don't even know why.

"The next thing I know, we're leaving the building, getting in a car to drive out of town, and she's telling me I'm a freakin' vampire. For a minute, I thought someone's got to be playing, like, the most elaborate practical joke ever or I must be in the Twilight Zone or something. I'd wake up and it would turn out to be some kind of bad dream or whatever, but I've been living the same nightmare ever since. She took everything from me that night — my life, my family, my friends, my name, my career, even the daylight — and now you don't even believe me."

I paused, waiting for her to speak, but she just looked at me, open mouthed, not saying a word. The way she stared unnerved me. I couldn't stand it. I'd never said any of that stuff out loud to anyone. Not even to myself. It made me self-conscious, and I hated myself for feeling so vulnerable.

"Look, I'm just going to go, okay? I'm sorry I fucked up your life. Just pretend you never met me. Want me to glamour it out of you, I will. I just…you were the first person in the last twenty years — hell, the first person ever — who made me feel something other than empty and lost. But I made a mistake, all right? I shouldn't have ever let this happen. You don't need me screwing up your life too."

She crossed the balcony, and when she reached where I stood, she lifted her hand to touch my face. "You really are him, aren't you? No bullshit."

"No bullshit. But it doesn't matter. It's just a name." Everything in me wanted to push her hand away, but my feet froze in place.

"No," she shook her head. "It does matter. It's so completely you. I don't ever want to forget you, so don't you dare even think about trying that glamour stuff on me. I will kill you."

I couldn't help but smile and laugh, wiping away the last of my tears. "You couldn't if you tried."

"Shut up." She took my face in her hands and kissed me fiercely.

My arms wrapped around her, and I held her body close to mine, wishing I could be the man she needed and this kiss wouldn't mean goodbye. Only her shivering made me pull away. "You're freezing."

"I don't care."

"Yeah, well, your chattering teeth say otherwise." Taking her face in my hands, I kissed her forehead, then the tip of her nose, and then her lips. "Look, I…I've got to go anyway. I don't want to, but I don't have a choice. I love you, Sybill."

"I love you...Raul." The way she looked into my eyes made my dead heart swell as though it might beat one more time just for her. "Go. I'll see you soon."

We walked inside as I nodded, giving her the lie again. "Soon."

Once more I kissed her, savoring the taste of her lips, fixing it in my memory forever, and then I pulled away and left her standing in the doorway, as I turned away from the apartment.

The elevator ride downstairs felt like the longest of my whole life. I wanted to go back up to her, take her in my arms, and...and then my realistic self took over and told me thinking I could ever have her was just a foolish dream. I couldn't condemn her to this life. Hiding in the shadows, the hunger always lurking beneath the surface, having to give up her whole life, her family, her home. No. I could never ask that of her. Better for her to remember me this way.

On the street, I reached into my pocket and called Marie's cell phone. No answer. Could she still be sleeping? I doubted it. She had probably gone on to the shop and had simply forgotten the phone at home.

Before I faced her, I needed some answers. I told myself I'd just swing by the crime scene and make sure I hadn't left any evidence behind. I told Marie's voicemail I had to run a quick errand and then I'd meet her at the shop. Shouldn't be long. Maybe twenty minutes at the most. I hung up and headed toward the park, hands in my pockets, trying to walk off my fears and decide exactly what I would say to Marie. I needed to tell her. We would have to run.

Out of Time

Chief Inspector

I flashed badges at the police who were huddled around the crime scene in the dark. Yellow crime tape encircled the area, and plastic tenting covered the ground to protect it from the rain. It only took a little glamour to convince them my team and I were part of a special task force.

My team went to examine the crime scene while I canvassed the perimeter, looking for evidence the humans might have overlooked.

Suddenly, in the tree line, I saw a young man, and I knew right away he wasn't a man at all. He gave off no heat and didn't react to the cold, though the rain slowly turned to snow. He obviously had come to observe the crime scene, just like me.

161

Swifter than shadow, I fell upon him, my hand on his throat as I shoved him back against a tree, fangs out. "Don't make a sound, and don't struggle," I said. "Or I will kill you right now. I'm older and stronger. You can't fight me. Nod if you understand."

He nodded, eyes wide with surprise and fear.

"Good. Now, I'm going to have some questions for you. Understand?"

He nodded again.

"Good boy. Now, you're going to walk with me calmly and go get in that van by the crime scene. Don't make a scene or try to run. You can't escape me, so don't even try. If you make the humans question your presence, I'll kill you and make them forget you even existed. Understand?"

Again, he nodded, and I let go of my hold on him. "Now walk."

The two of us walked side-by-side, as though we were simply out for a stroll, back toward the van. I smiled at the human police officers and said, "I think we've found what we need." Then I snapped my fingers, and the evidence team emerged. With one look from me, the entire team climbed inside the van with me. The door slid shut behind us, and we drove away.

C'EST LA MORT

Marie

I waited all night for Fin to appear at the shop. As each hour ticked past, I became more concerned. Finally, just before dawn, I decided he must have gone to see his human without telling me. The thought irritated me beyond measure, but I had given him permission, so I had to let go of my anger and allow things to take their course. Besides, he would tire of her once she was no longer shiny and new in his eyes. I returned to the house alone just before dawn.

My dreams, however, were far from restful, and I woke screaming his name. The house answered only with silence. I could sense dark had just fallen, and in a panic driven by dread, I threw off the covers and dressed quickly. He was definitely in danger. I felt equally certain if I didn't act fast, I might never see him gain.

I tried to reach my mind out to him, but I could no longer sense his whereabouts. He was too far away from me. Frustrated and filled with a rising sense of fury, I knew I would have to use my other senses to track him. In my hurry, I left behind my coat, determined to follow his scent wherever it might lead. Because of the cold, I must have looked bizarre to the humans on the street, but I paid them no mind.

Letting the monster in me guide my steps, I followed the faint smell of him, still barely perceptible despite the rain the night before. He had taken a path I didn't know, and his scent ended at an apartment building. He had been inside that place, and it only took a moment for me to know the reason why. His human. I detected her perfume, though I saw the building could not be accessible through the locked and guarded front door.

Without an invitation, I would never get inside.

I paced, fury mounting. With each moment that passed, he slipped further away. I felt my fangs descend and a blood-lust come over me. He would have been safe with me if not for this human. My mind ran wild. What if she had captured him? What if she had done something to him? What if, what if, what if? I blamed her for all the imagined evil that possibly could have befallen him.

Just as I made ready to break down the doors with my bare hands and glamour the guard into giving me access to the building, I saw a young woman exit the elevator and walk across the marble floor toward the entrance. She had strange, wild hair and silver in her nose and ears. I pulled back to stand in front of an automatic banking machine at the next building, pretending to make a withdrawal, but as soon as she emerged from the building, her scent blew toward me on the wind, unmistakably the same cloying smell that had clung to Fin.

Snarling with fury, I rushed forward and shoved her to the alleyway, pressing her body to the wall. I bared my fangs and growled, "Where is he?"

She squeaked, eyes wide like a deer in headlights, shocked into silence. Her reaction only infuriated me more, and I shook her fiercely, my hands gripping her shoulders like a vice. "Do you know who I am?"

"You-you're her," she whispered, nodding. "C-Claire Marie. Please, don't kill me."

"You're in no position to ask anything of me!" I saw her wince, and I moved in until we were eye to eye. "I want him. Where. Is. He?"

She trembled with fear. "I don't know, I swear. I was just going to go looking for him, myself. He said he'd come back after he talked to you, but he never showed up."

"When did he leave?" I didn't back off, and my eyes flashed. "Tell me quickly!"

"Last night! Early, maybe ten o'clock? He said he wanted to talk to you about the murder."

"What murder?" I snapped.

"The one in the park. The vampire killing. I saw it on the news. I told him about it, and he got all worried. Said he needed to talk to you right away."

Her answer made the hair on the back of my neck rise with alarm. I knew Fin. I knew his haunts. I knew exactly what

165

this meant. This human girl had cost me my companion, my son, my Fin, and I directed all my fear-driven anger at her.

With one swift motion, I bit her throat and drank deeply. Her blood filled my mouth, and I swallowed in greedy gulps. I wanted revenge, to feel her die in agony. She struggled at first, but then grew weak.

At last she fell limp in my arms, and I could feel her life fading. Then, as always happens, I felt her soul and mine mingle. I could see into her deepest desires and knew with a flash of understanding I had made a horrible mistake.

She loved my Fin, body and soul, just as he was. She had a fierce loyalty to him. I could see that too. I saw in her mind's eye the memories of all that had passed between her and Fin. I saw he had given her his true name. He had trusted her. I knew he felt that way with good reason. He loved her. I knew for his sake, this girl, this Sybill of his, must not die.

Her blood loss, however, became more than her frail body could sustain. I'd taken her past the point of no return, and only one way lay open to me now. She must become one of us.

I pulled away my fangs from her skin with a sigh and bit into my wrist. I pressed the wound to her lips, letting my blood pour into her mouth. "Drink," I whispered, and she did.

Slowly, she took her first swallow, and then she latched onto my arm. I could sense the change in her, and when I knew she had had enough, I drew back from her. She reeled and collapsed to the ground, groaning as her humanity fell away, her body died a human death, and she began the transformation.

Standing over her, I watched, a ghost of a smile on my lips. "Don't be afraid, ma chére. We will find him, you and I. Wherever they have taken him, we will find him. Together. This I swear to you."

PART II

Blood Will Have Blood

Sybill

I felt so strange and new, like my body had become lighter, faster, stronger. Colors were brighter, and scents were richer. I had a craving greater than hunger or thirst, and whatever would fulfill it, I wanted it now, now, now!

Rising swiftly from the pavement, I stood in one motion, an animalistic growling escaping my lips, and for the first time, I felt my fangs. I could taste the scent of humans on my tongue, making me suddenly certain what my body desired. However, when I moved to begin pursuit, a short blonde woman, not a woman at all, stood in my path.

"Not yet. Not here." She looked me in the eye as she spoke, and I had to obey, though I snarled in protest. "I know what you need. Come."

She led me further into the dark of the alley, and I struggled to remember the particulars of my identity.

"You're disoriented. Don't worry, it will pass. You need to feed. If there had been time to prepare, I would have planned for it, but we shall have to make do. I am sorry I brought you to this life this way, but one day I hope you will forgive me."

We reached a cross street, and she halted, raising one hand to stop me, and sniffed the air. I followed her example, and she turned to smile with approval. "Good. Now, because we are trying to avoid discovery, we must take someone the world will not miss. Ignore the ordinary humans. Concentrate on the scent of despair, of the desire for death and oblivion. Sift it out from all the others. Do you smell it?"

I raised my head, closed my eyes, and breathed deep. Yes. The scent seemed faint but easily detectable now I knew what to seek out. My eyes opened, and I practically salivated. I caught her gaze, and she nodded approval. "Yes, ma chére. Now we hunt."

We moved so fast, it seemed the rest of the world stood still, and in moments we were blocks away by a dumpster near a pile of boxes. I knew inside would be the thing I sought, a human, homeless and without hope or desire to continue. He reeked of Listerine, which he'd been drinking to stave off the cold, and I took him in his sleep. Each swallow brought back more and more of my memory. I drank deep until only an empty shell of flesh remained.

Looking down, I could pity him now my thirst had been satisfied. I covered him with the ragged blanket by his side, closing his eyes gently and whispering, "Thank you."

The woman beside me laughed. I remembered her name, my brain dredging it up from the depths of memory, and said it aloud. "Claire Marie."

I lifted a quizzical brow, and she laughed all the more. "That man should be thanking you, my dear. You gave him what he wanted. He wished for death. Couldn't you hear it?"

I looked back down at the body, already growing cold, and I knew she was right. Still, some part of me felt I ought to have a sense of guilt for what I'd done. Ought to, and yet I didn't all the same. My eyes lifted to meet hers again. "I…what did you do to me?"

She smiled. "You are a vampire. I am your maker."

"Why?" I said, tilting my head at her with earnest confusion.

"Why what, ma chére?" An edge of condescension under her question irritated me.

My eyes narrowed as I gave her a piercing glare. "Why did you do it?"

Giving me a hurt little smile, she raised a hand to my cheek, "For Raul. You needed to live for him."

Then the last of my memories flooded back, her questions, my worry for Fin…no, that wasn't his name. I remembered her accusations, my fear, and then my death. "You…you killed me. He will never forgive you."

She bit her lip, and I felt genuine sorrow coming from her. How could I feel her emotions? I don't know, but I did all the same. "I hope you are wrong. But whether he does or not, the fact is he is in great danger, and we are the only ones who can help him."

"Danger?" I felt a surge of adrenaline rush through me, and I balled my fists, ready to take on anyone who might hurt him. My Raul. That was his name, the one only I called him. She knew his true name, but he gave me permission to use it. "Where? How do we find him?"

"Steady. If we are to find him, we must first be sure we ourselves escape the trap into which he has fallen. Today is not the day to fight. Today, we run."

"Then what? We just abandon him? I can't do that!"

She placed a hand on my shoulder and shook her head. "No. Not abandon him. We plan. We will need to gather our strength and be cunning. That is the only way we will succeed."

"How do you know they haven't killed him already?" The idea threw me into a panic.

"Because they haven't found me yet." She smiled and took my hand. "Come. We need to gather your things and escape this place. Take me to your apartment. Quickly. We have wasted too much time already. We can talk more once we are away from here."

"I can't leave," I said. "My family is here. My whole life. I can't just run off without even saying goodbye."

"If you love them, you must. Those who have captured Raul, who are after us, you have no idea what they are capable of. Once they know about you, no one you know or care about is safe. You must cut all ties as of this moment."

I could see the sincerity in her face, and I felt my heart

break at the same moment I felt strangely liberated, free from my father's world forever. Isn't that what I'd always wanted?

As I stood hesitating, puzzling through my emotions about this catastrophic rebirth, she tugged at my hand. "Come, child of mine. Now is the time, or the net will snare us as well. You will have time to mourn once we are away."

Though I comprehended the pragmatic urgency for her argument, I knew once we were out of immediate danger, she would have a lot to answer for. I took a deep and unnecessary breath, swallowed down all my questions for the moment, and followed her.

As we approached my building, we slowed our movements to human speed in order to avoid attracting attention. Emerging from the alleyway, I took the lead, walking with her to the main doors. I swiped my card, and we headed confidently past the guard to the elevators. We rode up in silence, and then strode down the hall to my door.

That place, which had felt so comforting and safe to me, now seemed foreign. Even the size of the rooms had changed, or to be more exact, my perception had shifted. I could smell Raul ever where, and it made me stop in my tracks to breathe him in. Claire Marie wrinkled her nose, but said nothing, passing me and going straight on into my bedroom.

"Hey!" I said, startled into action and following her. "You can't just barge in like you own the place. This is my apartment."

She dug in the closet for a suitcase. "Not for much longer, it isn't. Here." With an effortless movement, she tossed a large red suitcase in my direction. "Pack some things. Whatever is most important. We must hurry."

I caught the suitcase and opened my mouth to object, only to find clothes being flung in my direction one after another. "Hey! Cut it out, okay? I'll pack my own shit."

"Tsk," she paused, looking at me. "There is no cause for cursing."

"What, are you my mother?" I rolled my eyes.

"Yes," she frowned." Now, pack."

"Fine. Just let me do it myself." I placed the suitcase on the bed and opened it, then began shoving clothes into it as quickly as I could, not bothering to fold anything.

"Honestly!" She threw up her hands in exasperation, watching me with supreme disapproval.

"Hey, you said to hurry. I'm doing it." I shoved some underwear into the front pocket. "Don't you have something else you can do?"

She thought for a moment. "Your phone. Where is it?"

Taking off my messenger bag, I dug in the front pocket, pulled out my iPhone, and handed it to her. "Here. Knock yourself out." Claire Marie shook her head at me, and then with a smirk, she crushed the phone in one hand, reducing it to a pile of glass, twisted plastic, and broken metal on the floor. I gasped in horror. "What the hell did you do?"

"Saved you from being tracked," she replied smugly. "Tell me something, did Raul ever contact you on that thing?"

I nodded, still staring open-mouthed at the debris.

"Well, then your number is in his phone. They will know who you are. They will put a trace on that machine, and they will have us both, quick as you please. I've saved you from that." With a smile and a bow of her head, she went on, "You can thank me later. Do you have a house phone as well?"

Knowing she was right didn't make me feel any relief at all. "In the kitchen. Don't destroy it too."

"I have no intention of it. I need to make a call." With that, she walked away. "Shower and change."

Though I felt annoyed, I went into the bathroom and took one of the fastest showers of my life. As I toweled off, I could hear her talking from the other room. I could hear everything now I had become a vampire. I could hear the conversation as well as if I stood in the room beside her. Claire Marie told someone named Crystal she'd had a death in the family and had to go out of town. She asked Crystal to put a "closed" sign on the front door of her shop and then go by her house to pick up her dog and take care of it until she returned. The call didn't take long, leaving me just enough time to throw on a sweater, some leggings, and a short black skirt. I heard her hang up and then she came back into the room to watch me pull on my socks and Doc Martins, leaning on the door-frame, arms crossed.

"Who were you talking to?" I said.

"My assistant."

"Do you really think we'll be back?" I paused, looking up at her.

She shrugged. "I don't know. I rather doubt it. There is only one way that can happen. That scenario seems highly unlikely."

Sniffing with annoyance, I stood and shoved my toiletry bag into my suitcase. "Anyone ever tell you you're kind of cagey?"

Chuckling, she nodded. "There is no 'kind of' about it. I have good reasons for my secrets, and once we're safe, I'll share those reasons with you. At least as much as you need to know. Your hair is still wet."

"I'll have it under a hat." I grabbed a gray fedora off the dresser, pulling it on at a jaunty angle. Then I closed my suitcase, snapped it shut, set it on the floor, and pulled out the handle so it could easily be dragged. "Okay, done. Now what?"

"Now, my dear," she said with a clap of her hands, "we get 'the hell out of Dodge' as they say in the movies."

"How old are you? Nobody says that anymore. I swear, you've got the weirdest way of talking." I followed her out into the living room, and I scanned the room for anything I might be leaving behind I'd regret. I felt tempted to take family photos, but I knew that could be dangerous. Then I dropped the bag, thinking quickly. "Wait. Give me a second."

While she stopped by the kitchen bar, I ran into the other bedroom, the one I used as my studio, and came out with a sketchbook and some charcoals. I shoved those into my messenger bag and slung it over my chest.

"You're an artist?" She raised an eyebrow. "Interesting. Very well. Shall we go?"

Glancing toward the kitchen, I paused. "Do we need to take snacks or anything with us?"

She gave me a quizzical look. "Are you hungry?"

"Well, no. I just didn't know...well...am I ever going to eat food again?"

Caught off guard by my question, she laughed, covering her mouth in amusement. "You just let me know if you actually feel hungry for human food, all right?"

"You're making fun of me. How am I supposed to know

these things if you don't tell me?"

Nodding, she looked serious again. "You are quite right. I shouldn't have laughed. No, you will not ever need to eat or drink again. The blood will suffice."

"But if I wanted to, could I?" I thought back on those espressos Raul had ordered in the coffee shop. Had he ever actually drunk any of it?

She shrugged. "Quite honestly, I have no idea. I have never tried, though if you did eat, I can't imagine it would sustain you for long and might make you ill." Looking down at her watch, she frowned at what she saw. "We must go. The longer we delay, the further we are from getting Raul back."

One last look around. I would never be here again. The rooms already felt as though they no longer were mine. I sighed and then looked back at her. "I'm ready."

"All right. I need to stop by my shop. There are some items there I don't want anyone to find. Plus, we will need all the money we can get. Come." She opened the door and gestured for me to follow. "Time is wasting."

That's how I left my place, with nothing but one suitcase, my purse, and a pair of Doc Martins. "You're not going back to your house for anything?" I said as we waited for the elevator.

"It's easier if I walk away. Plus, I've run away frequently enough to know when it's time to leave. There is nothing there I cannot get back with enough time."

In the lobby, she whispered, "Watch this" and then walked up to the guard. She proceeded to tell him we hadn't been there, he'd been alone and bored all day. He stared deep into her eyes and nodded. Then, as though he no longer saw us, he looked down at his phone and started playing Angry Birds.

We walked out, and once the door shut behind us, I said, "What did you do to him?"

"I glamoured him," she said simply. "He won't remember us."

Color me impressed. We started down the street toward an area of the Central West End I almost never went to. "How did you do that? Just where exactly are we going?"

"I'll teach you how to do it, don't worry," she assured me. "As for where we're going, I told you before, my shop. I have a few things to pick up. It's not far."

Curiosity got the better of me. "What kind of shop is it?" I couldn't imagine this woman working.

"Antiques and Interior Design. This will likely be the last time I see the place. Ah well. Nothing lasts forever. Except us, of course. We needed to move on anyway, I suppose. If I'd stayed much longer, people would have started to ask me for the name of my plastic surgeon. Never let them notice you don't age. Otherwise, you'll find yourself at the wrong end of a stake." She made a sad face and turned left to cross the street, while I scrambled to follow.

We passed two more blocks before she halted and began digging for keys in her pocket. "Ah, here we are."

I read the sign aloud. "It's All In the Past?"

"Indeed, it is. In more ways than one." Within a few seconds, she opened the door and led me inside, locking it back behind us. "It's just through here," she said.

"What is?" I peered around at the glass cases and display

of artistic antiques.

"My office." Passing the jewelry case with several expensive pieces, she walked to the back of the store and opened a door. "Well? Come on, then. Don't stand there idling. We're in a hurry, or didn't you hear me before?"

Thinking better of my tart remark, I did as she asked, following her into a poky little room with papers scattered about on a cheap 1980s style office desk. A computer filled up a good portion of it, and as she walked past and bumped one corner, the mouse moved slightly and the screen came to life. I saw an online auction site on the display with a contact form as yet still blank. "Buying something?"

"Not anymore," she said, snatching a canvas shopping bag from a desk drawer and then walking over to a safe which stood in the corner. She entered the password, and I heard a click. Then she turned the handle to open the safe door. I couldn't see what she had inside, but she scooped it up into the bag and closed the door once more. Then she grabbed a bank deposit bag from the desk drawer. Without saying anything, she headed back out of the office into the shop, and I took that as my cue to do the same.

Back in the main area of the shop, I saw her emptying the cash drawer.

The bag already had several bundles of hundreds inside, and she added to it until the bag bulged and hard to close. Taking another sack from the register area, she opened the jewelry case and took out several large pieces, leaving others behind. She made a quick scan of the room and then packed up three other small pieces which I assumed either had sentimental value or were worth a great deal. At last, both bags full, she set them down next to me, then ran back to her office one more time. She emerged a few moments later in a fur coat.

"Shall we?" she said, stuffing the bank bag into the back of her shirt, tucking part of it into her waistband before pulling the shirt back down to cover it.

"I'm guessing this isn't your first hasty exit," I replied as she picked up the two shopping bags.

She laughed. "Not exactly."

"So, how are we leaving town? What's the plan?"

"Bus," she said, striding across to the front door and unlocking it. "Two tickets to wherever is out of the way, then we change buses and go somewhere we really want to be."

I stopped her in the doorway. "You're kidding, right?"

"I've done this before, you know," she said, pulling away and stepping out onto the stoop.

"In this century?" I said, ignoring her scowl. "Because they've added security video cameras, and unless you're going to dye our hair and change our looks between here and there, you need a better plan."

Her frown deepened, and she snapped at me in frustration, "Fine then. What do you propose?"

With a quick glance down the street, I walked over to a generic white paneled van in front of a flower shop, looked both ways to see if anyone could see us, then I broke the passenger side window and unlocked the door. "Get in," I said, climbing over to the driver's side, throwing my suitcase in the back. I reached down and pulled the wires out under the dashboard, clicking them together until the engine roared to life.

She stared at me for a second from the sidewalk. "Where did you learn to do that?"

"You're not the only one with secrets," I told her. "Now hurry up and get in before someone calls the cops."

ATLASTA MOTEL

Marie Antoinette

When we were far enough from the city to satisfy my fears of immediate discovery, I turned to Sybill and smiled. "You did well, my dear. I need a few items to help ensure our escape. When we reach the next town, we need to stop at a dry goods store of some sort."

"A what?" she frowned.

"No need to sound so perturbed," I laughed. "I believe a Walmart or Walgreens will have the variety of inventory I require."

"Uh, okay. So you need someplace with a little bit of everything. Is that right?" Her eyebrow raised at me as she peered in my direction.

"Precisely." I nodded. "This sign indicates there is a town three miles from here. There seem to be several eating establishments at this location, thus I believe it would be safe to assume such a store would likely be in the vicinity as well."

"You talk so weird, you know that?"

I winced at her slang. "My family raised me to speak properly. I find no ill in that."

"Hmm," she grunted. "Whatever you say, I guess. No one talks like you, though. How friggin' old are you, anyway?"

"Old enough your asking my age is more than a little bit impertinent, my dear. But I shall overlook it." I turned away then, facing out the window once more. "This is our exit."

"I see it. Jeez. Keep your panties on." She signaled and veered off the highway and as we reached the overpass, I saw a Walgreens on the right.

"You have a strange idea of proper conversation, my dear." I pointed toward the store. "Please take us over there, if you would. Park under the shadows toward the rear. I would prefer to avoid security cameras in case someone is looking for this stolen vehicle."

We turned into the parking lot, and she did as I'd asked, stopping the van under an overhanging tree whose limbs had been weighed down by last week's heavy winter snow.

"What is it you want from here?" she said as we clambered out and shut the doors.

Smiling fiercely at her, I started toward the automatic doors at the front of the building. "You shall see. I told you I have had a great deal of experience with disappearing. This is not, as they say, my first time at the rodeo."

She burst out laughing. "Who says that? Cowboys?"

I rolled my eyes and gave a low chuckle. "Just trust me."

The glare of the fluorescent lights hurt my eyes as we entered the store, and I pulled a pair of large sunglasses off a display and placed them on my face, not bothering to remove the tag. Then I snatched up a shopping basket and headed directly back to the health and beauty area. Out of the corner of my eye, I saw her blink at the brightness of the store just as I had, and she soon followed my example before scurrying after me.

"We're trying to hide, and you want to buy cosmetics? Seriously?"

"Hush." I waved my hand dismissively at her before pulling some new makeup from the shelves – mascara, eye shadow, blush, and tanning liquid with makeup base to match. She sighed in annoyance, but I ignored her as I went next to the hair care aisle. It only took me a few seconds to choose hair-coloring kits, red for me, blonde for her. I also picked up a pair of scissors and a comb, along with some finishing products.

"You can't be serious?" she whispered.

"Deadly serious," I assured her, turning away in search of the office supply area. "Now if I were duct tape, where would I live?"

"Duct tape? You planning to tie someone up?"

Annoyed, I stopped and turned to face her. "No, though I might put some over your mouth if you do not learn to be quiet."

"Fine." She scowled and pushed past me, snatching a roll of duct tape from a display at the end of an aisle. "Here. Happy?"

I took the roll from her and nodded, saying nothing further, scanning the signs for the last items on my mental want list. When I saw a shelf with inexpensive blankets in the home decor section, I smiled and scooped up three of them. "I think that should do," I said. "We can go."

And without looking to see if she followed or not, I took my items to the checkout. As the cashier began scanning the bar-codes on my purchases, I felt her close behind me. "Sunglasses," I said, holding out my hand to take them from her. I could feel her annoyance as she passed them over to me, but again I ignored her attitude and placed both her sunglasses and mine on the counter to complete the sale. I paid for the items in cash, then smiled and met the gaze of the cashier. "Thank you. You've been quite helpful," I said, seeing his eyes glaze over. "You won't remember our faces or be able to describe us if anyone asks questions about our time here in your store. You only know we were a couple of nice women who were passing through. Please, can I have the keys to your car as a token of neighborly kindness?"

He nodded and dug in his pocket, then handed us his car keys along with our bags, a hazy smile on his face as he told us to have a nice day.

"Good boy. Now run along and destroy the video recordings of our visit here," I told him. Taking the keys and smiling as I turned to walk away. Sybill and I replaced our sunglasses and walked through the doors without another word.

Once we were outside, she turned to look at me. "That is so creepy, what you did back there. Now what? How do we know which car is his?"

I pulled down my sunglasses and winked at her over the top of them as I pushed the lock button on his car remote. A horn sounded from a RAV-4 in nondescript black, parked in the back row. "Be a dear and go get our bags, would you, please? I will bring the car around."

For a moment, she looked at me, and her mouth opened as if she planned to speak, but quickly she thought better of it. Her mouth snapped closed, and she turned, making quick strides toward the van. I couldn't help but laugh a little as I got behind the wheel of our new conveyance and turned the key. She might be young, but this rebellious questioning of hers would lessen now she could see I was more aware of the modern world than she had given me credit for. I brought the car to the rear of the van, still hidden beneath the tree and out of sight of the security cameras, I hoped. She loaded our things in quickly, and then we sped away toward the highway once more. Sybill became quiet, mulling over recent events. I didn't interrupt her thought, keeping my mind focused on my own plans.

The clock in the dashboard told me we had about three more hours before dawn. Time enough to put some more distance between us and any pursuit. I drove for a little less than an hour, then pulled off the interstate onto a minor highway running north.

"Where to now?" she said. "You looking for something in particular or just bored?"

"We are simply less likely to be found by the human police if we go this way," I said. "Changing our direction is a good idea."

I saw her put her elbow on the armrest and begin gnawing at her thumb nail absently, her mind obviously turning over the rapid change of events since our paths met.

"Penny for your thoughts?" I said.

"Hmm? I'm just wondering where Raul is and when the hell we're going to stop long enough for you to explain what is going on." She didn't look at me, but the tone of her voice let me know she felt both worried and angry. "I mean, how do I know anything you've said is true? You could just be lying to me. To Raul too, for that matter."

Her accusation made me furious, and I jerked the wheel and slammed on the brakes, pulling to a sudden stop by the side of the road, a cloud of dust rising from the gravel shoulder. "Listen to me, right now. I have had enough of you questioning my motives and my intelligence. If I'm going to keep us both safe and somehow manage to save Raul, you're going to have to shut up and do what I tell you. I've been running from these monsters a long time. The only way I have survived is with my wits. You're going to have to trust me, or you will find yourself being tortured by them, and believe me when I tell you the worst you can imagine does not even begin to describe the horrors they will put you through if you're caught. Am I clear?"

Eyes wide, she stared at me as though I'd slapped her in the face. I saw her gulp and then nod slowly.

"Good. Don't ask me about what they might or might not be doing to Raul. I don't want to think about it. If I stop for even a moment to be afraid for him, it will put us both in jeopardy. I'm going to save him. Period. You are going to help me. Got it?"

"Yes," she said.

"Good. Now, it isn't long until dawn, and we need to rest. We're going to look for an old seedy motel where it's not surprising if people stay for only an hour or two. A place where the clerk is trained not to notice who is staying and knows better than to ask questions. Yes, it will be less than pleasant surroundings. But in terms of our safety, it's what the moment requires. Keep your eyes peeled for that sort of place and be ready when I say. Understood?"

Again she nodded, and I looked away once more, pulling out onto the deserted highway, tires flinging gravel in our wake. We rode in silence, and I felt the tension in her as though she were a guitar string stretched to near breaking.

At the next town, we passed by a faded stucco-covered motel with a neon sign flashing "ATLASTA MOTEL." The pool had chain link surrounding it and advertised weekly rates just above the vacancy sign. Dilapidated cars were in front of some of the doors, but there were still several empty spots, making it clear the place was not even half-full.

"That's perfect," I smiled, and drove on past into the dark at the edge of the city limits.

"Hey, aren't we stopping?" she said, looking over her shoulder.

"I thought I told you to stop asking questions," I said, pulling over again. "Get out."

"What?" She stared at me, agog.

"You heard me. Take your things and mine and get out of the car. Now."

I felt the fear and panic rising in her like a wave, but she did as I said, dragging all of the bags with her. She looked like a frightened child as I rolled down the window. "Don't move. I'll be right back."

Pulling out onto the highway, I shut off the headlights and drove on a little further. My vampire sight let me see perfectly in the dark, and about half a mile down the road from where she stood, I saw a ravine. Bracing myself, I drove straight for it, and just before the car went over the edge, I opened the door and jumped free, rolling on the asphalt until I came to a stop. The car didn't survive the impact. I heard a crash and a splash and the sound of breaking glass and shearing metal. Brushing myself off, I rose to my feet, already starting to heal, and I could see the vehicle thirty feet below, the front bumper wrapped around a tree, though in order to see it there, one would have to know to look. The brush would keep the wreckage well hidden from human eyes, and it would likely take several days, perhaps even weeks, before anyone noticed it.

"Perfect," I smiled, then I turned and ran at vampire speed back to where Sybill waited on the side of the highway in the dark.

"Why did you do that?" she said, panic rising in her voice. "I thought you were leaving me here."

I picked up my bags and grinned. "I told you I'd be back. We needed to lose the car for our own protection. Come. Our room awaits." She blinked with surprise, but as I walked away, she gathered her own things and followed in my wake back toward the neon sign.

Strolling up to the main office, I muttered, "Follow my lead," and then walked inside with Sybill at my heels. A bored red-faced older man sat behind the desk, and I could see him playing online poker by the reflection in the lenses of his glasses. Perfect. He would be in too much of a hurry to finish our transaction to pay any attention to us.

He handed me the requisite forms, and I filled them out with an innocuous smile. When I reached the line for our car's license plate, I looked up at him and gave him a sad expression, then said with a heavy Russian accent, "Car is kaput. We wait here for brother, yes? He come tomorrow night. Is okay we wait in room for him?"

Nodding, he assured me we could stay, but we would have to pay for two nights, even if we didn't sleep.

With an exaggerated pout and a sigh, I looked over at Sybill and whispered some words in Russian to her. Though she didn't understand them, she did comprehend my purpose and went along with me, nodding her head and replying, "Da."

"Is okay," I told him, and he gave a smarmy smile. He told me the amount we owed and asked for the money up front. I bit my lip as though it were a heavy burden to pay so much, then dug in my purse, crumpling up some twenty-dollar bills before pulling them out and handing them to him. He passed me the key and pointed vaguely to his left, telling us we would be in room number 17. Only one bed, a double, but it would be cheaper. I nodded and thanked him, then Sybill and I walked back out with shoulders hunched as though we were tired and sad. In the security mirror's reflection, I saw him immediately return to his online poker game without a second glance in our direction.

As soon as we were inside, "Do Not Disturb" sign on the doorknob and the bolt thrown shut, Sybill tossed down her bags and put both hands on her hips. "What was that about? We're Russian now? He's going to think we're prostitutes."

I laughed, digging out the blankets and duct tape. "I certainly hope so."

"Why is that a good thing, exactly?" Her voice sounded testy, and I knew she feared we might end up with unwanted visitors.

"Because two Russian prostitutes could never be mistaken for an antique dealer and a college student on the run for stealing a car three hundred and fifty miles away, now could they? Here, hold this a second, won't you?" I handed her the blankets and began unrolling the tape.

She made a little noise of surprise, but her argument had ended.

Pulling one of the cheap chairs toward the door, I stepped up into the seat and began duct taping across the top of the door and covering the door-frame, sealing it shut. "The key to staying in human lodgings," I said, pressing the tape down well, "is to make sure no sunlight can get in. That would be unfortunate. I'm sealing all the possible entries for light in this room and making sure no one opens the door to clean."

I climbed down and taped the sides, then took one of the blankets from her arms. While she looked on, I rolled the blanket and put it at the base of the door to shut out any light that might enter at the threshold. I finished by putting a small piece of tape over the peephole in the door. Next, I started with the curtains, taping the sides and bottom to the wall, sealing them together at the center. At the top, the rod held the curtain a couple of inches from the wall, so I took another blanket and rolled it, then placed it on top of the rod, taping it securely in place. No light could enter that way either.

Turning back to look at Sybill, I smiled with satisfaction. "There. Now we're secure."

"You've done this a few times, I guess, huh?" she said, unable to hide her admiration in spite of herself.

"Once or twice," I laughed, tossing the roll of duct tape back into the shopping bag. "Now, shall we?"

She raised an eyebrow. "Shall we what?"

"Well, we can't exactly keep wandering around looking like ourselves, now can we? That wouldn't be much of a getaway." I pulled out the hair coloring kits and scissors.

"Nuh uh," she said, backing away and shaking her head. "You do not want me cutting your hair, Miss Soccer Mom America. Looking this fierce is not cheap. I just had it done." I couldn't help smirking, and she caught the look on my face. "Hey, just because it isn't your taste doesn't mean it isn't awesome."

"Look," I said, stepping forward, stern and serious again, "we are not on a girl bonding road trip. I'm not asking, I'm telling. That signature style you love so much is going to get us caught and killed. Get this straight right now. You are going to have to leave behind your life, your name, and your look. For good. You're going to have to walk out of this room as someone else. Otherwise, you may as well go right back home and wait for them to show up at your apartment, capture you, and make you watch them kill everyone you've ever loved before they flay you alive. Got it?"

The shock on her face told me she hadn't realized until just that moment she couldn't go back to her former life. Not ever. Her bottom lip quivered, and tears welled in her eyes.

I pitied her, but I had no time to coddle her. With a sad smile, I reached out to touch her cheek tenderly. "I am sorry, Sybill. I wish it didn't have to be this way. If I could change it, I would. But Raul is depending on us. And I'm the closest thing you both have to a mother, now and forever. We're family. I'm going to do whatever it takes to keep you safe just like I…" my voice broke, and I had to clear my throat before continuing, "like I wish I could have done for my children. I lost them to these people, and I'll be damned if they take you from me too."

"It…it's only hair," she said, letting the tears fall, and I could see her acceptance and understanding in her eyes. I knew she truly cared for Raul, and I prayed it would make her strong enough for what lay ahead.

"Good girl." I smiled sadly and leaned in to kiss her cheek. "Now, who's going first? You or me?"

She sniffled and wiped her eyes. "I'll do yours first."

Reaching up, I pulled my long blonde hair out of the clip that held it and let it cascade down my back. With a deep breath, I looked at her resolutely. "All right then."

Putting on a brave face, she wetted it down, and began snipping. By the time she finished, she'd given me a Bettie Page cut, and then we dyed it a deep auburn. When I caught a glimpse of my reflection in the cracked bathroom mirror, I barely recognized myself. The style looked modern, and while it would take some time to adjust, I found it strangely becoming.

Because Sybill had so many layers, in order to change the style, I had to make the cut more drastic. I had always had a knack with hair, and when I stepped back to let her see, she smiled at what she saw. I'd given her a spiked pixie cut. "I love this!" she exclaimed.

"Good, but we still have to make you a blonde," I reminded her. She looked at me hopefully, eyebrows raised, and pleaded. "Can we just make it blonde streaks?" Clearly, she wanted another way to make herself look unique.

I rolled my eyes. "The idea is to blend in, remember? Not stand out. Sorry, but it all has to be bleached blonde."

"Ugh." She sighed. "Okay fine, but one day when this is all over, I'm changing it back to black."

Humoring her, I nodded, and she went to apply the color while I started sweeping up the hair off the floor. I gathered it all into the trashcan, then removed the liner and tied it up neatly to burn once we were safely away.

While she rinsed, I got out the fake tanning spray, and she and I took turns spraying one another until we looked like we'd just come back from a vacation in Cozumel. I made her remove all of her piercings and jewelry since they were too easily recognizable. We would also have to cover her tattoos with makeup since they were identifiable markings.

Finally finished, we stood side by side, gazing at our new faces in the mirror. "We'll change our makeup styles tomorrow

196

night before we leave. We'll also need to pick new names. We will have to buy some new clothes soon. But this is a good start."

"Well, I don't look like myself anymore, that's for sure."

"You look stunning, my dear," I told her, brushing her hair back from her forehead, and I meant it.

She blushed, gave a deep sigh, and then yawned hugely. "Sorry. Didn't mean to yawn right in your face. I'm suddenly worn out."

Taking a look at the clock on the bedside table, I realized how near dawn we were. "Don't worry about it. This has been a long night, and you've been through a great deal of heartache, loss, and confusion. Time for rest until tomorrow. Then we'll get out of here."

We lay down side-by-side on the bed, still fully clothed, and I switched off the light. As I closed my eyes, I heard her sniffle, and I could feel her sadness coming over me in waves. I stretched my hand across to take hers and give it a squeeze. "We will find him, Sybill. Don't worry."

Something in her finally relaxed then. She'd been defiant with me, I knew, because she felt frightened, and the little girl in her wanted reassurance. Squeezing my hand back, she whispered, "Thank you."

I smiled in the dark, and we both drifted off to sleep at last. Before losing consciousness, I thought of Raul, and I prayed wherever they'd taken him, he would be safe.

OUBLIETTE

Raul

When they captured me, they'd cuffed me and covered my head with a hood, then stuffed me in the back of their van. I don't know how long we drove, but at last we stopped, and they brought me out. I stumbled blindly as these people pulled me along by the arms, then lifted me bodily into a seat and strapped me in place. I heard a voice tell someone to close the door, and next I heard the whine of an airplane engine. When we lifted off, I felt my heart sink, knowing my last hope of Marie finding me had been destroyed. At that moment, I gave in to despair, imagining the look on Sybill's face when she realized I wouldn't come back to her apartment.

I berated myself for being so easily trapped. Consoling myself with the knowledge they had let me live, I held onto the hope perhaps they were not going to hurt me either.

No one spoke as we flew. At last, I felt us descend and touch down, and then they led me to another vehicle, shoved inside, and driven again. This time, the ride didn't take long before we stopped. Still hooded, they yanked me out and walked me into a building. We passed through several doors, and I heard the sound of security equipment beeping as each one slid open and then shut again behind my back.

Finally, they brought me into a room, and my cuffs and the hood were taken off. The woman who had captured me in the park stood there alone. I blinked in the blinding fluorescent light and looked around. I was inside a concrete cell. On one wall I saw a one-way glass window. A bench stood along the wall with a blanket and a small pillow.

"Where am I?" My voice cracked slightly, and I struggled to maintain my composure.

"Sleep. It is dawn now," she said, ignoring my question. "This room is vampire proof, so forget trying to escape."

She started to walk toward the door, and I begged, "Please, what am I doing here?"

Without a break in her stride, she continued out the door and shut it behind her. I heard several bolts slam at once, and then she left me there alone.

"Wait! Hello? Is anyone out there?" I hammered my fists on the door, fighting down my panic. "Face me! You said you had questions. Well, I've got some for you. Who the hell are you people? Where am I? What do you want with me?"

No one came.

I banged on the two-way glass. "Let me out of here! What is this place? You hear me? Let me out!"

The fluorescent light went off with a click, and I stood there in the dark.

No answer came to my cries, and so at last, exhausted, I lay down on the bench and pulled the blanket over me, not for warmth but for comfort. First I dreamed of Sybill, of her face, the feel of her hair in my hands, the touch of her skin, her lips on mine. Those dreams then faded over the long hours as I became anxious nearly to the level of paranoia, imagining somehow my dreaming of her would lead my captors to her door. Striving to keep my fear from driving me to insanity, I consciously pushed her from my thoughts, meditating on the emptiness, trying to make my mind a blank.

At one point, I thought I heard something outside my door, but when it didn't repeat, I began to think I'd imagined it. I called out, but no one replied. The lights remained off. I remained alone.

Lying there in the silent darkness, I gave up on the idea anyone even remembered my existence in that place. I began to believe I might never get out or hear another voice again. Would this be the way my life finally ended, alone, forgotten, left to starve?

Hunger came next, and my mind ran over all of the kills I'd ever made in succession. Initially, I felt guilt, but the longer I sat, the more my mind and body began to crave the blood. I felt my fangs lengthen, and my stomach churned with need. I became the monster, struggling to keep from flinging myself at my prison door like a bird caught in a room, beating its wings against glass windows in a desperate attempt to escape. I roared and shook and hugged my arms around my knees, curling up into a ball and rocking.

Still, no one came.

I began to sing to myself. Singing every song I'd ever known, even those I'd forgotten the lyrics to, even songs with no words at all. My voice broke, my thirst making my throat burn, and at last I could only whisper.

When singing failed me, I closed my eyes again, and fell into a fitful sleep, dreaming once more. This time, I dreamed of Marie. I first found comfort in her, imagined she would arrive, beat down the door, and rescue me. That she would take me in her arms and hold me like her favorite son, protecting me from danger. Soon, however, a deep resentment took hold and in my dream, I questioned her with suspicion and growing anger. I wouldn't be in this place if it weren't for her, would I? I had kept her secret for so long, and I could no longer remember why. Loyalty? Fear? Loneliness? Or had I done it simply because I had no choice? She made me. Could I have defied her? Had she trapped me in this life against my will? Kept me bound to her from selfishness?

I woke up in a bloody sweat once, terrified I had talked in my sleep. For a while afterward, I tried to stay awake. However, the silence and hunger were more than I could bear. Sleep became my only solace. I sank back into it like a drowning man, giving up hope of rescue.

Then finally, I stopped dreaming altogether.

I might have been in that room for three days. It might have been three years. Without a way to record the passage of time and with nothing but my own thoughts to keep me company, I have no way to know for certain.

Just as I had given up the hope of escape and stopped expecting someone to finally appear, the lights suddenly came on with a loud click and a hum. I squinted and blinked, unable to bear the brightness. I shielded my eyes with my hands, groaning.

"State your name," came a voice, the same woman, her words booming through the loudspeaker so my ears rang with the sound.

Grimacing, I hunched my body and covered my ears to block out the painful noise.

"Your name. Now." The voice meant business, and it wouldn't stop the assault on my senses.

My voice cracked as I choked out, "Fin. Who are you people?"

"That is not your name. State your name." She ignored my question altogether.

"Fin. I told you. I don't know who you think I am, but you've got the wrong person, I swear." I pleaded, hugging myself with pain. "Please, I'm so thirsty. Please."

The voice insisted. "We know that is a lie. Your name! Now!"

I bit my lip and shook my head, repeating the same reply once more. "I'm Fin."

"She won't come for you. You have to know that.

She doesn't care for you at all. You're fooling yourself if you think otherwise. She cares for no one but herself." Like a snake, those cold words slithered around my heart and tightened there.

I wouldn't give her up. I told myself the voice lied. Trying to force me to reveal her name to her enemies. "I don't know who you're talking about. You have the wrong guy, I'm telling you. Please, I'm so thirsty!"

"Lies again. So be it." With a resounding click, the lights went out once more, darkness enveloping me like a shroud.

"No! No, please! I'm thirsty! Please!" My words were a ragged sob of desperate hunger.

No answer came. Only silence and dark. She'd left me alone again. This time, I knew they were watching. I had no idea if I would ever hear from the voice again, or if I would be left here in this dark and lonely tomb to waste away until nothing remained in the cell but the monster. I roared with frustration and cursed the voice and my hunger. I banged on the door and begged for release. No one came, and after a while, I just gave up and sank to the floor in defeat. A keening cry came from my body, unbidden, and I hate to admit it, but I wept like a lost child, arms around myself, without any hope of comfort left.

A Good Wench for this Gear

Sybill

That evening, I awoke with a burning in my throat, and it felt as though I'd slept on a nest of fire-ants, my skin aching from head to toe. I roared in agony as I sat up, ripping the bedclothes with my bare hands. I wanted something to stop the pain, and though I couldn't even make coherent speech, nearly blinded by my need, my sense of smell had heightened to astonishing levels. One whiff and I knew on the other side of the wall stood the thing I desired. Like a starved animal, I bared my fangs and rushed to the door, only to find myself clasped around the waist and held in a grip of iron.

"Not like that!" Marie said in my ear. "I know the craving,

but you must not give yourself over to the monster so easily. You must learn to control it, or you will lose yourself forever."

I struggled in frustration, groaning, and only one word found it's way to my lips. "Blood!"

Marie brought her wrist to my lips. "Here, this will calm you. Drink. Then we will hunt, but not as savages."

I didn't crave her blood, but once I bit down and tasted it on my tongue, I felt flooded with instant relief. She held me until I felt like myself again, then pulled back and whispered gently, "Enough. Better, yes, ma chère?"

Licking my lips, I nodded. "Is it always like that?" I found it terrifying to contemplate spending an eternity waking up that way.

"No," she laughed, touching my cheek as though I were a child. "No, it isn't. You are new. This will pass once you have learned to tame the creature within."

I wanted desperately to believe she told the truth, but I didn't know how I'd be able to manage it. Certainly, if she had not been with me, I would have slaughtered everyone in the place without a thought. I could still smell the human in the room next door to us, but I no longer felt driven mad with the urge to rip his heart out and drink it dry. The image in my mind's eye made me shiver. "How do you do it?"

She backed away and began to pack up our things. "I've had a long time to get used to the monster in me, my darling girl."

"Do you hunt every night?" The thought seemed simultaneously appalling and fascinating, and I could feel my fangs extend again.

"Not anymore," she replied, stuffing her clothes away. "I used to, though. And it is hard to avoid when away from home. When you run, you must do whatever is necessary to survive. But if you stay long in one place, you cannot live that way. People will notice, and it will catch up with you."

"How long were you in St. Louis?" I said, tilting my head with curiosity, perched on the edge of the bed as I listened.

She shrugged. "Twenty years, I suppose. Not long."

"That's almost as old as I am." The thought made me pause. "Did Raul stay with you that whole time?"

"Mmm hmm. He was new then, just like you. Full of questions and learning to control the dark side of himself." Her face softened as she spoke, though she didn't look up, and I sensed a sudden sadness in her. "I found ways to get blood from the blood bank. I made sure he always had it within his grasp when he needed it, so he never succumbed to the urge. At least, almost never."

I took a moment to absorb her words. *Almost never.* That caveat spoke volumes. "What about the boy they found in the park?"

Stopping to raise her gaze to meet mine, she frowned. "I don't know. That kill was sloppy. Only a vampire who waited too long to feed would do such a thing. We hide our kills, and if we can drink without killing, even better. It will be hard for you at first, but I will teach you. We must at all costs, avoid detection. Understand?"

I nodded my assent. When I thought back on my observations of Raul, I had always thought of him as so tightly in control of everything. But he admitted to me his emotions were taking him over when it came to me. Were his other drives as out of balance as well? I began to feel indirectly guilty for that boy's death. I hated to believe it. And yet, now the monster lived in me, I could understand.

"There is no more time for questions now. We need to leave this place and get to somewhere safe. While you slept, I made my decision. There is a coven in Chicago that will take us in, at least temporarily. We will go there and ask for aid." I could see her set her jaw and knew she put on a strong face for me.

"How are we going to get there? You wrecked the car."

I stood, reaching for my bag to take out a change of clothes, trying to keep my voice even.

"Same way we got here, my dear." She winked at me, then put on a heavy Russian accent again. "We take car, yes?"

I couldn't help but laugh. "Yes."

"Good. Now get dressed so we can paint our faces for the part, and then we will leave this place once you've fed."

It didn't take long before we'd both transformed ourselves into the role of mail-order brides down on their luck. After removing the duct tape and blankets, we walked out of the room and knocked on the door beside us. A weather-beaten man in a dirty t-shirt holding a beer opened his door and asked us what we wanted, giving us both the once over with his eyes.

"We need borrow ice...how you say...bucket?" Claire Marie made a gesture to indicate the item in question, seeming to struggle with her words.

I could hear his wicked thoughts as he watched her, and it disgusted me to know what he wanted to do to her.

To both of us. "Yeah, sure. You girls come on in. I'll take care of you."

Claire Marie looked over at me with a sideways knowing smile, then we both entered the room. He closed it behind us, and we heard the lock click.

He thought of himself as the predator and us the prey. He could not have been more mistaken.

In less than a heartbeat, we were both on him, feeding until we heard his pulse go still along with his body. She pulled me off him, then. "He is gone, my dear."

I wiped my mouth with the back of my hand. "Did you know his thoughts? What he wanted to do?"

She smiled. "I can always sense the wickedly deserving. You will be able to sense them just as I can. That is, in fact, why his blood drove you wild earlier tonight. It called to you. You simply didn't know why."

With a lick of my lips, I nodded and smiled back. Knowing I didn't have to kill innocent people gave me a surge of confidence and surprising pride along with this realization. "And now?"

"We hide the body and take his vehicle, of course." She bent over and began digging in his pockets, and in a few seconds she stood again in triumph, keys in hand. "Stay here. I'll be just a moment."

While she slipped outside, I stood beside the body, trying not to look down at his eyes staring up in blank and deathly horror, his body already getting cold. I could sense the change in his body temperature even from a distance. I wondered which of my other senses were magnified. I didn't have long to ponder, however. Claire Marie knocked on the door a few minutes later. When I opened it, I saw she had broken the bulbs of all the lights by the doors so we could bring the body out into darkness.

"I put the bags in his truck. Let's get his body into the seat on your side. Just sit in the middle, and hold him upright against the door."

I wrinkled my nose. "How long are we riding with him?"

"Not long." She grunted, picking the body up under the arms. "Grab his legs."

We hefted him into the cab of the truck and put the seatbelt on him to hold his body in a seated position, then I rode beside him just as she told me, keeping his head leaned against the window as though he were sleeping.

About a mile down the road, she turned off the headlights and pulled over to the shoulder next to a deep culvert beside the road. She reached across me and unbuckled his safety belt, then opened the passenger door. His body fell out and down into the darkness below, landing with a thud and a splash. Straightening back behind the wheel, she smiled at me.

"Scoot over, dearie, and shut the door. We've got a long way to go."

I did as she asked, then pulled my sunglasses out of my pocket and put them on. "It's a hundred and six miles to Chicago, we've got a full tank of gas, half a pack of cigarettes, it's dark, and we're wearing sunglasses. Hit it."

She chuckled. "*Blues Brothers*, eh? You're going to be all right, kid. You're going to be all right."

She put her foot down on the gas, and we sped off into the night.

Sweet Home Chicago

Marie Antoinette

"So tell me about Chicago," Sybill said.

Confused, I looked over at her from behind the wheel. "What sort of information do you want, exactly? It's been a few years since the last time I visited there."

"How many years?" A tone in her voice told me she didn't believe I could navigate my way around.

"I visited in the 1980s, but I used to live there for a few years."

Sybill leaned back in the seat, curling one leg under her, hoping for a story. I glanced over at her quickly, then gazed back out at the road before us. "The 1920s, though, was a good time to be a vampire there, let me tell you. Oh, what a place Chicago seemed to me. The city really came alive at night. Dancing and music. And the dresses. I'd never worn a dress that showed my ankles before. I felt positively wicked."

She laughed. "You? It's hard to imagine. Weren't you born wearing winter white sweater sets?"

"Oh, ha-ha." I winked and smirked over at her across the seat of the truck. "This is my antique dealer costume. I've had to reinvent myself many times over the years."

"Oh really? And who were you in the 1920s?" Her eyebrow quirked up as she asked her question.

"They called me Goldie. Goldie O'Shea." I smiled, remembering.

"Where'd you come up with that name?" she said. "You're not Irish."

I shrugged. "My hair color. Everyone back then was named after a color or a jewel or a flower. As for O'Shea, well, there were a lot of immigrants in the city at the time. I thought it would make it easier to blend in. I also found it easy to explain the fact I had no other family." I put on an Irish accent as I continued. "They all died in the potato famine, don't you know?"

Laughing again, she shook her head at me. "You sure are a good mimic. Where are you really from, anyway? You never have said."

Her question made me pause and bite my lip. "That's a story for another time."

"When?" I could hear the exasperation in her voice. "Do you seriously not trust me? After all this? Come on.

211

You told me you would tell me the truth. No one else is here to hear you, and I swear to keep a secret."

For a moment, I considered answering, but then I stopped myself. "Not yet, please. It's a long story, and we aren't far from our destination. I want to tell it straight through without stopping, and I can't do so and concentrate on the road at the same time."

She sighed loudly. "Okay fine. But I want to hear it once we get wherever we're going."

Without speaking, I nodded agreement, and our conversation ended for some time. She sat staring out the window at the passing lights, and I kept my eyes on the road. I wasn't ready to reveal everything to her. I needed to do it in layers. I felt too emotional to do it all at once, and I couldn't stand to seem weak in her eyes.

The city has changed so much over the years. I remember the years before the Sears Tower (now called the Willis Tower), Trump Tower, and the Hancock Building. Chicago always had been a city of high rises, though, even back in the days of Prohibition. That status became a matter of pride. Chicago was a city of industry, slaughterhouses, and self-made men. Where St. Louis is soft with wide avenues and large green spaces, Chicago is steel and concrete, the buildings looming overhead and making even the greatest of men feel small.

We turned down Lakeshore Drive, and then I made a left at the Field Museum, followed by a right onto Michigan Avenue toward the Magnificent Mile. Sybill gawked openly at the view. I could tell she had never seen it before except perhaps in movies. When I turned again, I almost heard her sigh with disappointment.

"We will be here for a few days," I said, pulling into the parking garage for the Palmer House Hotel. "You'll have a chance to explore, don't worry."

I stopped the truck in front of the valet parking booth. I tipped well, knowing we were going to be ridding ourselves of the vehicle at the earliest opportunity. The flash of cash did not go unnoticed, and porters came from out of the woodwork to help us bring our bags inside toward the main lobby. I heard Sybill gasp at the architecture. "Beautiful isn't it?"

"Uh huh," she nodded, agog. She stared up at the marble and gilded details throughout the enormous space. Her jaw dropped, and I chuckled at her childlike innocence.

"Close your mouth, dear." I leaned in conspiratorially to whisper, "It's the oldest hotel in the city. I've stayed here many times." I smiled again, remembering how it looked when everything seemed shiny and new.

We reached the registration desk, and the concierge asked for our reservation. I could sense Sybill's apprehension, but I beamed across the counter and replied, "We are guests of Mister DeLuca."

He took only a moment before he blinked and smiled back. "Miss O'Shea. Of course. I'm sorry. I didn't recognize you. It's an honor. I believe you know my father, Carl. I'm Bobby. Bobby Franks. At your service. Your usual room, I presume?"

"Yes, thank you, Bobby," I nodded, and I stepped on Sybill's toes before she vocalized her astonishment. "Can you please notify Mister DeLuca I'm here? I would love to see him and catch up on things while I'm in town."

"Of course, Miss O'Shea." He handed over the keys. "I'll have your usual sent up to your room as quickly as possible."

"Excellent. Please be sure there is a little extra for my growing girl here, if you don't mind."

"Understood, madam." He bowed his head. "Please, if there is anything else you need, I am happy to provide it."

I backed away to start toward the doors but gave him one last smile. "Thank you so much, Bobby. And please give my regards to your father."

Taking Sybill's arm in mine, I pulled her with me toward the elevators. Her eyes were wide in shock. "What the heck was that all about? Who the hell are you?"

I chuckled softly, then looked back at the porters bringing along our bags. "All in due time, my dear. I told you I'd been to Chicago before."

"Yes, but you didn't tell me you had some secret code to get us a fancy room in a swanky hotel where people know who you are."

The elevator opened, and we stepped inside. "I'm not who you think I am. That's all you need to know for now. Once we meet the others, everything will be clear."

"The others?" she said, but I poked her in the ribs hard since the porters were following us into the elevator. They pushed the button for our floor, and we rode the rest of the way up in awkward silence. I could hear her mind screaming questions at me, but she knew better than to say them aloud.

Our room was on the twenty-second floor, and Sybill gasped again when the door opened. The suite had a comfortable seating area with a wide screen TV, and there were two bedrooms, each with a king-sized bed and private bath. I tipped the porters, and once they were safely out of the room and the door shut tight behind them, Sybill flopped down on the sofa with an exclamation. "Phew! Now, you want to tell me what the hell is going on? I'm about to burst!"

I walked into one of the bedrooms and began opening my bags. "We are here to seek refuge with the coven. Vincent DeLuca used to be my paramour at one time. He owns the hotel, though don't tell the IRS since he's officially dead."

"You dated Vince DeLuca? The guy who worked for Al Capone? Any other surprises you've got in store for me?" I didn't look up, but I could feel her eyes boring holes into me from across the room.

"I'm full of surprises, my dear. As for Vincent, I wouldn't say we dated, exactly. We danced. Had a few laughs. I played hostess for some of his parties. He gave me certain things I needed that weren't easy to procure. He never judged me or asked questions. I did the same for him."

She fell silent for a moment. "I swear, it's a small world, isn't it?"

That made me lift my head to meet her gaze. "What do you mean?"

"I told you, you're not the only one with secrets." I sensed a sadness in her I didn't understand. "My family, they're in The Family, if you know what I mean."

Suddenly, I had a much fuller picture of her as more than just some pretty rebel artist. Those walls she'd built around her heart had been put there early in her life. I understood why she hadn't questioned me when we'd had to change identities and disappear. She'd lived under the shadow of that possibility since childhood. She knew the fear of discovery just as I did. Perhaps that is why she and Raul had understood one another so well.

"Yes, I know exactly," I told her, not wanting to reveal to her how moved I felt by her admission.

"So Vince, he's a vampire?" she said, forehead furrowing as her mind spun a thousand questions.

"Yes," I said. "Though I didn't turn him."

"Do you have others you've turned? Besides me and Raul, I mean." Biting her lip, she leaned forward, straining for answers.

"Only one," I said softly, looking back down and continuing to unpack.

She frowned. "Well, where is he now?"

With a sigh, I glanced over at the clock and saw the night had almost ended. "That's enough questions for now. I need some rest. We'll have a lot of excitement tomorrow, and you and I will need to save our energy."

I heard her grumble, but she didn't ask me anything more. "Fine. I get it. You don't want to answer me. What else is new? Good night."

"Good morning, you mean," I corrected.

"Yeah, yeah. Whatever." She trounced off into her room and slammed the door.

Angry as she felt, it didn't take long before I sensed she had gone to sleep. When at last I had washed my face and curled up in bed, I closed my eyes, hoping the welcome we'd received tonight would still be there tomorrow once Vincent knew the reason for our visit.

A Leopard Does Not Change Its Spots

Chief Inspector

Only two numbers were in the phone I had pulled from the young vampire in my custody. No one answered either of them when I attempted to call. My techs were able to track down the address under which the phone was registered. One other phone matched the address, and it corresponded to the number at the top of the missed call list. Someone had been looking for him and then had inexplicably stopped calling. A Claire Marie Hapsburg. Lips curling into a smile, I rejoiced. Hapsburg. She made my job easy.

I also had them track the address for the second number, registered to a Sybill Lysander. The techs were able to get into the

Department of Motor Vehicles' database and pull her driver's license and ID photo. Black goth hair and makeup with tattoos? The face looked more like a vampire wannabe than the real thing. Still, she might be a minion. She might know something useful. No record of a vehicle existed under that name, but we had an address.

Leaving guards to watch the prisoner, I returned to St. Louis with my team and, in a rented vehicle, drove first to the house in question, though with no expectation of finding my quarry within.

Only blocks away from the discarded body, the house stood hidden in a gated community of wealth and privilege. I sniffed with derision as I gazed up at the facade. "A leopard does not change its spots," I said, stepping out of the car and leading the group toward the front door. It stood unlocked.

Suspicious, I pushed the door open and listened carefully. I could sense no one inside, living or dead. My eyes narrowed. "Scour the place. Find me information. Places she might be hiding."

Leaving my team to complete the search of the house, I then drove alone to the second address, a high-rise apartment listed under this Sybill person. I could see a guard at the desk inside and cameras in the lobby. This would take some finesse.

I buzzed for entry and, putting a full glamour on the guard who let me inside, I convinced him I had a delivery for the tenant in 404. I explained I had legal documents only the tenant had authorization to sign. He gave me no real resistance, and I could tell from this fact he had been glamoured before. Curious. Some other vampire had been here already. This Sybill was turning out to be interesting after all.

The elevator took me up to the fourth floor, and I stepped out into the hall, quickly finding the apartment I sought. It took me only a second to pick the lock, and when I walked inside, I could smell both vampire and human, though neither were currently present.

I scanned the living room then walked into one of the bedrooms. The scent of linseed oil pervaded, and paintings in various stages of completion were stacked around the corners of the room. An artist? Unexpected, but not useful information.

Immediately, I knew I had found something important as soon as I went to examine the other bedroom, however. Clothes hangers were strewn across an unmade bed. A towel lay on the floor of the bathroom beside a pile of bloody clothes covered with street grime. One quick whiff told me there had been a turning. I could smell the human and the vampire in this woman. That meant only one thing. Marie had gone on the run with a vampire child. But why this tattooed girl whose face I saw in several framed photos in the apartment? I gathered a few up and stared at the face peering back at me. She seemed an odd companion for the queen.

I pondered the connection. Then I smelled it. The faint scent of the male vampire already in my custody. He'd been with this Sybill. They'd been together on the bed. Had he turned her? If so, then why would Marie have come to claim her? Unless....

Yes. I had it. I knew exactly what to say to make him give over everything I wanted to know. By the time I returned to the house on Westmoreland Place, my team had found an address for an antique store not far away.

219

Certain of myself, I assured them, "She won't be there anymore. Still, we should examine the area for evidence. Perhaps we can find where they might have gone."

"They, mistress?" said one of the team members as we all climbed into the van.

"She has another vampire with her. A newly turned one." I handed over the framed photos I'd taken from the apartment. "Sybill Lysander is her name, and for some reason, she is connected with our fugitive. Find out who she is. I want names. Family. Associates. Everything you can get me."

When we arrived at the antique shop, a blonde woman with a butterfly headband, clearly an employee, switched the sign from Open to Closed on the front door. Holding a shrilly yapping little dog, she blocked our entrance to the shop, saying, "We're closed. Sorry, but you'll have to come back another time. There's been a death in the family."

I chuckled, putting my hand on the door to push it open. "Yes, I am certain there has been."

"Excuse me, but you are just plain rude! Somebody died, or wasn't I clear?" The blonde woman's forehead furrowed, and her blue eyes flashed with annoyance.

"When will your mistress return?"

The blonde woman's scowl deepened. "I don't know all my boss' business, but it's sure as heck none of yours either. Y'all better just clear on out of here and go back to wherever it is you came from."

Stepping forward, I caught the blonde woman's gaze. "Enough talking. You will let us inside."

Her eyes widened, and she slowly opened the door,

though she clearly struggled against the command to keep quiet. The little dog, held firmly in her arms, whined in confusion while my team swarmed into the building, and one of my men held the blonde woman still while the others began the search of the premises.

A quick look around showed someone had emptied the cash register and stolen several items from the display cases. In the back office, a safe stood open and empty. On the desk, the computer still showed the online auction page with the shoes. We were one step behind, and I became enraged, knowing once more the fugitive queen had slipped through my fingers. The Master would be enraged unless I could gather information to lead to her apprehension.

How did they leave? Searching through the papers in the office, I could find no record of a vehicle registered under the name of Claire Marie Hapsburg.

"Secure the human," I said, gesturing toward the shop girl. "We can question her later."

One of my assistants tossed the yappy little dog out of the blonde woman's arms onto the floor. It yelped once before crumpling on the rug and lying mercifully silent and still. The woman gasped, helpless to say anything more. Instead, we marched her out and pushed her into the back of the van. Though she didn't struggle or speak, behind her eyes I saw a strong spirit of rebellion. Clearly the fugitive queen had found her independence of mind endearing, as she had with others in the past.

Just as we were about to leave, one of my men spied some broken glass on the curb. It must have come from a shattered car window. Someone had stolen a vehicle here. Excitedly, I instructed them to search for reports of a stolen car in the area within the last two days. Perhaps the fugitive queen hadn't gotten away after all.

With renewed hope, I headed back to the command center with my team to interrogate the human woman and the vampire prisoner, hoping that, paired with the information my techs could recover, I'd be able to set a trap to catch Marie Antoinette once and for all.

An Audience at Last

Sybill

Claire Marie shook me awake with a cup full of blood in hand. She wore a crisp white double-breasted suit and looked like an angel leaning over me. "You were talking in your sleep, my dear." She smoothed back my hair from my face as though I were a child. "Here. The staff brought up a carafe full of fresh warm blood. I took the liberty of bringing it to you myself to avoid any unpleasantness with the wait-staff."

Pulling myself up to a seated position, I took the cup from her without a word and drank it all down. She watched me with a soft tender smile that made me feel self-conscious.

When I had finished swallowing the last drop, she took the cup back from me. "Good. Now get dressed, dear. We have a lot to do tonight."

Her tone and behavior annoyed me, and I snapped back, "Look, I'm not a baby, okay? Don't treat me like one."

With an eyebrow raised, she looked back over her shoulder at me. "In human years, no. But as a vampire, you are a newborn. You are my child, and it is my duty to care for you."

"Duty, huh? Bet you're sick of it already." I threw back the covers, and stomped over to my suitcase, only to find it empty. "Hey! Where's my stuff?"

"I awoke early and put it away for you. You'll find your clothes hanging in the closet and folded in the dresser drawers." She walked away, and I saw her put my cup down on the room service tray, then take up a cup for herself and pour the bloody contents of the carafe into it.

"Hmpf," I sniffed, turning to stride over to my dresser. Just as she said, she'd folded everything neatly, organized by color. "Anyone ever tell you, you're a little too...I dunno...just too much."

I heard her laugh. "Clothes are my thing, dear." Then she took a sip from the cup. "Mmm...tasty. Vince always did know how to get the good stuff."

Rummaging through the drawers for a pair of tights and underwear, I replied. "Yeah, how did he...."

"Don't ask, don't tell," she interrupted.

"But it tasted really..."

"Fresh? Yes. Let's just leave it, shall we?" She took another sip, and I knew better than to pursue it further.

I sighed and let it drop, walking instead over to the closet, but when I opened the doors, I stood there staring in shock. "Uh…these aren't my clothes."

She chuckled again. "I knew you'd react that way."

"Well, then you shouldn't have put someone else's clothes in here. Seriously, where's my stuff?"

"Tsk, what kind of a disguise would it be if you wore exactly the same things you'd have worn at home? Honestly! I told you we'd need new things." She took another drink, and I could feel her rolling her eyes at me even with my back turned.

"New things?" I whipped around, holding up a couple of hangers. "This makes me look like some kind of rich celebutante. I am not Paris Hilton!"

"No, but you can't be Sybill Lysander from St. Louis anymore either. After all, you're supposed to be missing. I'm sure by now your parents will be looking for their little girl. We'll need to pick a new name for you." Not meeting my eyes as she dealt out this harsh dose of reality, she placed her empty cup back on the tray with a clank.

"Oh my god." I sat down heavily on the edge of the bed. "I've missed my dad's birthday party. He's going to be so pissed."

"Darling, your father's birthday is the least of our troubles. Now, get dressed. I went to a lot of trouble to get that new look for you. We have business to attend to, and you can't just keep lolly-gagging around all night."

I saw her primping her hair in the mirror in the other room, and it chilled me to the bone.

"Don't you have any feelings at all?" I sobbed. "I've lost everything!"

Her face looked pale as she turned to look at me, and for a fleeting second she looked as though she might cry, but then I saw her clench her teeth, and her expression took on a fierce determination. "You don't know what it is to lose everything. Don't you dare talk to me of loss. You have me, and if that isn't enough for you, well, then you have Raul, or have you forgotten him already?"

I shook my head. "Of course not. It's just...."

"It's just you want to sit here and feel sorry for yourself for a few days. Well, we do not have time for self-indulgence. Grief makes you weak, my child. Give in to it, and you may as well lie down and die your final death right here and now. When there is time and we are safe, then you can grieve all you want, but not here. Not now. I've been through too much and run too far and struggled too long to let your self-pity get us both killed. Now get dressed."

Her tone made me lash out, wanting to hurt her. I stood up, balled my hands into fists and faced her in defiance. "What do you know about loss? I'll bet you never cared about anyone but yourself, did you?"

I felt the air move as she bore down on me with a roar, fangs out, slamming me to the wall. "I have lost more than you could ever dream in your worst nightmares. If you ever speak to me that way again, I will kill you myself!"

"Oh yeah? What have you lost that's so precious? How do I know you're telling me the truth? You won't even give me your name." I glared, trying not to tremble, trying to keep my voice from shaking.

"I'm Marie Antoinette, you ridiculous child, and the only

thing I haven't lost is my own head, though they certainly tried."
She let me go then, and I stood there in shock.

"You're...what? That's just...no. That's not possible."
I blinked at her, staring her up and down.

"Why? Because she's dead?" She scoffed at me. "Darling,
it happens to the best of us."

I gaped at her open-mouthed, stunned speechless.

"You're going to catch flies. Close your mouth, and don't
look so shocked. You knew I had to come from somewhere.
Now I've told you. Satisfied?" I had definitely hurt her. Bitterness
dripped from her voice like venom.

"But..." I started.

She sighed, one hand on her hip. "But what?"

"How did you escape? Weren't you a prisoner? The
schoolbooks all said...."

"History books are rubbish. They teach you what they
want you to believe, not what really happened. If they told you
what really happened, you'd never believe it. The truth is more
horrible, more bloody, more disgusting and dangerous and cruel
than any schoolchild is prepared to comprehend. The truth
is also richer, fuller, more breathtakingly beautiful and liberating
than they want you to realize. They give you only the tiniest
pieces of fact, facts you can wrap your mind around and accept.
And they want you to feel lucky to be living in whatever era
you're in now. If they paint the past with a rosy hue, you'll realize
just how much humanity has lost. Better to keep you happy and
ignorant than tell you what really happened."

I took in her words and then said, "Then what was
it really like?"

"What was what like? Being queen? Being a prisoner? Watching my entire way of life crumble? Be more specific, my dear. I can't answer your question like that."

"Tell me the worst of it," I replied, biting my lip. "I really want to know."

"You don't." She closed her eyes for a moment, and I thought she might break then.

"You're telling me I don't understand. How can I understand if you don't explain it?"

For a moment, she didn't speak, and I thought she felt angry with me, but then she opened her eyes and looked back at me steadily. "All right. But don't ask me this again. Not until this is all over and Raul is safe. Understand?"

I nodded and sat back down on the side of the bed to listen.

"I'll tell you the short version for now. We don't have time for more. Vince is waiting for us. He'll be patient for a little while longer, but I know how he is, and we can't trespass on his kindness. I'll skip the things everyone knows. Captured. Imprisoned. Tried. You can look those things up for yourself. What they don't tell you is what all that did to me." She began to pace, not looking at me while she spoke, and I found myself leaning forward as she explained. "My time in the Tower had been designed to break my spirits. First, they separated me from my husband, Louis, not such a great loss to me as perhaps it should have been. Ours had been a marriage of state, you see, never one of the heart or mind.

"Next, they severed me from my friends, but as I only had a few companions I truly trusted, this did not distress me much either.

"The separation from my children nearly drove me mad, however. They took them from me, though they were still so small, and they left my son, my little one, only six years old, in the chamber just below my own. I could hear his cries for me for days. I begged their mercy. I would have given them anything. Signed whatever they'd demanded.

"When he finally stopped crying for me, that is what broke my heart. He had given up on me. Given up on his mama. That cut me to the core, and they knew it. They never came to question me, however. They didn't torture me for the sake of information, but rather used torture as an end in itself."

She paused in her telling, and I said, "You had a daughter, didn't you? What did they do to her?"

"I never saw my daughter again. History books will tell you they released her after three years and sent her into exile, but that story is not the one they told me at the time. I begged for news of her each day, and finally they told me she had died. I will never forget the face of the priest who informed me – cold, impassive, and without sympathy of any kind. He told me as though it were simply a casual matter for conversation. I collapsed and had my hair cut in mourning. Such display of motherly grief, however, earned me nothing but ridicule and derision from everyone. They accused me of faking my attachment to my own children. Of pretending to love them, and trying to play on the sympathies of the public. Sympathies indeed. None had pity or sympathy for me. Animals. I practically begged for Madame Guillotine by the time my moment came. Indeed, I do not know what made me resist death at the last. I had not planned my escape at all. Perhaps that is why it succeeded. If it had involved anyone else, I would surely have been recaptured and executed on the spot."

I leaned forward, hands on my knees. "But people saw your execution. They saw the guillotine cut off your head."

Her eyes caught mine. "They saw an execution. They saw someone's head. It didn't belong to me."

Blinking, I furrowed my forehead. "Whose was it, then?

"My poor lady in waiting." She sighed before continuing. "I glamoured her just as I glamoured that man in the pharmacy a few days ago. She exchanged dresses and wigs with me, walked out onto the scaffold, and died in my place. I pray she never became aware of what was happening to her. That she felt peaceful unto the last. I have never stopped feeling sorry for her, and I have tried to live my life in such a way as to be worthy of her sacrifice."

I fell silent for a moment, trying to understand the enormity of what she'd told me. "Well," I said at last, "at least her death was quick, right? I mean, they invented the guillotine to be merciful and painless."

Her eyes flashed in anger then. "Merciful? No. The guillotine had nothing to do with mercy. It killed efficiently, pure and simple. It sanctified the slaughter of scores of people with cold and gruesome precision. Execution became a spectator event. People came to watch the deaths of whole families, all beheaded at once. But the machine was designed with a specific purpose. Not just for simple execution, but for the execution of the vampires the public realized had taken over the country. Almost all of the nobility of France were of the blood. Beheading was the only way to ensure their deaths."

I gasped. "The French nobility…were vampires?"

"Oh yes. Why do you think we made face powder so popular? If everyone looked pale, it became easier for vampires to blend in." She smiled then. "I held the distinction as the queen of fashion. Others emulated my every choice of gown, shoe, makeup…. At least until they understood my true nature."

"Hmm." I shook my head trying to wrap my mind around what she'd told me. "Yeah, you're right. The history books kind of left that stuff out."

"Well, they would, wouldn't they?" She patted my shoulder signaling the end of our conversation. "Now, get dressed, please. We have a lot to accomplish tonight, and we've wasted enough time as it is."

With that, she walked out and into her own room, shutting the door behind her. Our audience had ended.

My mind still reeled, but I got dressed, this time without saying another word. I could only imagine all the things she'd been through, all the things she'd seen and experienced. And yet here she stood, still working hard to stay alive and keep going, even after all that loss and horror. She must have become amazingly resilient and smart to survive so long.

I hadn't been able to ask, and perhaps by her design, who pursued us and why. Undoubtedly, she knew, at least she seemed to. Even if the identity of the individuals in pursuit were unknown to her, I knew the person giving the orders couldn't be unknown to her. If we were going to rescue Raul and bring him back safe, she needed to share that information with me. But I knew better than to push her any further right then.

She'd kept secrets for hundreds of years, so expecting her to suddenly become forthcoming with information well, that just wouldn't happen.

Still, all in all, we'd made a good start. She finally opened up to me and started to trust me, and I could understand now why she'd been so secretive before, like I suddenly had found the crucial piece of a puzzle to make everything else fit with patience. Even without knowing it all, I knew enough to give me confidence and trust one day it would all make sense.

I did my makeup, consciously choosing not to do my usual smoky eyes, but instead, I thought about who this new me might be. A new me who wore pink. By the time I finished, I barely recognized myself in the mirror. When I stepped out of my bedroom into the sitting area, I could see Claire…no… Marie (That name would need time before I'd feel comfortable with it.) had done the same.

"Well, aren't you a picture?" She beamed at me. "Have you chosen a new name yet? Jessica is a popular name for women your age, but if you have another idea, well and good."

"Evangeline," I said, and somehow the name fell from my lips as though I'd been saying it my whole life, though in truth the name simply popped into my head on impulse. "Evangeline Mars."

"Eva Mars," she ruminated, tapping a finger on her lips. "I like it. Sounds like a movie star or a model. It's perfect. Nice to meet you, Eva. I'm Goldie O'Shea."

As she said her new name, her voice changed so she spoke with a different accent, smiling, sweet, and bubbly like an audition for Miss America. Her chameleon-like transformation amazed me, and at the same time I found it more than a little unnerving. If I hadn't witnessed her change from Claire Marie into this Goldie person, I'd never have believed they were one and the same. If I wanted to keep up with her, I had a lot to learn. She held out her hand, and we shook on it smiling. It felt like a contract we'd just agreed to.

Taking my arm in hers, she pulled me close as though we were old schoolgirl friends. "Come on. Let's go meet Vince You're in for a treat."

We took the elevator up to the penthouse suite, and arm-in-arm we strode up to the doors. Two guards stood at the entrance. They waved a metal detector wand over us both.

"Find anything you like, boys?" Marie said. "Don't rough up the merchandise. Vince wouldn't like it."

They ignored her question, and one of them spoke into a Bluetooth earpiece, "They're clean, boss."

"Hmpf. No thanks to you and your grubby paws," muttered Marie as the door opened, and we passed through into the room opulently decorated in white and gold. In the corner, a man in a tuxedo played Gershwin on the piano. Two bodyguards stood behind the sofa where a dark-haired man in a double-breasted black suit sat sipping from a champagne glass, though the liquid was definitely not champagne, however. I could smell the blood from across the room, rich and enticing. He stood when we walked into the room, setting down his glass on the coffee table in front of him.

"Vince. Darling!" Marie, separated from me and walked across to him, opening her arms to hug him lightly and kissing both his cheeks. "Is that any way to treat an old friend?

We were such good friends, weren't we? I hope we still are, you dear boy."

He pulled back, obviously flattered but trying not to show it. "Goldie baby, you always were a doll, you know, but I gotta be careful. That ain't never changed. It's been a long time. I have to say, hearing you showed up here after all this time, well, I was mighty surprised." Looking her up and down appraisingly, he tilted his head to the side. "You did something to your hair."

"You like it?" She patted the red locks and posed with a giggle. "A girl's got to keep trying new things, you know."

"Yeah. It's okay. I'm partial to blondes, you know, but red's a good look for you. Different, but good." He glanced over at me and then back at Marie. "Listen, I ain't gonna beat around the bush, doll. You're bringing me an awful lot of trouble this time."

"Me?" She feigned shock, laying it on thick. "Why whatever do you mean, Vince? I've been a good girl for years now. Good as gold. Cross my heart." She crossed it, making doe-eyes so obviously, I nearly laughed aloud.

"Don't tell me you don't know. Maybe you hadn't heard, but this girl you got with you," he pointed in my direction with a hammy finger, "she ain't just some sweet young thing you can just walk away with and not have people asking questions. The wrong sort of people. The wrong sort of questions. Capiche?"

I stared at him in confusion. "Who me?"

"Yeah, you," he said, annoyed. "Now, I ain't gonna say nothing to nobody, and I will help you because of old times, but you better get this girl out of here, pronto."

"But Vince, we've only just arrived," Marie protested.

"Yeah? Well, unarrive," said Vince. "Anyone finds out this girl is here, and I'm gonna have a mess to clean up. A big one. You know how those types of messes get handled, don't you? I got a lot of people on my payroll. You don't want that on your conscience."

She sat down heavily, all the smiling demeanor gone. "What's happened? Please tell me. I honestly have no idea what you mean."

Vince looked up at me. "You ain't told her?"

"Told her what?" I said, baffled at his question.

"Oh jeez." He rolled his eyes and gestured to the sofa. "Sit down, and I'll show you what I mean."

I sat, and he took his seat once more, reaching for the remote control for the television hanging from the opposite wall. He clicked it on, and my face appeared splashed across the screen in a photograph on CNN. Anderson Cooper stood asking questions of the on-the-scene reporter who stood outside my apartment complex. They were discussing my disappearance. I gasped. "Oh Jesus."

"Oh yeah. You better be praying. I know I am." He clicked off the screen, and it went to black. "Now, maybe you ain't told the whole truth about who you are, am I right?"

"She…she told me her family had connections to…you know…" Marie stammered.

"Yeah? That how she put it?" Vince said sarcastically. "Connections?"

I bit my lip and looked down at my hands, clasping them on my lap. "Oh, don't play the innocent, with me, sweetheart. I know you ain't stupid." Vince took a sip of his blood and stared me down. "You better start singing like a fuckin' bird, chickadee. Now."

"My father is the head of the St. Louis arm of the mafia," I said, my voice flat and emotionless. "He's on the top ten most wanted list by the FBI."

Marie stared at me, her turn to be shocked.

I shrugged. "I told you, you weren't the only one with secrets."

Vince laughed. "Understatement of the year. You know your face is on all the cable news channels from sea to shining sea? You're famous. Which makes a problem for me, which I'm sure you are starting to understand."

I nodded, looking down at my lap once more. "My daddy, he's looking for me, isn't he?"

"You just said a mouthful, kid." Vince sat back and gazed back at me. His body language seemed lazy and casual, but I knew looks were deceiving. At any second, he could leap over like a tiger and rip my throat out without blinking an eye. "But that ain't the worst part."

Marie and I both looked up, but she spoke before I could. "There's something more?"

"Oh yeah, doll. And this one's a doozy." He smiled, and I saw a hint of his fangs. "See, this girl's father, he thinks maybe someone kidnapped his kid. You know, like a revenge kind of thing. Now he's got his boys looking into it. If he finds out any of us got your girl, he's gonna start a war to make the Valentine's Day Massacre look like an Easter Sunday church picnic."

Marie gasped, but I swallowed hard. I could picture

my father's face, and I knew it would be a horrible thing to behold. "Oh god."

"You betcha. Now, I'll help you, like I said. I never renege on a promise. But that help is gonna mean getting you both the hell out of here, and when you're gone, I ain't seen you. None of us has. You get me?"

We nodded. "I'm so sorry," I started.

He waved his hand. "Ah, save it, sister. You ain't sorry. You're just scared. And you should be. But now you know what kind of a bind you're putting me in." He turned to look at Marie. "Hope she's worth it to you."

Marie took my hand, and I couldn't have been more surprised as she gave it a squeeze. "She is."

My eyes teared up as I realized she really meant it when she said we were family. She planned to be there for me, in spite of all of this.

Vince nodded. "All right then. I'll take your word for it. So, what is it that brought you here? I know you ain't here to make romance with me again, Goldie. You ain't got to pretend. I know it's business. I'm all right with that. Just give it to me straight."

"I don't know where to start," she said, licking her lips thoughtfully.

With a shrug, he smiled at her. "At the beginning is good. Boys," he said, turning to the bodyguards still standing at attention, "go get these ladies a drink. Take your time."

The two men nodded and walked out of the room. As soon as the door closed, Vince looked back at Marie. "There. Now we're alone. You can tell it like it is."

She took a deep, unnecessary breath, gathering herself, and then she said, "They've taken him, Vince. My darling boy. They've got him, and they're coming for me next."

His eyebrows rose with curiosity. "The actor guy…what's his face? The looker? Well, that is a shame. Who they got on the chase now?"

Shaking her head, she sighed. "Raul, yes. I don't know who is taking the lead this time. I do know they're getting close. I acted recklessly. I just never thought…."

"Yeah, well, that happens. You have been a little quiet for a while, and you start thinking maybe they've given up, right? But they ain't never giving up on you, doll. You know I'm right. Catching you would be the biggest thing they ever done. A real coup. Ain't nobody more important to them than you."

Her eyes downcast, she sighed again. "I know. I just… I wish they'd leave me alone. Haven't I gone through enough? Haven't I paid whatever blood price they think I owe?"

"Hey, now, pity won't keep neither of you safe. But I gotta tell you, running won't either. It ain't easy hiding these days. All this modern technology is a bitch. Facial recognition, DNA…it's a bitch, I tell you." He leaned forward. "You know what you need to do? Stop letting them make all the rules. Take the fight to them. Show them you ain't scared no more. Quit running. Let them see why you're the queen and always will be. Capiche?"

"But…"

"Ah no. No buts. I'm right about this. Trust me. I've been where you are, doll. Hunted. Hiding. It sucks, am I right?" He looked over at me, and I nodded agreement. "See? She knows what I'm talking about. You do too. You just tried to forget you were running for a while. But doll, you ain't never stopped. They will never, ever give up on the chase until you end it."

"I know you're right, Vince." Her voice sounded low but serious.

"Of course I'm right. I didn't get where I am without being right. I'm always right. Ain't I, Wolfie?" He turned to look over at the piano player still sitting in the corner. He'd kept playing all through our conversation, the sound so like a recording, I'd forgotten about his presence entirely. The sandy-haired, long-nosed little man, wasn't really handsome, but something about his eyes, a kind and lively playfulness, made him seem attractive all the same, and I couldn't help but smile.

"Hello, Marie," he said softly. "It's been a long time."

"Wolfgang?" Her eyes were huge and full of surprise, and I blinked as she leapt from her seat and threw herself into his lap, her arms around him, and kissed him firmly on the lips.

"Well, I didn't rate that kind of a how-do-ye-do, even in my own place," laughed Vince. "How do you like that? You could at least pretend to be happy to see me."

Marie pulled back with eyes sparkling, grinning from ear-to-ear. "Oh don't be jealous, Vince. We're old friends, Wolfie and me, aren't we? I haven't seen him since I was a young girl. I thought he died."

The little man laughed, his arms around her waist. "Well, technically, I did. But the how and why of it doesn't quite match with the storybooks. You look beautiful, Marie. Immortality looks good on you. That marriage offer still stands, if you'll have me."

Giggling, she shook her finger in his face. "You're a bad boy, Wolfie. Letting me mourn you all those years and not a word."

"You weren't exactly easy to find, my dear," he replied, and then he gave her a little slap on the behind, making her squeal and jump up from her seat.

"See? So naughty. Now you cut that out or I'll…"

With an impish grin, he turned back to his piano. "You never could resist me, Marie. That's why they had to separate us. Couldn't have you running off with the help, now could they? You'd been promised to France."

"You know it wasn't my idea," she retorted, hand on her hip.

"Mmm. I knew you weren't in love with your fop of a husband. You never could get over me, could you?" He winked, and I couldn't help but laugh. His eyes turned to look at me, and then he rose and made an archaic bow. "Wolfgang Amadeus Mozart. At your service."

I gaped. "No way."

He laughed again, and with a waggle of his eyebrows, he sat at the piano bench once more to begin playing the opening bars of Eine Kleine Nachtmusik. "Way."

"Show off," said Vince. "These musician types, they're all the same." Marie stood on tiptoes and kissed Vince's cheek. "Oh now, boys. Let's not fight. Wolfie was my first love. You can't blame me for a little lingering crush."

"Crush, huh?" Mozart laughed. "Here I still hoped for our wedding day." Then he looked at me and smiled. "It's nice to meet you, Miss....?"

Flustered, I blurted. "Sybill Lysander." Then I remembered I couldn't be her anymore. "Well...now it's Evangeline Mars. Sorry. I almost forgot."

"Nice to meet you, Miss Mars. It's out of this world, in fact." He chuckled at himself and gave me a saucy wink.

"Why are you here, anyway? I mean, you're not even playing your own music. What's that about?" The questions tumbled off my lips before I could stop them.

"Really, my dear!" Marie interjected. "There's no need for rudeness."

Mozart shook his head and looked up benignly from the keyboard. "No, no. It's fine. I don't mind answering. I came here looking for a job. Mister DeLuca offered me one along with a place to stay, and in exchange, I play whatever he asks me to whenever and for as long as he likes. He prefers Gershwin to my, as he calls it, 'hoity-toity stuffed-shirt music,' and I learned long ago to give my patrons what they want. Plus, I've learned to kind of like it." His fingers began moving swiftly over the keys playfully, and he crooned, "Nice work if you can get it, and you can get it if you try."

"Wolfie, you don't have to explain yourself to her." I felt Marie's eyes boring into me, disdain dripping from her lips.

Vince cleared his throat. "Ahem. Not to put a damper on this whole reunion thing, but we really do got to get down to business here, if you can both put that lovey-dovey stuff on hold."

Mozart bowed. "Of course. Until later, ma chère." He blew Marie a kiss and then went back to playing softly, withdrawing himself from the conversation once more.

"Look, doll," said Vince. "I'll talk to some people. Pull a few strings. I'll get you new papers and a ticket out of town. After that, you're on your own, right? No offense, but I can't let my name get tangled up with yours. Not this time."

She nodded and took his hands in hers. "Thank you, Vincent. You're a good man."

"I definitely am not," he said. "But I owe you. I ain't no welcher. This puts us square, though, right?"

"Absolutely," she said. "I won't forget it."

"Yeah, yeah. You just lie low, and I'll take care of it," he told her. Then he turned to face me. "You, missy, get your new name straight, see? You slip up again, and you'll both end up killed, and me along with you. I am kind of partial to not being dead, get me?"

"I got you," I nodded. "Won't happen again."

"Better not," he said, and I saw death in his eyes. I knew if I did anything to lead my father back to him, he wouldn't forget it. Not ever. He looked back at Marie once more. "You girls, you stay in that room, you hear me? You need anything, I'll make sure you get it. No going out on the town and stirring up trouble. I mean it."

"Cross my heart," said Marie, and she actually even did it.

"Good." Just then, the door opened, and the bodyguards came back into the room carrying a tray with two champagne flutes and a carafe of blood. "You guys get lost or something?

Jesus. I nearly sent out the cavalry. These girls are ready to go back to their room. Why don't you escort them there, huh? Make sure they get there okay."

I knew Vince really just wanted to be certain we didn't try to leave the building. Marie knew this also, but rather than complain at being under house arrest, she smiled and kissed Vince's cheek one more time. "Thank you, darling. You always did take such good care of me."

"Uh huh. Okay. You girls go cool your jets while I make good on that business of ours." Though he knew she flirted with him, I could see for a split second his expression soften. He still cared about her, more deeply than he would ever let on. Even though he sent her away, I could see he wished things could be different. I felt partly to blame. When he pulled back from her, he looked over at me. "Nice meeting you, kid. Don't fuck up."

I nodded. "Yes, sir. I will try."

"Don't try. Do." Then he winked at me in a way that reminded me of my father, a friendliness, and yet a hint of a threat behind it.

"Got it." I nodded again, letting him know I'd received is message loud and clear.

"Goodbye, Wolfie," Marie said with a wistful smile, taking my arm in hers to start toward the door.

"Oh, you can't run me off so easily, sweetheart. Now I've finally found you, I can promise you, you'll see me again." He grinned up from across the top of the piano, still playing.

"I'm going to hold you to that," she said, walking away.

"I can die happy then, so long as you hold me," he said.

243

She shook her head, laughing as she opened the door. "You are a wicked little man."

"You like it," he said just before we walked out and the door closed behind us.

If she could have blushed, I'm certain she would have. "Mozart, huh?" I teased.

Marie laughed as we walked to the elevator, followed by the bodyguards, one of whom still carried the tray. "Oh, it was ever so long ago. I was just a girl, still living in Austria. He came to the palace to perform. So talented and charming. A prodigy. I'd never met anyone like him. He made me laugh like no other. I fell in love on the spot. Of course they put a stop to it right away."

"Who did?" I said. The doors to the elevator opened and we stepped inside.

"Oh everyone. My family. His. But not before he asked me to marry him."

My jaw dropped.

The elevator doors closed and Marie pushed the button for our floor. "Don't look so shocked. He was only joking, of course. But why else do you think he couldn't leave Vienna? My brother kept him there at court and refused to allow him to leave his service. Joseph knew, of course, I would have made him a home in Paris. That would never do. They expected me to produce an heir, and that child could not exhibit any musical skills."

"You wouldn't really have..."

"Had an affair? What do you think?" she said with a secretive smile.

"Wow. Just...wow." The doors opened, and we walked to our room.

Marie turned to the bodyguards as we reached the door and opened it with the key-card. "Just set the tray down over there, please, gentlemen. We'll be just fine from now on."

Clearly, her words were a dismissal, and the men did as she asked. I wondered once the door closed behind them whether or not they'd be guarding our door to keep us from leaving. Marie didn't seem so concerned, however, though perhaps she simply hid it well. She walked over to the tray and poured some of the blood into her glass. "Mmm. Well, we may as well settle in for the night. Want to watch some old movies on TCM?"

I shook my head. "No thanks. I think I'll go take a nap for a while."

"Suit yourself," she shrugged. "If you change your mind, I'll be in here."

"Thanks. Goodnight," I said, then turned and walked into my room, closing the door behind me firmly. I had a lot to think about, and I needed some alone time to process everything I'd learned.

I might never get used to the idea the woman who'd turned me, my mother of sorts now, was the Marie Antoinette. She behaved nothing like I'd thought, and yet when she'd been in that room with Mozart (another overwhelming event), no one could deny her identity. I could see the flirtatious and beautiful woman of legend. I had a lot to take in all at once. I also felt torn about what I'd learned about my father. I hadn't really thought about his reaction to my disappearance. My mother must be out of her mind. I'd been so wrapped up in events, I hadn't imagined what they'd be going through until now. I felt guilty, but at the same time, the idea of what my father might do frightened me. When faced with this much grief, my father became capable of anything. I'd always be his little girl, and he would never rest until he knew I came home safe. But I couldn't give him that assurance. I couldn't reach out at all. Too much hinged on secrecy. Then there were the people pursuing us. I couldn't help wondering about this shadowy group were and why they wanted us so badly. What would they do to us when they found us? And what were they doing to Raul? He just had to be okay. The idea of anyone hurting him made me sick.

Darkness, My Only Friend

Raul

"Tell me about Sybill Lysander."

My eyes flew open to see the woman from the park staring at me through the thick glass. I blinked in the harsh brightness. My lips were chapped and cracked, and though I no longer felt hunger, it had been replaced by a deep emptiness that fogged my thinking. It took a moment for her words to filter through to my mind. Sybill. My Sybill. How does she know that name? I sat up, shaking my head to fight off the sluggishness, stuffing down my panic with denial. It's a bluff. Has to be.

"Who?" In a croaking whisper, I blinked up at her, and it didn't take much acting to seem confused.

247

"Stop pretending. We know her name. Sybill. Pretty girl. Shame about the tattoos." The woman sneered at me, and I felt a surge of anger, though I refused to let it show on my face.

"I like tattoos. Don't know the girl, though. Sorry." Though I forced a disaffected air into my voice, I suddenly had visions of Sybill in a place like this.

Confidently smug, the woman crossed her arms over her chest. "Of course you do. We found your scent all over her apartment. Nice place. Her paintings aren't bad either."

This woman had been in Sybill's apartment. The shock of that thought made me sit up straighter, and I looked back at her in defiance. "If you've hurt her...."

She laughed. "So now you know her?"

I turned away, furious with myself and wanting to rip out the woman's throat for forcing me to reveal anything at all. Just then a pang of hunger made me clutch my stomach, grimacing with aching need, and I groaned.

"You must be hungry."

Through gritted teeth, I growled, "You think?"

I heard her whisper and realized there must be others in this place besides her. Before I had time to process this information, I heard a clank near the door, and I looked up to see a small panel open in the wall. Inside the opening were several pints of blood. With a feral lunge, I sprang forward and took them out, piercing the plastic with my fangs and draining them dry one after another in greedy desperation. All too quickly, they were emptied, and I sighed with relief before dropping the containers on the floor and sinking back down onto the bench.

"Better?" she said, and I looked up to see her lip curled

with disgust at my hasty blood-lust.

I sniffed, biting back all the things I wanted to call her, looking away again into the corner.

"Good," she said, as though I'd replied and thanked her. "Now, let us get down to business. This sullen silence of yours and insistence on perpetuating long-held lies is pointless. Tell us what we want to know."

"Right." I spat. "Because you've been such a great hostess up to this point."

Her tone seemed suddenly soft and almost pitying. "If you think by protecting her secrets you will earn her gratitude, you are mistaken. You are a smart young man. You know she is full of her own self-importance. She's never been grateful for anything. She has used people as pawns to suit her whims for centuries. You aren't the first to be used by her, and you won't be the last. Not unless you help us stop her."

"Who's us?" I looked up to stare straight into her eyes, trying not to let my expression show how much her words affected me.

A hint of a smile passed her lips before she replied. "If you choose to join us, I will tell you everything."

I snorted in derision. "Sure you will. As long as you get what you want. Then you'll decide I'm not worth anything to you and kill me off. Forget it, sister."

She paled for a split second, then her eyes narrowed at me. "I can understand your mistrust. You've been lied to for twenty years. You've been brainwashed by the queen of lies. But I'm offering you a way out of that nightmare. All you have to do is work with me."

"Save your breath. I'm not giving you shit." I lay back down on the bench and closed my eyes.

"Sybill and Crystal will be sorry to hear you say so."

I opened my eyes once more, and, in a flash, I crossed the room and stood with my nose to the glass, glaring at her with fangs out. "You leave them alone, you bitch!"

With a shrug, she shook her head, "You're not giving me much choice. Someone has to help me. If you won't, then maybe they will."

The lights went back out, and I bellowed in fury. Only silence answered me as I beat on the window until my fists bled.

An interminable time later, a light interrupted my defeated sleep. It shone not in my room, but only in the room beside mine. Sitting up blinking, I looked over and realized I could see into it through the one-way glass. A table with two chairs sat in the center of a gray concrete space. I walked over to look closer, and just then I saw a woman, her head covered with a dark hood, being led inside by two men in black suits. One of the suited men pulled back one of the chairs with a scrape across the floor, and then the other pushed the woman down. Her wrists were next zip tied to a couple of metal loops built into the chair legs, and then they removed her hood Crystal, her hair tousled and her face streaked with tears, sat with her hands trembling and her eyes darting around in fear.

I cried out and beat on the glass, but again no one answered or heard me.

The woman from the park, wearing all black with a badge pinned to her top, walked into the room and sat at the table opposite Crystal. She folded her hands in front of her on the tabletop, and I saw her say something to the guards who then walked out of the room. Once they'd left, I saw the woman reach one hand over to the edge of the table and flip a switch.

Suddenly, I could hear Crystal's sniffling and rapid breathing.

"Crystal, isn't it?" said the woman with a dispassionate sneer.

"Y-yes," she replied, nodding. "I'm Crystal Kirby. What do you want with me?"

"Do you have any family, Miss Kirby?"

Crystal blinked. "My parents died in a car accident five years ago. Why?"

"Routine questioning," said the woman dismissively. "Tell me the name of your employer, Miss Kirby."

In spite of her fear, Crystal spoke with shaky defiance. "If you don't know who she is, then I'm sure as heck not telling you anything. I want my lawyer. You can't just grab people up like this. No one read me my rights. I didn't do anything. Am I arrested, or what? Who the heck are you people anyway?"

Calmly, the woman raised her hand, gazing back at Crystal. "I'll be the one asking questions. Now, tell me her name."

Crystal shook her head but didn't answer.

Slamming her hands down on the table with sudden force, the woman leaned across the table with a fierce snarl. "Who is she? You answer me!"

With a jump that scooted her chair back a little, Crystal squeaked, "Claire Marie Hapsburg."

"Lies." The woman pounded the table again. "What is her real name? We know that's a fake."

"I don't know!" cried Crystal, fresh tears streaming down her cheeks once more. "I swear to god. Please, let me out of here."

"Who are her associates? You're going to tell me right now."

Poor Crystal sat shaking, petrified, and I felt helpless to save her. I could barely stand to look at her face. It broke my heart. I knew she didn't know anything. The questions were useless. Marie had kept her life so secret, Crystal had nothing of use to these people.

I saw Crystal shrug. "I don't know. There's Raul. He lives with her. They used to be a couple, I guess, but now he just lives with her."

"That isn't his real name. I think you knew that, didn't you, Crystal?" The woman sat back, keeping her voice even, speaking with calm decisiveness.

She shook her head again. "I always thought he looked familiar, but I never could figure out how I knew him. Is he missing or something? I thought maybe he was a runaway she took in. Is that what this is? You think she kidnapped him?

The woman gave her a steely smile. "Is that what you believe?"

"No, I mean, they fought sometimes, but that didn't seem strange to me."

"How would you characterize their arguments?"

"I don't know what you mean," Crystal said, sniffling and looking away.

"What kinds of things did they argue about? Did you ever feel like she kept him against his will? Controlling him?

That sort of thing?" The woman leaned forward, making Crystal squirm.

Crystal licked her lips. "I…I don't know. I mean…I guess sometimes. She'd get this look, and she'd tell him what to do, and he'd just…do it, you know? Like he had to, even when he didn't want to."

I didn't like this line of questioning, and I wanted to scream at Crystal to stop talking, but I knew it would do no good. She'd never hear me.

"I see," said the woman with a satisfied smirk. "Like he seemed compelled, would you say?"

"Compelled? I…I guess." Crystal started squirming in her seat, pulling at her wrists. "Listen, I don't know anything else, I swear."

"Where did her money come from?" said the woman.

"How should I know? Please, I need to go to the bathroom." Looking down at the zip-ties binding her tightly, Crystal began pulling a little more, and I could see the plastic digging into her skin.

"Not until we are through. You worked for this 'Claire Marie' for how long?" Tapping her fingers on the table, the woman ignored Crystal's growing anxiety.

"Five years. Lady, I've really got to go…"

"In all that time, you never wondered how she kept the business afloat? We've looked at her financials, and frankly they just don't make sense. She never made enough to even pay the rent, much less to pay you. Didn't you ever wonder about that?" Crossing her arms over her chest, the woman sat back in her seat and stared Crystal down.

"I guess I figured she had a lot of money, and it didn't matter to her if she made any or not." Beads of sweat were breaking out on Crystal's forehead, and I could hear her heart beating faster.

"Did she ever mention her past? Any previous associates?" Tilting her head to one side, the woman in black watched on with amusement at Crystal's discomfort, and I suddenly recognized the predatory expression on her face.

Oh god. I thought. She's a vampire. She can hear the heartbeat just as I can.

I banged on the glass again with renewed desperation. "Leave her alone! God damn it! Let her go!"

Crystal obviously couldn't hear me, though a fleeting look in the other woman's eyes let me know she herself had heard every word I said.

"She never talked about her past with anyone," Crystal insisted. Then she paused before continuing. "I mean, I know she said she used to live in Chicago. We had this client once who came from there, and I heard her say she used to live there. But that's all I know."

I cringed and shouted even louder and more frantically. "Listen to me! Let her go!"

"Chicago. I see. Did she ever mention a name? A place, perhaps?" That dogged woman wouldn't let it go now.

"I really have to use the bathroom," Crystal said, and then she hissed as one of the zip-ties cut into her wrist. "Ow! This hurts."

Blood dripped onto the gray concrete floor, and I saw

the woman's face change suddenly as she caught the scent. Her eyes grew large and dark. Her lips curled back to reveal her fangs. Crystal stared and screamed, pushing her chair back to the wall, then she fell over with a crash as the seat kept her pinned to the ground. She kicked and shrieked as the woman lunged over the table toward her.

"No!" I roared. "Crystal! No!"

I saw the woman rip into her throat and drain her right before my eyes. Crystal struggled only for a moment, and then went still.

My knees buckled then, and I fell to the floor in a heap, sobbing. Agonizing guilt flooded me, and I berated myself. I couldn't save her. She died because of me. If I had just controlled my urges and gone home instead of to the park that night, Crystal would still be alive. I ruined everything, and Crystal paid the price. And I despaired thinking next I'd have to watch the same scene play out before my eyes with Sybill.

Through my shuddering cries, I heard the woman's voice echo in my cell through the speakers, "Now you understand how far I will go to get to the truth. Think about that for a while. When I come back, we'll talk again."

I heard the woman walk out the door, slamming it behind her. When at last I could bear to look up, I saw she had left the light on in the interrogation room. Crystal lay in a mangled pile in the corner, arms still strapped to the chair.

"I'm sorry, Crystal," I whispered. "I'm so sorry."

Hours later when they finally came to remove the body, I hugged my knees, curled up in the corner and rocking myself for comfort, deliberately staring at the wall, though I couldn't see anything in my mind's eye except the terror I'd registered in Crystal's eyes just before she'd died.

This time when the lights went out, I felt grateful to be left alone in the dark.

THE SALT OF OUR YOUTH

Marie

About thirty minutes after Sybill had gone to lie down, a soft knock came at the door of our suite. I unfolded myself from the sofa, switched off the television (I'd been watching *Cleopatra* with Elizabeth Taylor and Richard Burton for the hundredth time and laughing at its garish costumes), then tiptoed over to look through the peephole.

Wolfie, stood there, rocking on the balls of his feet impatiently. I had known from the moment we saw one another again, he'd never be able to stay away.

"Let me in," he whispered, knowing I could hear him through the door.

"Quick, before these thugs tell Vince we were canoodling." His nervous, infectious laugh, high and unpredictable, burst out of him in waves.

With a soft chuckle to myself, I unlocked the door, opened it about a foot and said, "We were not canoodling. Got it? No canoodling of any kind."

I frowned at the guards who were posted on either side of the entrance.

"Don't you boys have better things to do?"

They didn't answer me but looked back down at Mozart who covered his mouth with his hand and giggled. "I don't think they do. Won't you let me in, sweetheart? They're starting to look hungry."

I rolled my eyes and opened the door. "Get in here. Goodness, but you're presumptuous. You'd think I came to Chicago just to see you rather than because I ran for my life."

"Are the two reasons mutually exclusive?" he said as he walked past me, grinning.

Closing the door, I turned to face him, "I didn't realize you were here. In fact, I didn't know you weren't dead. Don't think I've forgiven you yet, because I haven't."

"Darling, I didn't know about you either. How would I have written even if I had?" He put on a mocking grin and pretended to write with an imaginary quill, "'Ma chère Marie, I'm a vampire now, but don't worry, I'm happy about it. Shame about your husband and kids. Still, now we can be together at last since you're undead too. Send money, and I'll meet you in Switzerland once your people are through killing one another.'"

I crossed my arms over my chest and narrowed my eyes. "Must you make a joke of everything?"

He shrugged, throwing the invisible quill over his shoulder. "It's better than the alternative, isn't it? You endured enough seriousness with that dour hubby of yours, didn't you? Come on, my darling little girl. Say you forgive me." Dropping down on one knee, he clasped his hands together and looked up at me with a fake pout, batting his eyes. "Please?"

"Oh, just stop it. You're ridiculous, and I am not a little girl anymore." I said, trying to keep from laughing. "You'll ruin your tuxedo, and I'm sure Vince paid for it. He won't be happy with you if he has to replace it because you were here making goo-goo-eyes at me."

He hopped back up with a grin. "Not quite forgiveness, but since you're concerned for my well-being, I'll take it as a given. But, more importantly, you didn't say you're not my darling, and that is even better."

He stepped in close, wrapped his arms around me, and swept me up in a kiss that made my toes curl. I should have pushed him away, slapped him, or told him in no uncertain terms to get out. I should have done a lot of things, but instead, I kissed him back with all the fervor of the young love I'd never had the chance to show him.

At last, we pulled apart, and he whispered softly, stroking my hair, "Now, that's some canoodling."

I couldn't help but laugh. "You are such a wicked little man. You'll be the death of me, I swear."

My words made him frown, his expression suddenly serious. "Don't swear to that. I'll never joke about that.

Don't you know I mourned you all these years? My darling girl. I felt devastated."

The hurt in his eyes made my heart ache, and I caressed his face gently.

"I never stopped missing you. I blame myself for your financial troubles. To think you'd have been buried in a pauper's grave. You. I cried when I heard of it. I know my brother did that to you out of spite because of me."

"Shh..." he said, placing a finger to my lips. "Don't be so hard on him. Your brother treated me well at first. There were others at court whose jealousies led him to change his mind, however."

"Yes, but he knew I wanted you in Paris with me."

With a sad little smile, he shook his head. "You couldn't have me, my darling. You cannot blame a brother for wanting to protect his sister from ruin and scandal. He had a duty to you and to himself. I understood, even if I didn't agree."

He sat then on the sofa, pulling me into his lap, and we held one another there for a long time. I had missed him for so long, I found myself wanting to touch him just for confirmation this wasn't a dream. "So how did it happen?" I said, placing my hand on his cheek.

"The usual way," he laughed, showing me his fangs. "Same as you."

"Yes, but I mean...."

"Oh, don't let's get into all that unpleasantness from the past and spoil the present. Let's just say my turning wasn't an easy thing for me and leave it at that, shall we?" He kissed my neck, trying to distract me.

"Was it really so bad?" I said, sighing softly at the touch of his lips.

"Well, my dear," he said, his words punctuated with kisses, "if you saw my Don Giovanni, you would know the answer to that question."

"You wrote that about your turning?" I said, my fingers sliding into his hair.

"Mmm…I'd have thought anyone like us would find the correlation obvious." He kissed his way over to the hollow of my throat and for a moment, I couldn't speak.

"I couldn't bear your Requiem," I said at last, pulling back and lifting his chin to look him in the eye. "It broke my heart."

"You told me once you didn't have one." His mouth had a teasing smile, but his eyes were soft and tender.

"I said my life didn't allow me to have a heart. That's not the same thing." Leaning forward again, I brought his lips to mine. When we broke the kiss again, I whispered, "Did you really miss me after so long?"

"Darling, you never forget your first love, do you?" Our noses touched as he said the question.

"No," I said. "No, you don't."

One more kiss, and then, without another word, I took him by the hand and led him to my room. He closed the door behind us with a smile, humming a Gershwin tune, dancing me in his arms all the way to the bed.

TELL ME SOMETHING GOOD

Chief Inspector

I licked my lips as I sat back in my office chair. I should not have lost control like that, but I couldn't bear the scent of her blood. The blonde woman, Crystal, had no family, and therefore no one would notice her absence. That's what I told myself as I tried to dismiss my concerns about having killed her. My team would dispose of the body. She would be just another missing person.

Still, if The Master got word of my outburst, he would not be pleased, and the thought of making him angry worried me. More importantly, any information I might have been able to get was lost for good. I told myself Crystal's death had given me leverage over the prisoner, however, which ought to prove of more value. It had certainly better be, at any rate.

My team had lost the trail of the stolen van, and I felt furious about it. I needed results, not more disappointments and dead ends.

A knock at the door drew me out of my thoughts. "Come," I said, gathering myself once more.

The door opened and a young assistant peeked inside. "Madam, you ought to come and see this."

My forehead furrowed. "What is it I'm supposed to see?"

He stammered and then backed his way out of the room. "I think it is better if you just come and take a look for yourself."

I leapt from my chair with annoyance and walked out into the central office area. Several lab techs and some agents were standing around in a semi-circle, staring a television screen. There, on the twenty-four hour news channel, for all to see, the face of that tattooed young woman we had been seeking, Sybill Lysander, smiled from family photos, and news crews were describing her as missing. Experts were speculating as to whether to categorize her disappearance as a kidnapping or a simple runaway situation. One of the talking heads mentioned the possibility she might be the next victim of the "St. Louis vampire."

A cold rage bubbled up inside me, and I walked over to the screen and turned it off, then looked around at the group and said, "Get back to work! We don't have time for you to be standing here. You've got a job to do!"

They scattered hurriedly, and I stormed back into my office and slammed the door.

The timing couldn't have been worse. I picked up a red glass paperweight off my desk and hurled it across the room where it smashed into blood colored slivers which scattered all over the floor.

Just then, my cell phone rang. Gathering myself, I pulled the phone out of my pocket, dreading it would be The Master calling. What I saw on the display made me relax just slightly. My field operative. I pushed the button to answer.

"This had better be good news," I said coldly.

What I heard made me raise her eyebrows in surprise, and I even smiled a little. "Chicago. You're certain it's her?"

The operative's reply made me smile even more. "You'll receive your payment as promised."

Without another word, I hung up and then gave a sigh of relief. A lead at last.

I walked over to my desk and lifted the phone to dial another office, and when the other person picked up, I said, "She's been sighted in Chicago. I am going to intercept her. Transfer the prisoner to our headquarters immediately. The Master will deal with him there personally."

No Strings Attached

Sybill

W hen I awoke the next evening, I heard humming in the outer room. Bleary-eyed, my hair a tumbled mess, I shuffled out into the seating area in my sleep shorts and tank top, still rubbing the sleep away. There on the sofa sat Mozart, his fingers tapping in time to a song I'd never heard before.

"What time is it?" I yawned, covering my mouth with my forearm as I flopped in the seat opposite him.

"Half-past seven," he answered, continuing to tap his fingers. "Did I wake you?"

"A little," I said. "Don't worry about it."

265

"I do apologize, my dear. It's the most wonderful thing. I've begun a new composition. It's been years. I couldn't help myself." He put his hand to his chest and gave a half bow from his seat, his other hand still tapping in time to the music in his head.

I blinked blearily. "A new composition? That's the noise I heard?" I knew I sounded rude, but I felt too sleepy to stop myself before the words tumbled out of my mouth.

He laughed then, his voice bursting unexpectedly into high pitched squeaks of delight so he almost seemed to be hiccuping. I reached over and thumped him on the back. "You all right there? Need a glass of water or something?"

"Hee-hee!" he tittered. "No, no. I only drink one thing these days, same as you. You'll have to forgive me my hilarity, I'm afraid. I have always been inclined to laughter. It's one of my foibles." His eyes were rimmed with tears, and he wiped them away as he gradually began to wind down. "Would you like a beverage yourself, my dear? There is a delightful vintage over there on the table. Hee-hee!"

Though I couldn't see why he found my words so amusing, his giggle was infectious. I smiled at him, laughing just a little. With a shake of my head, I got up to pour myself a glass of blood, still warm, and I shivered with delight right down to my toes. "Mmm…delicious."

"Yes, no one procures quite the same quality as Vince. I don't know how he does it." Mozart turned his body to face me as I took my seat again.

"So…" I began, looking around the room, "…you're here early."

He began the hysterical chortling all over again, covering his hands with his face as he snorted and whooped.

"Uh, was it something I said?" I raised my eyebrows and looked at him in confusion. He waved his hand to stop me from talking while he tried unsuccessfully to compose himself. I took deep droughts from the glass, watching on silently as wave after wave of giggle fits took him over. "Okay. I'm just going to stop talking and drink my blood over here."

By the time I'd emptied my glass, he finally managed to calm himself enough to speak coherently again. "Sorry. It's just, it's the funniest thing, you see. So amusing. You'll die when you hear…"

But before he could explain, a knock at the door came.

"You expecting anyone?" I said.

He shook his head and stood, suddenly completely serious, all hint of laughter gone.

I rose from my seat and walked toward the door. Through the peephole, I saw Vincent standing in the hallway. "Great," I said. "Just great."

Putting on a smile, I opened the door halfway and leaned on it to block his view into the room. "Vincent. Nice to see you again."

He rolled his eyes. "Can the small talk, kid. Lemme in. I gotta talk to our girl, pronto."

"Charming," I sighed, pasting on an even wider fake grin and opening the door completely. "Come on in. Join the party. Make yourself at home."

Vince walked inside while I closed the door behind him. When he saw Mozart there, he did a double take. "You? I thought I told you to lay off the dame."

Mozart giggled once, and I glared at him. "Oh no. Not again. You start laughing again, swear to god, I'm going to slap you in the face. I am not in the mood, mister."

Peering at me sideways, Vince gave me a knowing look and nodded. "Amen, kid. Now where is she?"

Before I could answer, the doors to Marie's room opened, and she stepped out wrapped in a fluffy white bathrobe, her hair bound up in a towel. "Vince, darling. What an unexpected delight to see you again so soon."

He looked her up and down, then his eyes narrowed, and he turned to look at Mozart, his nostrils flaring. "Why, I ought-a —"

Marie stepped between them before Vince could go any further.

Mozart's eyes were wide, and he shrugged, grinning mischievously and attempting miserably to stifle his nervous laughs. "Now, now. We're past all that, aren't we? Please, Vince. Just tell me what you found out."

He scowled muttering, "Goddamn musicians."

I poked Mozart in the ribs to make him stop giggling.

With an irresistible smile, Marie took Vince's arm and led him to the sofa, sitting down beside him. "Oh now, Vince darling, please."

She leaned over and kissed his cheek, and he sighed heavily. "Fine, fine. Whatever. It's none of my business anymore, I guess." He looked up at Mozart and shook his finger. "You're fired. You hear me? That's the last straw. You're done in this town."

Mozart shrugged. "I thought you might say that."

"Yeah? Well, you were right." Vince gave him another scowl, then sighed again before looking toward Marie once more. He dug in his inside suit coat pocket and pulled out a large envelope. "All right, here's the deal. I got you gals new papers. They're done by my best guy."

Pulling the towel off her head and letting her wet hair fall to her shoulders, Marie took the proffered envelope and then dropped the towel to the floor at her feet. She opened the envelope carefully and pulled out the passports, one for me and one for her, as well as an itinerary for a private jet inside. She examined the paper before looking back up. "Venice? Why Venice?"

Vince shoved his hands down into his pockets casually. "I thought you might ask me. Well, it just so happens I got some associates on the continent who said the guy you was looking for a few years back...he's been seen there."

Her eyes grew wide with a shock and emotion I didn't understand. "Oh, Vince!"

"Look, I don't know any more than that, and I ain't makin' you no promises." He shrugged, but his smile revealed his pleasure at her reaction. "My people will meet you there and give you more details once you can talk to them face-to-face. I know how much you wanted to find him way back when. I can't help you with this missing actor of yours, but I figure, hey, maybe your guy can help you once you find him."

"Oh, Vince!" she exclaimed, and her voice choked as she threw her arms around him and held him tightly. "Thank you. Oh, thank you."

He patted her on the back awkwardly. "There, there. It's the least I can do."

"It's wonderful." She sat back up, and her eyes were filled with tears. "I can never repay you for this."

With a wink, he touched her nose with one finger. "You don't owe me a thing, doll. Just don't get killed. Got it?"

She nodded, and sniffled, smiling from ear to ear. "I'll do my best."

Mozart peeked out from behind me. "I'm going with you."

"Say what?" Vince said.

"You what?" I said, wheeling around to stare at him. "You've got to be joking."

"Oh no, I couldn't ask you to do that." Marie shook her head.

"Nonsense. I just happen to be a free agent at the moment, in a manner of speaking." He stepped forward with a swagger. "I think you need someone to help make sure nothing goes wrong."

"You doubting my associates?" Vince began to stand up with a warning in his eyes.

"Oh, no." Mozart waved his hands and bowed. "I would never call into question their motives or yours. I'm sure they're lovely fellows, just like yourself. But who knows what could go wrong? I'd like to be of service. Plus, I can't bear to lose you now after we've only just found one another again, my dearest."

He took Marie's hand and dropped to one knee. "Please, let me do this. I would brave any danger for you."

Vince rolled his eyes. "Give me a friggin' break."

But Marie seemed truly touched, and she smiled at him and squeezed his hand. "My sweet Wolfie."

I thought I would gag, but then she looked up at me, turning those same irresistible charms in my direction. "Would you mind, dear?"

"Who me?" I blinked at her. "You're finally asking me what I think now? I want to know one thing: will this trip help us save Raul? Tell me the truth."

Marie gazed back at me with complete sincerity. "The truth is, I don't know. But it's the best option I have. Unless you know how to find these people and bring him back on our own, we are going to need help."

"This guy we're going to try to find, whoever he is, he's just going to drop whatever he's doing and help us both? What makes you so sure he'll be willing, even if we do find him?" I crossed my arms over my chest and glared at her.

"Because…" she said, "…he's my progeny."

The whole room went silent. Vince had a knowing look on his face, but Mozart stared back at her in as much surprise as myself.

"I told you I had another," she said quietly, standing up. "I lost him years ago."

"Lost?" I said. "People lose keys or phones. This is modern times. How did you lose a whole person?"

She looked down at me steadily. "It wasn't modern times."

271

"Right. Well, that answers that." I threw my hands up and glared. "Should I be worried? Because this is starting to seem like a bad habit or a curse or something. I think I'm your only kid who hasn't disappeared."

Her face grew pale as though I'd struck her, and I frowned, angry with myself. "Sorry," I said. "That wasn't fair."

"No, you're right," she said. "You are the only one. I am not going to lose you, understood?"

She held out her arms and threw them around me, gripping me tightly, and I couldn't help but embrace her right back. I felt moved by her show of real emotion, and we hugged for a minute or two before Vince cleared his throat.

"Not to break up this tender moment or anything, but your plane leaves in two hours. If I'm going to get this bozo..." he gestured to Mozart with his thumb, "...a seat, I've got to make some calls, capiche?"

Marie pulled back from me, smiling. "Thank you again, Vincent. For everything."

"Don't mention it," he said, moving toward the door. "I just hope one day we'll meet again under better circumstances."

She followed him, and when he reached for the door handle, she stretched out her hand to touch his shoulder. "You've always been good to me, Vince. I will never forget it."

"Only the best for my Goldie." Eyes softening, he leaned forward and kissed her forehead. "Take care, doll. Come back in one piece."

With that, he left.

Marie sighed softly as the door closed, then she turned back around and smiled at us both. "Pack your things, darling.

272

We haven't a moment to lose. Wolfie, you'd better go do the same."

He nodded and walked over to her, taking her face in his hands. "I will see you soon, my angel." Kissing her softly, he held her close, and I decided to remove myself from the room.

"Can't wait to watch that all day long," I murmured as I walked away, and I heard Mozart giggle as I closed my bedroom door.

Beyond the Edge

Raul

They came for me in the dark. Weak from lack of blood and emotional exhaustion, I couldn't have fought off a small child, but there were four of them who came to "subdue" me. They shot me with a tranquilizer gun, then shackled my hands and feet, gagged me, and covered my head with a hood.

They hoisted me into a wooden box, perhaps a coffin, and then screwed the lid down tight over me. The sedation wore off quickly, but it had been potent enough to last until they secured the final screw. It seemed like overkill to me, but I had no resistance to tell them so.

I fully expected to be buried that way or to be thrown off a cliff into the ocean to lie at the bottom of the sea for who knows how long until the wood rotted away and let me escape at last. After what had happened to me, I would have welcomed the former. The latter was the thing of my nightmares, and I lay in the box in dread.

Neither of those scenarios happened, however.

Instead, they carried me onto a vehicle, bumped along for ten to fifteen minutes, unloaded, and then loaded into, as I soon realized, an airplane. I heard and felt it taxi down a runway and lift off. Too busy thinking about being dumped at sea, I couldn't pay much attention to the small details that might have told me the type of plane. At some point, I drifted off to sleep, so it must have been day, which meant the pilot had to be human. I awoke, still in the box, being carried along in another vehicle up what must have been a mountainside. The road full of switchbacks, we rode at a fairly steep angle. I found myself continually fighting to stay on my back as gravity kept rolling me onto my side, each turn knocking me into the wood with a painful lurch.

At last, the vehicle stopped. They unloaded me again. I heard gravel crunching, then a steel grate squeak open. Next, there came the echo of sound on stone, and I felt myself being brought down a series of steps, further than I'd have believed. More steel doors opened and closed, they carried me through, then set the box down abruptly. I heard an electric screwdriver remove the screws, and then the lid slid off. The air smelled damp and musty, like the wetness of a cave. Before I could take in any more information about the place, however, they shot me once more with a tranquilizer.

I came to, lying on a bed of straw in what could only be described as a dungeon. I'd only seen them in movies, but when you're in a place like that, it's unmistakable. I felt as though I'd stepped onto the set of *The Count of Monte Cristo*, but this place was horrifyingly real.

Shackles attached my wrists to the wall with a long length of heavy chain. The cold stone walls were made of massive blocks, laid together without mortar for the seams. There were no windows. I heard water dripping somewhere in slow drops, and I heard the moans of what must be other prisoners through the small opening in the steel door. A pale light flickered just beyond it, and the tiny square opening gave the only illumination. This place, I felt, was where people were brought to be forgotten. Forever is a long time, but facing the real possibility this cell might be where I'd spend the rest of my immortal life seemed a devastating prospect.

What had these people done with Sybill? Did they have her in this place too? I held onto a desperate hope she still lived. I closed my eyes and imagined her face. I couldn't stand to think she had suffered as Crystal had. I couldn't bear the idea I wouldn't see her or hold her in my arms once more.

My mind began racing, full of all those questions I hadn't let myself ask until now. What about Marie? Had they found her? I had to believe she remained free. Otherwise, what would they want with me? What had she'd done to warrant such violent means of seeking her out? What might they do to me in order to capture her?

My heart sank. My dreams of being rescued by her were foolish. She must think I'd died by now. I couldn't see how anyone could escape such a place. Each moment, Marie and I grew further apart, and the likelihood of my release became more remote.

Opening my eyes, I gazed around the cell again in dismay. I'd exchanged a modern prison for an ancient one, and I feared my terror had only just begun.

Blood Makes Noise

Chief Inspector

At the Palmer House Hotel, I entered wearing dark sunglasses, six-inch heels, and a black tailored suit, walking purposefully up to the desk and trailing a hard -sided suitcase.

The concierge at the desk gave a welcoming smile and asked for my name. I raised my glasses and looked the man in the eye, and with my voice low but firm, I said, "Tell Mister DeLuca an old friend has arrived."

His eyes grew wide and disconcerted. "Just a moment, ma'am. I will be right back," he said, and immediately went to the back to make a call. I could see him through a window looking into the manager's office, talking quickly and making frantic gestures with his hands.

When he returned from the office, face flushed, beads of sweat stood out on his forehead. I could smell the blood pumping through his veins, and my nostrils flared as he spoke to me, "I have a room for you, complements of the management, Miss...?"

"Ernestine Lambriquet." I gave the man a fixed stare. I could hear his blood pulsing, the sound of it nearly ringing in my ears, and I let my face become a predatory mask while my voice dropped to a low growl. "I believe Mister DeLuca and I have some important business to discuss."

"Oh, I'm sorry. I hate to be impertinent, madam, but I'm afraid Mister DeLuca is a busy man, Miss Lambriquet. He never sees anyone without an appointment." The little man began typing furiously into the computer, trying not to look up, but his hands shook, and sweat began to drip down his neck.

"He'll see me," I said, reaching over the counter to lift the man's chin, forcing him to meet my gaze. "Tell him to make room in his schedule. You will see to it he knows I'm here. He will make time for me. Tell him the people I work for insist upon it. He will know who I mean. They aren't happy with him, and they can make his situation here uncomfortable if he doesn't cooperate. Understood?"

"I...I'll tell him you are here. That is the best I can do, ma'am," the man said with extreme agitation.

"Do it." I let him go, annoyed at the man's resistance, and he breathed a sigh of relief as he finished his entry into the registry.

He asked for my signature and then handed over my room key-cards. As soon as I took them from the counter, he turned to call over a porter for my bags, but I waved my hand dismissively. "I can find my own way, thank you. Be sure to tell Mister DeLuca he won't like me if I wait long."

I walked away toward the elevators, and as soon as I stepped out of his line of vision, I could hear the nervous concierge return to the office to make another urgent call. When the phone picked up, I overheard him say, "Mister DeLuca? Sir, I hate to bother you, but there is a bit of a situation."

A few hours later, as I sat on one side of a long sofa, wearing a smart suit and a pair of black Louboutins, texting on my phone, a knock came at the door. I set the phone down on the coffee table before me, then rose and swished across the room. After looking out the peephole for a moment, I opened the door and glared at the gentleman standing there with an iPad tucked under his right arm.

"Miss Lambriquet?" he said, smiling.

My eyes narrowed with irritation, sizing him up and down, recognizing him as a young vampire. "You're not Vincent."

"I'm sorry, ma'am," he said, "but Mister DeLuca is a busy man, and without an appointment, I'm afraid…."

"Oh, you should be afraid," I said, reaching out one arm to take the man by the throat and drag him into my room, slamming the door behind me. The man dropped the iPad and struggled to pull my hand away, but I kept my iron grip, and he gagged in pain. I bared my fangs. "He thought I couldn't glamour you if he turned you. I won't need glamour. You're going to tell me right now what I want to know, or I swear you won't be leaving this room alive. Have I made myself clear?"

He nodded frantically, and I let go then, stepping back while he coughed and loosened his tie.

"Now," I said, crossing my arms over my chest, "I am looking for someone. I know Mister DeLuca is protecting her. She is a dangerous fugitive, and the people I work for want her in custody. A blonde woman about so tall." I gestured with my hand to show the height, then went on. "She's perhaps changed her hair color, but she has striking blue eyes. She'd be traveling with another woman. Dark hair. Tattoos. The two would have arrived in the middle of the night in a stolen vehicle with almost no luggage. They'd have been paying with cash, and whatever names they gave are false. I can assure you, they may be beautiful, but they are deadly. They're wanted in connection to two murders just in the last month, and there may be others."

The man shook his head. "I haven't seen anyone who meets that description, ma'am, and even if I had, I couldn't divulge that information. Mister DeLuca takes the privacy of his guests seriously."

Giving him a fanged grin, I stepped forward into his space and said, "Yes, I'm sure. You know what I take seriously? Lying." With one swift motion, I pinned him to the wall, fixing my eyes on his. "Two women. Where are they? Tell me, or I start removing body parts."

"They left!" he squeaked as my hand found its way to the bulge in his pants and squeezed.

"When?"

I dug my fingernails in, and he cried out. "Oh god! An hour ago!"

"Where did they go?" I said, twisting my hand until he made a tortured scream.

"Europe somewhere! I swear, that's all I know!" Tears were streaming down his cheeks, and his face contorted with pain.

A wave of fury washed over me, but I let go my grip and took a step back. The man sank to his knees, doubling over. "That's all I know. Please, that's all I know."

"Too bad," I said, reaching forward to take his head in both hands and, with a roar, ripped it from his body before flinging it into the corner with rage. Blood splattered everywhere, and I licked my lips as I kicked the body away from me. Then I turned on my heel and walked to the bathroom, slamming the door shut behind me.

Twenty minutes later, I emerged, freshly showered and clothes changed, holding a large duffel bag in one hand and a white bath towel in the other. The pool of blood around the body had begun to congeal, and I wrinkled my nose in disgust, talking to the corpse as I gathered my phone and a small bag, leaving the rest of my belongings behind. "Never send a baby vamp to do your dirty work, Mister DeLuca. That's just sloppy. And you should have known better than to mess with me. You've made your last mistake."

I pulled a pair of latex gloves from my pocket, put them on, and then picked up the dead man's iPad from the floor, wiping off the blood with a corner of the towel. Quickly, I brought the screen to life. A series of floor-plans of the hotel appeared, detailing the employee spaces on every floor. I scanned through, and what I saw made me smile. "Gotcha."

Tossing the iPad back onto the floor, I bent over and searched the body, pulling a security card and a cell phone out of the front lapel pocket. I cleaned them both with the towel as well before I laid it down over the pool of blood then walked across it toward the door, my shoes leaving red impressions on the white fabric. I placed a pair of sunglasses on my face, then opened the door and walked out.

The elevator at the end of the hall took me down to the lower level basement. I exited into a corridor and turned left toward a locked door.

Swiping the key-card I'd stolen, I made it through to the next hallway and found my way toward the room I remembered from the floor plans. One more swipe of the key card brought me inside, and there, I saw a row of cages on the right hand side of the room. Those cages held young human men and women. Above each cage door hung a sign which designated the blood types of the humans inside. I tilted my head in curiosity as the humans began to rattle the bars and call out to me for help. Shaking my head, I chuckled softly, then looked away to search the rest of the space.

A quick scan on the other side of the room revealed test tubes and gurneys and medical equipment, and beyond stood a row of confinement rooms with observation windows, each again labeled by blood type. In these rooms, I saw groups of pregnant women, their eyes full of defeat.

At the rear of the place, I could see a set of hooks hung from the ceiling and a drain in the floor. A tub stood nearby.

This was a slaughterhouse. But how did he dispose of the bodies? It only took a second for me to realize the truth.

I had to admire Vincent's ingenuity. No need to worry about being caught killing off humans on a regular basis. He had a self-contained herd of humans which he maintained for harvests. He bred them, then killed only the offspring. The women could then be bred again. Smaller amount of waste. Renewable source of blood. It made perfect sense, from a vampire perspective. Ingenious.

Still, I had a job to do. I wanted to punish Vincent for his disrespect to me and to The Master. He should have known better.

Stopping in the center of the room, I brought out the stolen cell phone and scrolled down to find Vincent's number. I opened a new message to him and texted, "The people I work for are not forgiving, Mr. DeLuca. Game over." With my thumb, I clicked send, then tossed the phone to the floor carelessly.

Placing the duffel bag on the floor, I opened the zipper and brought out several bundles of plastique and some remote detonators. It only took a few minutes to place the explosives on support pillars throughout the basement room. Then I picked up my duffel and exited the place, returning to the elevators. As I walked down the hall, I gave a wink to the security cameras, knowing I would make it out of the building before anyone could reach me.

Vincent hadn't planned for this sort of attack from inside. He had insulated himself from direct assault from armed killers, but he hadn't anticipated a lone assassin targeting spaces of his building he didn't occupy.

Removing the latex gloves and stuffing them into my pocket, I took the stairs up to the lobby and then walked out the front doors of the hotel, smirking at the concierge who stared at me in confusion. On the sidewalk, I turned away to the left on Monroe Avenue toward the L train lines.

Two blocks away, I climbed the steps to the Deerborn Station and hopped on the last of the Blue Line trains where I took a seat in the front car. As the doors of the train closed, I reached into my duffel, and inconspicuously pushed a button on a remote device, smiling to myself before I zipped the bag closed again.

A series of low rumbling booms began sounding, and the people on the last car of the train just had time to see the front windows of the Palmer House Hotel explode with flame. By the time the news stations were showing images of the building's collapse, I had departed the train and disappeared.

This is not a Fire Drill

Marie

Vincent had been better to me than I ever expected. He agreed without question to dispose of the truck Sybill and I had driven to his hotel. He had arranged for his driver to deliver us to O'Hare. Most touchingly, he'd reserved for us a private jet with a windowless cabin, designed to his specifications for his own personal use.

The crew welcomed us on board and saw us to our seats while the bags were loaded. Sybill seemed delighted with the accommodations. Vince had thought of everything, and I knew he had gone far beyond what he owed me in this. Clearly, he had a personal interest in seeing us well away and out of his area, but he'd gone to great lengths in order to ensure our comfort, quite

286

obviously due to his lingering feelings for me. I had small twinge of guilt I could not reciprocate those feelings, but having my dear Wolfie beside me after so many years during which I'd thought him lost to me forever…words could not describe my joy.

I knew Sybill didn't care for Wolfgang much, but I hoped she would come around once she knew him better. I put it down to a jealousy at no longer being the center of my attention. Such emotions were common for children upon being presented with a mother's new suitor. I resolved to demonstrate my dedication to her safety and to spend some time with her, training her in her new powers once we arrived at our destination.

On board the plane, Sybill settled into her seat with headphones on, closing her eyes right away and losing herself in the musical selections on board the plane. Wolfie, on the other hand, clearly found flying disconcerting, but he bore it well, holding my hand and putting on a brave face for my sake.

As for me, I felt relieved to be putting so much distance between us and our pursuers, and I tried not to dwell on my fears about Raul. It would be so easy to give over to despair, but for his sake I had to believe it would still be possible to find and rescue him.

I also felt elated beyond measure at the prospect of finding the child I'd thought lost to me forever. I could never have hoped for such a gift, and I could barely believe, after all this time thinking him out of my reach, I might finally lay eyes on him. Would he forgive me for what I had done to him? Would he be as overjoyed as I hoped to be at a reunion? What would be his reaction to my companions? Jealousy? Indifference? Anger? What if he had found a companion of his own by now? I didn't know how I would feel about that either. I hoped my fears were unfounded. Moreover, I hoped beyond everything else he would be willing and able to help us find Raul. I needed help so desperately. I needed someone strong to rely on. He had always been that. I hoped he could be that for me again.

When we lifted off, I waited until we reached altitude, then lay back to get some rest while I could. I knew once we landed we'd be off on another adventure, and I needed all my strength if I wanted to tackle what still lay ahead. I didn't know if we would find what we sought once we arrived in Venice, but I held onto hope.

I was first and foremost a survivor. I'd been through so much heartbreak, and yet I had never lost my sense of self. I'd never given myself over to the creature. Where others had lost themselves to the hunger and the rage or allowed themselves to fall victim to the slaughter of the Revolution, I had escaped and found a way to retain my soul and sanity. My resolve was stronger than the monster within, more resilient than anyone had ever believed I could be, and whatever might happen, I had to believe I would continue not only to endure, but to come out even better than ever before.

My house, my shop, and my peaceful life back in St. Louis I felt certain I would never see any of it again. I would miss those things. I hoped Crystal was happy, and I resolved to contact her once we'd found a safe haven and sign over the business to her care. It was the least I could do after all her hard work.

I tried to remember the sound of Raul's voice and the smile on his face.

I told myself I'd see him again. That we'd make a life together once more. I imagined the joy we would both feel when he knew I'd made sure he would never lose his beloved. I pictured them together. I wished for a wedding that would make them both happy forever.

Just before I drifted off to sleep, my head on Wolfgang's shoulder, I whispered a prayer to the Virgin Mary, praying for her intercession on his part. "Keep him safe, Holy Mother. Hold him in your arms until I can bring him home again."

The plane bore us over the waters in the dark, pointing over the horizon, traveling inexorably toward whatever came next.

APPENDICES

Afterward by the Author

Cast of Characters

AFTERWARD BY THE AUTHOR

This book has been a long time in the making. I kicked the ideas around in my head for about two years before I finally started turning my ideas into written form.

Claire Marie started as a standalone role-playing character long before I ever had a book planned around her. Yes, I said it. Role-playing. I just loved the idea of Marie Antoinette as a vampire. My premise began with a simple "what if," but the more I explored her character, fleshing her out in my mind, the more I realized she had a complex story to tell. There is so much intrigue and mystery and such a vast wealth of history to draw on for her. As the series continues, you'll see many more facets to her, and I hope her past will continue to surprise and frighten you in turns.

Raul Griffin came next, and what a great tragic and romantic figure he's turned out to be. He nearly met a grisly end in this first book, but I had second thoughts about losing him so early. He's got a reprieve...at least for now. I'm not promising he will survive till the end of the series, but he does have a lot more of his own tale to tell, and I'm definitely not finished with him yet. If you are like me, you'll have a hard time letting him go as well, and I may just find he'll make it through after all. However, the poor guy is going to have a seriously rough time of it, let me tell you, and if he does survive, he may not be the same person he is at the beginning, though we can all hope for it just the same.

As for Sybill Lysander, I knew as soon as I introduced her as a love interest for Raul and foil for Marie, she would turn out to be so much more than that. She has expanded far beyond anything I foresaw when I first started writing, and I absolutely love her. What a fantastically fun character to write! She has so much depth, and she's constantly surprising me. I loved exploring her family life and thinking about ways that might change her. Sybill will keep on surprising us, and I look forward to showing just what she's capable of as the story continues.

The Chief Inspector has a convoluted back-story, and we will learn much more about her in the next book. Is the name she gave in the hotel her true identity or not? You'll have to wait and find out. I don't want to give too much away too fast about her. I'm enjoying the cat and mouse. She's so deliciously dangerous.

Just who is The Master? Well, you're going to have to wait to find out. All I can tell you is when I finally reveal the identity, it'll be a game changer for all the characters in the series. He adds a whole new element of mystery, suspense, and horror in the next book I think will shock and excite you. I can't wait until I get to tell you his name...but I am going to hold onto the suspense little while longer. Sorry! It's worth the wait, I promise.

Vincent DeLuca was so much fun to add into the mix. I'm not sure yet how much more of him we will see, but I've already got a lot of ideas for his rich back-story, and if there is a chance to add it into this story, I certainly will. He might merit his own standalone book, however. I'll just have to wait and see.

Crystal Kirby is based on a friend of mine. She asked to be in my book, and I was thrilled to let her personality flesh out a character I hadn't breathed life into yet. I hope she enjoys reading what I wrote and isn't too upset about the mess. I did warn you! I loved her character, and I think she really added an important grounding force as well as a power to the narrative that was missing before.

Finally, my darling Wolfie has been a lifelong fascination ever since I saw Tom Hulce's delightful portrayal in *Amadeus*. I am so pleased with his story arch, and I hope you will enjoy watching it progress through the series.

More characters will make their appearance in the next book. Their names and back-stories are all buzzing in my head and begging to be told.

As for the plot itself, it grew out of the characters themselves. I am an organized person, and I work best from a working outline that then can be modified or expanded as I go. I wrote a one page summary of what I thought would be an interesting story, then I broke that up into parts.

Those parts were then expanded, and a single book became two and then three. I listen to my characters, however, and am driven by their motivations and reactions to the events as they unfold, so my three book plan may expand before I finish telling the entire tale I have to tell. While completing this story cycle is planned as a trilogy, my characters lead me, and they may decide they want me to tell another story once this one is done.

To me, that is what storytelling is. It's about characters. I like putting my characters into settings that force them to react. However, I don't like to have long exposition setting those characters up in the beginning. I prefer for you to get to know them, just as you get to know people in real life. Your understanding of their history and motivations will grow as you learn more about them throughout the plot.

I also have a strong attention to detail, and I have always loved a good mystery. That's why the outline is so important. If you're going to hold the suspense and keep giving clues at just the right moment, you have to have a plan. Otherwise, those clues aren't leading to a satisfying denouement.

One of the things I've kept in mind as I worked is every action, every piece of the exposition, every word of dialogue, must have a purpose. It must be moving the plot forward. Anything that didn't move the plot forward in this book was ruthlessly cut. There's no fluff. It's important to me that the momentum of the story keep propelling readers forward and keep holding their attention from the first page till the last word, and I want them begging for more at the end. I wanted this book to feel satisfying, but compel readers to ask what's happening next. The drama and excitement will continue to build as the story progresses, and I think you'll find yourself as excited as I am to see what happens next in Book Two. Those are the kinds of stories I enjoy reading, and with this novel, I've written the book I'd want to read. I hope you feel the same way.

I grew up watching *Colombo* and *Quincy* and *Murder She Wrote*, and I loved reading the novels of Agatha Christie as a child. During my teen years, I devoured Stephen King's books, and loved the tight way he spins a horror story. I'd read them late at night, huddled in bed, unwilling to put the book down both in fear and full of the need to know how it was going to end. As an adult, I fell in love with vampires, especially those of Anne Rice, and at the same time I became fascinated with thrillers and forensic crime scene dramas. This book combines the best of all of those aspects, I hope, with some romance in the mix as well.

There's a lot left to tell in this series. I'm just getting started.

CAST OF CHARACTERS

MARIE ANTOINETTE
Former queen of France, now stripped of her titles. Aliases include: Claire Marie Hapsburg, The Widow Capet, Goldie O'Shea.

RAUL GRIFFIN
Former child actor. Turned by Marie Antoinette. Aliases include: Fin (French for "The End").

SYBILL LYSANDER
Art student, barista, and mafia princess. Turned by Marie Antoinette. Aliases include: Evangeline (Eva) Mars.

THE INSPECTOR
Lead investigator in charge of finding Marie Antoinette. Works for "The Master." Aliases include: Ernestine Lambriquet

CRYSTAL KIRBY
Sales assistant in "All in the Past," Marie's antique shop in the Central West End.

WOLFGANG AMADEUS MOZART
Former composer and musical genius. Aliases include: Wolf Weber.

VINCENT DELUCA
Former mafioso. Head of the Chicago vampire coven.

ABOUT THE PRESS

Eagle Heights Press, a division of *Eagle Heights LLC.*, publishes thriller, fantasy, science fiction, historical fiction, paranormal romance, speculative fiction, young adult, non-fiction, and more. We also publish classic literature and educational textbooks.

Find us on the web at eagleheightspress.com.

CPSIA information can be obtained
at www.ICGtesting.com
Printed in the USA
BVHW071150060619
550313BV00005B/23/P